The Riverhaven Years

RACHEL'S SECRET

BJ HOFF

HARVEST HOUSE PUBLISHERS
EUGENE, OREGON

All Scripture quotations are taken from the King James Version of the Bible.

Cover by Koechel Peterson & Associates, Inc., Minneapolis, Minnesota

BJ Hoff: Published in association with the Books & Such Literary Agency, 52 Mission Circle, Suite 122, PMB 170, Santa Rosa, CA 95409-5370.

This is a work of fiction. Names, characters, places, and incidents are products of the author's imagination or are used fictitiously. Any resemblance to actual persons, living or dead, or to events or locales, is entirely coincidental.

For my family…

I thank my God every time I remember you.

—Philippians 1:3

ACKNOWLEDGMENTS

As the Amish work in community to raise a barn, build a house, and supply the needs of their families and friends, so do the people who bring a book to its readers work in community.

It has been a very special blessing for me to work in *community* with Harvest House Publishers. More family than "company," more friends than "associates," and as much partners as publishers, the people who make up this remarkable team are among the most gifted, dedicated, and faithful folks with whom I've ever had the privilege of working. I owe you much, and I'm deeply grateful to every one of you.

Let me add a special note of thanks to Nick Harrison, my editor, who never ceases to amaze me with his seemingly bottomless well of patience and encouragement, a heartening love of a *good story,* and the unfailingly keen instincts and expertise that enrich that story in countless ways—most of which the reader may never be aware of, but for which this author is continually grateful.

To Janet Kobobel Grant, wise agent and faithful friend—thank you for all the things that, in the rush and clamor and "busyness of the business" too often go unsaid. I would never have lasted this long without you.

Special thanks to Dr. Richard Mabry for enlightening me about gunshot wounds and other medical issues.

And to my readers—for every note and email you've taken time to write...for every prayer you've offered in my behalf...for reading my stories and sharing my heart—God bless you.

THE RIVERHAVEN YEARS

Book One:
RACHEL'S SECRET

THE MEMORY BOOK

Fond memory brings the light of other days around me...
THOMAS MOORE

Amish settlement near Riverhaven, Ohio
November 1855

Every year at this time, Rachel Brenneman took out her book of memories. Memories of another cold, rainy November day three years gone.

Rachel's memory book wasn't stored in her chest of drawers but in her heart. She had heard that there were paper pictures some *Englischers* kept as memories—pictures taken by boxes called *cameras*—that captured the exact image of people and things, trapping them in a moment of time, so they could be looked at months or even years later.

This was a forbidden thing to the Plain People, of course. And yet what would it be like to have such a picture of her beloved Eli to gaze upon, rather than having to call forth the pictures stored away in her mind?

Not that she needed a piece of paper to remember her departed husband. His dear face was engraved upon her heart as clearly today as if he sat across from her, smiling, watching her mend one of his shirts or darn his socks. Yet at times she feared that one day the images now so vivid might fade and grow distant, making it more difficult to keep his memory close.

She was resolved that she would never allow that to happen. That's why this yearly practice of deliberately setting apart a time to reminisce was so important. True, along with the achingly sweet and tender moments stored in her mind, there were other memories not so dear. Some were painful, even frightening. Rather than warming her heart, they threatened to break it. But she would continue this annual ritual of sorting through them until it was time to put them away for another year. This was her way, the only way she knew, to keep Eli close and honor his memory.

Now that her day's work was finally done, the night growing late, the house hushed, she sat on a wooden chair at the kitchen table with a blanket wrapped snugly around her. The flame in the oil lamp flickered in the cold draft, dappling the table and the walls with shadows. In one hand she clutched the small, heart-shaped wooden box Eli had made for her hairpins. He'd made it "for pretty," he'd said.

Eli had loved her hair. Most nights he would remove the pins himself and let it fall free and then commence to brush it for ever so long.

Memories...

With her other hand, Rachel smoothed the material of one of the few pieces of Eli's clothing she had kept after his death, the dark blue shirt he'd favored for church services. The pin box and his favorite shirt—these were the most precious things she owned. Even though a Plain woman wasn't to count any worldly item as a treasure, she could not look upon these things as anything *but* treasures.

The loneliness that usually closed in on her at this time of night was held at bay by the sweet warmth of her memories. She knew, if she were to get up and look outside, the darkness would be just as black as any other night. The November wind would be as raw as ever, carrying the familiar brackish odor off the river.

But for these few moments, as she dusted off her memories and revisited the blessed hours she and Eli had once shared, she would not hear the wind or feel the cold or mind the solitary darkness. For now she would not bend beneath the heaviness of her grief, would not choke on the bitter taste of her loss, would not let the fear of the future—a future without Eli—leach into her pores and chill her hope like a merciless, debilitating disease.

For this time, at least, she would pretend the night that had shattered her life without warning, the night that had swept away her dreams, her hopes, her happiness like dust in a windstorm, had never happened. For now her memories would allow her to relive yesterday.

Reality would return soon enough with tomorrow.

I

STRANGERS AT THE DOOR

The night is long, and pain weighs heavily,
But God will hold his world above despair.

CELIA THAXTER

G ant was blind, and he was drowning.

He thought he was out of the water, but now he wasn't sure. He couldn't tell the river from the rain drumming down on him. The world had become nothing but a churning tide of red, a swirling veil of rain and river and hurt.

If he could fight his way out, break though the wall of water forcing him under, there was a chance he might still survive. Instead he went spinning, tossed farther out, away from land. He could feel his lifeblood draining out of him as weakness dragged him closer to unconsciousness.

He gasped for air but choked. His lungs caught fire, his heart exploded. The pain snaked its way up his leg, circling his thigh and hip, unleashing its venom in a quick, hot siege as it coiled upward on its relentless route to his brain.

He had thought death would be a gentler thing, quiet, even peaceful, not this freezing, stabbing assault. There was nothing now but the roar of the water and the steady ascent of pain—nothing but the numbing awareness that he was sinking into a mindless abyss. No strength left. Nothing but the weight of the water and the storm and the current pulling him below...

Fight. He should fight…else he would drag Asa under with him. And Mac…where was Mac?

"Captain! Can you hear me, Captain? Stay with me! You stay with me and Mac! You be all right now! We be safe. We got you now. We're out of the water! Just the rain now, Captain, and we'll soon be in a dry place. Look, look there—can you see? It's the light and the candle. And the quilt. We found it, Captain! We at the station. We at the safe place now!"

Somewhere at a great distance, Gant could still hear the river running…heard a man shouting, a dog barking…

A safe place. But didn't Asa realize? There was no safe place—not tonight.

Monday night, long after Rachel had finished preparing the food she would be taking to Maryann Plank's wedding the next day, she lay wide awake and restless, trying not to wake Fannie, sleeping next to her.

She was glad for her nine-year-old sister's company, glad their mother had agreed that Fannie could spend the night. They had had fun, the two of them, cooking and baking for the next day's celebration and then playing some pencil and paper games until bedtime.

It was a comfort, having her sister's warmth at her side. The bed Rachel and Eli had once shared seemed bitterly cold and too big by far even now, three years after his death. More than once she'd been tempted to ask if Fannie could live with her instead of at the family home, but that would leave their mother alone much of the time. For even though her brother still lived at home, he was gone more than he was there.

At nineteen Gideon was still in his *rumspringa*—his running-around years—and to their mother's despair, he seemed to have little thought of joining the church and settling down.

Rachel worried about him too, but she was hopeful that Gideon's good heart and personal faith would eventually win out. Surely it was only a matter of time.

In any event she didn't feel right about depriving her mother of Fannie's company for more than a night or two every now and then. Her father had been gone nearly seven years, but Mamma still missed him every bit as much as Rachel missed Eli. It would be selfish of her to inflict even more loneliness on her mother simply to ease her own. So after the wedding tomorrow, she would send Fannie back home.

The thought of the wedding stirred a sick feeling in her, a feeling she hated but couldn't seem to control. She was happy for Maryann and John, of course. She wished them nothing but the best. But ever since Eli's death, weddings were misery for her.

She was ashamed of this dark veil that seemed to fall upon her, shutting out the joy she knew she should feel when others found happiness together. She had told no one, not even her mother or her closest friend, Phoebe Esch, of this ugliness in her spirit. She forced herself to endure one happy event after another with a fixed smile, silently praying for deliverance from her inability to share another's joy. She went through all the motions, helping to prepare food and offering her gifts and good wishes as though she were thoroughly delighted for the happy couple. But all the while, something inside her felt as if it were dead and cold.

As much as she disgusted herself, she tried not to imagine how this darkness in her soul must grieve the Lord.

He burst into their world like an injured black bear blown down from the mountain by a winter storm.

Rachel was on the verge of sleep when a pounding on the door jarred her awake. She bolted upright, and beside her, Fannie also sat up, her eyes wide and startled.

"Stay here," Rachel told her as she shrugged into her dressing gown. Fumbling for the oil lamp, she lighted it and hurried downstairs.

When she reached the door, she hesitated, stumbling back a step when the hammering came again, this time accompanied by what sounded like the barking of a very large dog. The entire house seemed to shake with the racket.

Disoriented, Rachel still didn't feel fear at this late-night intrusion. She was more alarmed by the thought that something had happened to Mamma or Gideon. Even so, when she saw that Fannie had followed her to the door, she flung out her arm and pushed her sister behind her.

"Who's there?"

The pounding stopped, but no one answered.

"Who's *there?*" Rachel called out again.

Another long silence. Then, "A friend of friends, ma'am."

Rachel stared at the door. "What? Who are you?"

Again came the puzzling message. "A friend of friends." The voice was deep, laced with a strange, unfamiliar accent. "My captain is hurt. We need help."

Rachel glanced over her shoulder to make sure Fannie was safely behind her. Then, holding her breath, she opened the door.

A black man, slightly stooped from the weight of a white man slumped against him, faced her. Behind them, unmoving, stood an enormous dark dog, his tail held high, ears perked, watching Rachel closely.

The white man groaned. He looked to be barely conscious, held upright only by the companion at his side.

His right pants leg was soaked with blood.

"Please, ma'am. My captain is hurt bad. Will you help us?"

Rachel gaped at the two, her mind spinning. What had she opened her door to? She couldn't think when she had last seen a man of color in the area. And the wounded man hunched against him—he appeared more dead than alive!

"What...what do you want?"

The black man looked confused. "We...I saw the light in your window. And the quilt on the line."

"The light—" At her mother's insistence, Rachel kept a candle burning on the table in front of the window every night. Her signal that everything was as it should be.

"A woman living alone, Rachel. It's not so gut. If the light isn't on, I'll know to send Gideon to check on you..."

But the quilt? What about the quilt? She'd forgotten to bring it inside before the rain came, so she'd left it. But what did that mean to these strangers?

She knew she ought to be frightened. Yet something about the black man's strong features, the steady look in his eyes, was reassuring, not threatening. And clearly his companion needed help.

Even so, what could she do? "I'm sorry...I can't...let you in. You'll have to wait outside until I fetch my brother. My family lives just across the field. You wait here on the porch, while I get my coat and go for him."

"I'll go, Rachel. I'll go for Gideon."

The small voice behind her reminded Rachel that Fannie was also to be considered.

"You'll do no such thing! Not in this rain."

But Fannie had already grabbed her coat from the peg on the wall. "I'll just get my shoes!"

"Gideon might not even be at home—" Rachel protested.

"*Ja,* he is! He promised Mamma he'd stay in tonight because of the storm."

Rachel couldn't think what else to do except to let Fannie go for their brother. She couldn't very well go herself, now could she, and leave her young sister alone with these two strange men? And that giant of a dog!

"All right, then—but run as fast as you can and bring Gideon right back!"

Fannie shot out the door, turning back just long enough to eye the men and the dog. "Let them in, Rachel! It's awful cold. And let the poor dog in too!"

Rachel watched her take off across the field toward their mother's house and then turned her gaze back to the two men. Fannie was right. She couldn't leave the two men standing out in the storm any longer.

"All right, then, I suppose you'd better come inside. But I warn you," she added quickly, "it will take only a moment for my brother to get here."

"We mean you no harm, missus," said the black man quietly. "I want only to get help for my captain."

The dog came to the door, still watching Rachel. Then unexpectedly it turned, loped a few steps into the yard and stood watching Fannie as she crossed the field.

Rachel hadn't the heart to *make* the poor creature stay out in the cold wind and rain, but if that was its choice, all right then. She stood aside as the black man hesitated only a moment before tugging his sodden knit cap from his head and entering. Dragging the man at his side along with him, he followed Rachel as she led the way to one of the spare bedrooms.

When Eli had built their house, he'd insisted on at least three bedrooms. "Plenty of room for the *boppli* we'll have some day," he'd told her. But to Rachel's wrenching regret, there had been no children.

"You haven't told me your name," Rachel said, glancing over her shoulder. "And you called him 'Captain.' What kind of captain is he?"

"Asa, missus. My name is Asa. And Captain Gant here is a river man. A riverboat captain."

What an odd accent the man had! Rachel had never heard anyone talk the way he did. He sounded as if he must have come from one of those foreign countries across the ocean.

Quickly she turned down the bed coverings, but when she would have helped move the injured man onto the bed, his companion took over, lifting the other in his arms as if he were but a child—though he was actually quite a large man.

"You want to take the bed clothes off first, missus? The blood—it will ruin them."

Rachel considered doing just that, but the wounded man was clearly in shock. He needed warmth and needed it right away. "No, it's all right," she told him. "He's freezing."

She watched as the black man carefully lay his "captain" on the bed.

The man's face was gray, his lips blue, his eyes smudged so dark he looked to have been beaten. And his leg—it was twisted in the most terrible way! *Ach*, and the blood—his pants leg was soaked and glistening with blood.

"Is he...dying?" she whispered.

The black man straightened and turned toward her, not quite looking her in the eye. "I pray not, ma'am."

Caution gave way to concern as Rachel saw how frail the wounded stranger's hold on life seemed to be. "We'll have to send for Dr. Sebastian. My brother will go for him as soon as he gets here."

The man called Asa shot her a look of gratitude. "Thank you, ma'am. That is most kind of you."

Rachel leaned over and put a hand to the injured man's forehead, cringing at the heat that seared her skin. For a split second, his eyes snapped open, and Rachel caught a glimpse of the deepest blue eyes she had ever seen just before they lost focus and closed again.

"He's burning up with fever," she said, keeping her voice low. "What happened to him?"

The black man hesitated, glancing back at the stranger on the bed. "Captain Gant, he was shot, ma'am."

→ 2 ←

RELUCTANT HELPERS

*I was a stranger
and ye took me in.*

MATTHEW 25:35

"*Shot?*" Rachel stared at the man. "With a gun?"

The man Asa darted a curious look at her, causing Rachel to realize how foolish she must have sounded.

At the same time, the bloodied stranger on her bed suddenly took on a different appearance. In only a moment, he changed from an injured man who needed help to an outsider who was suspect, perhaps even a threat.

Why had someone taken a gun to him? Was he a bad man—a criminal? Was he dangerous?

What had she done? How could she be so naïve, letting two strange men into her home when she knew nothing about them? Who were they? Where did they come from?

Despite the almost dizzying surge of fear, she couldn't stop staring at the man's blood-soaked pants leg. A bullet had done that to him. He could die because someone had aimed a gun at him and shot him.

It struck her like a fist that he very likely *might* die if she didn't do something to prevent it.

But do *what?*

The stranger groaned and stirred. The sight of the black man whipping a kerchief from his pocket—a kerchief that looked none too clean—shocked Rachel into action. "No—wait. I'll get something else."

Hurrying to the kitchen, she grabbed a stack of freshly laundered dish towels and cleaning cloths from the sideboard near the sink. Scissors. She would need scissors to cut away the material from his trousers. And something to sterilize the wound. There was no alcohol in the house. The best she could do was boil water.

Back in the bedroom, she found the black man bending over his "captain," using a knife to slice away the bloody pants leg. As soon as he saw Rachel, he stepped away, wiping the knife blade with his kerchief.

The sharp metallic smell of blood stunned her, and she gagged on the hot surge of bile that rose in her throat. She clenched her fists against the trembling of her hands as she eyed the ugly, gaping wound just below the wounded man's knee. She managed to steady herself with the thought that the stranger on her bed was somebody's son, perhaps somebody's husband. If it were Eli, she would hope that another woman in her place would help him.

But there had been no one to help Eli...not until it was too late.

The stranger moaned, and she shot a quick look at his face. His skin was ashen. He was shaking so violently the bed quaked beneath him. His eyes were still closed, and Rachel was sure that he was now completely unconscious.

The black man crossed to the other side, bent low, and held the stranger in place while Rachel wrapped the dish towel above the wound and tied it. She placed another cloth over the wound itself and carefully applied pressure—enough, but not too much, she hoped.

"The bullet is still in the wound?" she asked.

The man, Asa, nodded.

"This is all I can do, then. Dr. Sebastian will have to remove the bullet and do the rest."

Relief swept through Rachel at the idea that she could do nothing more. Just as quickly she felt ashamed. Truth was, she didn't *want* to do more. She didn't want to touch this bloodied stranger who had breached the security of her home in the middle of the night. She was both afraid of him and repulsed by him. He was large and stunk of sickness and corruption. She hated the fear that gripped her, hated even more her aversion toward another human being, especially one in such obvious distress.

"It's very kind of you to help us, missus."

The black man's low voice yanked her out of her churning thoughts.

She looked at him. "Where are you from? And why are you out on such a night?"

A sudden blast of wind shook the house as if to give weight to her questions.

Asa lifted his head slightly. "We came many miles, first on the water. Once we were *in* the water. After that we followed the river to get here."

"Here? What do you mean, 'here'?"

"We came to this place to find—"

He broke off, a shuttered look coming over his features.

Rachel studied him. "What happened to this man?" she said, inclining her head toward the wounded stranger. "Who did this to him?"

He hesitated. "In Virginia," he said slowly, "we left the boat to get supplies. When we returned, men were waiting for us. They set the boat on fire and shot the captain."

"*Why?*"

For the first time, the black man met her gaze. Rachel caught her breath at the simmering well of anger looking out at her. "The bullet was meant for me. The captain, he pushed me out of the way and took the shot himself."

Rachel stared at him, her mind groping to take in his words. What kind of a man would place himself in harm's way for another? And for a man of color at that.

She disliked herself for the thought that entered her mind, but there was no denying the contempt some white folks held for those who were…different. And the idea of dying for one of another race—small wonder that this man's statement caught her by surprise.

"Are you a slave?" she blurted out.

His look remained steady. "No, missus. I am a free man. The captain, he paid for my papers. He gave me my freedom and a job on his boat."

"Who are these men who shot—what did you say your captain's name is?"

"Gant, missus. Captain Jeremiah Gant." He hesitated, obviously uncertain as to whether he should say more. Finally he added, "I think it would be best if Captain Gant explains everything when…he wakes up."

The wounded man groaned. Rachel studied him a moment, faced Asa and gave a short nod, then turned to moisten a cloth in the washbowl.

She placed the cool cloth on the stranger's forehead before turning back to Asa. "So, then," she said, "how long have you been…free?"

"I think maybe three years by now, missus."

Rachel thought about that. "If you're a free man—and for so long a time—why would anyone want to hurt you? You said the shot was meant for you."

Suddenly the man on the bed gave a jerk and cried out.

Rachel flinched but put a hand on his arm to calm him.

At the same moment, the front door swung open, and in seconds, Gideon appeared in the doorway to the bedroom. Rachel's mother and Fannie were right behind him.

Her brother looked from Rachel to Asa and then to the unconscious stranger on the bed.

"What's going on?" he said to Rachel.

As always his voice was deceptively calm, his words slow and easy. There was even a ghost of a smile touching his lips. But his eyes were everywhere and lit with fire as that quick mind of his took in the uncommon scene before him.

Rachel's mother quickly banished Fannie to the kitchen before coming to stand beside Rachel. "Are you all right, daughter?"

"I'm fine, Mamma. You shouldn't have come out in this weather."

"Of course I should have come," her mother said, touching Rachel's hand. "What is all this?" She frowned at the man on the bed. "Who are these people?"

Rachel gave her a reassuring smile. As always, Susan Kanagy's dark blonde hair was tucked neatly under her *kapp* and her bonnet, her brown eyes warm with concern for one of her children. Rachel knew that her long black coat covered her nightdress, but other than that, her mother appeared as alert and unruffled as if she'd been awake for hours. Always ready for anything, that was Mamma.

"Fannie told us you have an injured man here. We've sent Reuben Esch for Dr. Sebastian," Mamma said, stepping toward the bedside to have a closer look at the unconscious stranger.

"I could just as well have gone myself," offered Gideon. "No need running Reuben out in this weather."

"You need to be here with your sister," Mamma said in her no-nonsense tone. She bent over the wounded stranger, touched his forehead with the back of her hand, and frowned. "This man is burning up with fever! What happened to him?"

She looked across the bed at Asa, who dipped his head in a deferential nod but said nothing.

"He's been shot, Mamma," Rachel said. "He's in a bad way."

As if she'd done so dozens of times, her mother lifted the cloth from Gant's leg and studied the wound.

After a moment she fixed a sharp eye on Asa. "What are you men doing here, on our land, in my daughter's home?"

That was Mamma. No hesitating, no mincing words, no beating around the bush. If one needed to know, one simply asked.

If the big black man was taken aback by her bluntness, he made no show of it.

"This man's name is Asa, Mamma," Rachel put in. "The wounded man is his—employer. Captain Jeremiah Gant."

"Captain Gant? What kind of 'captain' is he?"

"Captain is a river man, missus," Asa replied. "A riverboat pilot."

Gideon, standing at the foot of the bed with his arms crossed over his chest as he watched in silence, finally spoke. "What does a riverboat pilot do to get himself shot?"

Unlike their mother, Gideon's tone was casual, his words almost a lazy drawl. But very much *like* their mother, his eyes probed the black man with a cutting intensity.

"That's not important at the moment, Gideon," Mamma said. "This house is cold. Go stoke the fire before Dr. Sebastian gets here. And, Rachel, put water on to boil."

"I already did, Mamma."

"Then see to Fannie. She needs to go to bed. She's lost enough sleep as it is. But first take a towel to her hair and make sure she puts on dry night clothes."

Guilt stabbed at Rachel when she saw the worry in her mother's eyes. Fannie had ever been a fragile child, prone to chest colds and sore throats. She hadn't *wanted* to send her sister out in the middle of a rainstorm, but what else could she have done?

No doubt Mamma would have an answer for that later, and it likely wouldn't do a thing to ease Rachel's guilt. She turned to go.

"And Rachel? Your hair. Where's your *kapp?*"

Rachel lifted a hand to her hair, only then remembering that it was still unbound, in a heavy braid. She felt heat rise to her face. No man except her husband was ever to see a Plain woman's hair unbound. "There wasn't time before, Mamma. I'll take care of it now."

With a quick glance at the dark-clad stranger on the bed, Rachel left the room. She was calmer now, though not altogether pleased with the relief she'd felt when her mother arrived and took charge. She had been a married woman and taken care of a husband and a home. But ever since Eli's death, she'd found herself shirking responsibility in difficult situations, content to let someone else deal with problems, even though she wasn't without a sense of shame over her avoidance.

She had never been able to dismiss the conviction that she had somehow failed Eli. Always the wrenching question nagged at her: What else might she have done to prevent his death? Had she waited too long to react? Should she have ignored his plea to go for help and instead stayed with him, fought for him? Had she shirked taking action that night too?

It occasionally entered her mind that Eli would have admonished her for such feelings, that he would have pointed out, albeit in love, that self-denunciation and self-disgust were self-defeating and futile to the extreme. But Eli was no longer with her, and Rachel couldn't seem to banish the nagging doubts that simply wouldn't go away. Instead they continued to lurk beyond the fringes of her mind, creeping in to plague her when she least expected it.

Perhaps that was why she went about her daily tasks, even the most routine ones, feeling heavy with fatigue and bowed with uncertainty.

How then was she to deal with a situation like the one that had visited itself upon her tonight—yet another calamity that might mean a man's life or death?

DR. SEBASTIAN

*There was a man whom
Sorrow named his friend…*

W.B. YEATS

Even before Dr. Sebastian arrived, Rachel's mother brought order to the earlier confusion, and, in the process, taught Rachel a few things about the treatment and care of a wound.

"I daresay we might not need Dr. Sebastian now," Rachel said. Clearly her mother's efforts to tend to the stranger's wound were much more thorough and expert than her own attempts

"Of course we need him," Mamma said. "I've done everything I know to do. Apparently there's still a bullet in this man's leg, and he's dangerously ill. Only Dr. Sebastian and the Lord God can help him now."

"I think I hear Doc," Gideon said, already on his way to the door.

"Missus?" The man Asa looked from Rachel to her mother. "I fear I have no money of my own—I lost everything in the river tonight. But I'm sure the captain has funds in his valise. I managed to hold onto it until we reached the riverbank. Its contents will be very wet, but I'm certain we can pay the doctor."

"You needn't concern yourself with that just now," Mamma said. "Dr. Sebastian will understand if you can't pay right away."

"But we *will* pay. Captain Gant would not have it otherwise. You can trust him." He stopped and then added, "You can trust us both."

Rachel's mother searched his face for a long moment and then gave a small nod. "*Ja,*" she said matter-of-factly. "I expect I can."

Dr. Sebastian entered the room in his usual reserved manner, his tall form slightly hunched, his eyes somewhat shadowed with fatigue. He gave a weary but warm smile to Mamma and Rachel. As always a shock of dark hair, fading to silver, fell over one eye.

"Susan. Rachel." In one movement he settled his eyeglasses a little higher on the bridge of his nose and brushed the hair out of his eye. He glanced at Asa for only a second before transferring his attention to the unconscious stranger.

"Well," he said and then again. "Well."

With his eyes fixed on his patient, he took off his coat and rolled up his shirtsleeves before opening his doctor case. His expression gave nothing away, but Rachel had known the physician for years, and she could sense his qualms for the wounded man on the bed.

David Sebastian was *Englisch.* And the irony was that the doctor was indeed *English.* He had come all the way across the ocean from the country of England many years ago with his wife—who passed on not long after they arrived in America—and his son. Over time he had become physician and friend to the entire Amish community of Riverhaven.

The early reservations of the People had gradually evolved to trust and then love for the quiet, unpretentious physician with the gentle ways and mild voice. There was no one outside the Amish settlement held in higher regard than Dr. Sebastian—"Doc" as he was known to most—and no one more dedicated to the well-being and safeguarding of the Amish families.

From time to time, Rachel wondered how such a highly educated man, rumored to be from an important and wealthy *Englisch* family, had ended up on a small farm near the Ohio River. Like the air of sadness that hovered about the doctor, mystery seemed to encircle him with a cloud of questions. Very little was known about him, other than that he was a good Christian man, a widower with a son who was now a doctor himself, and he was totally dedicated to his patients.

Rachel, however, knew one other thing about the kindly physician, something she was fairly certain no one else knew: Dr. David Sebastian was deeply in love with her mother.

As a physician, David Sebastian held to an unwritten policy of never forming a negative opinion about a patient. Dislike or distrust, at any level, could affect one's judgment and even the course of treatment, not to mention the fact that it was a distinctly unchristian sort of behavior.

At the moment, however, his emotions seemed intent on waging a battle between the rules he had set for himself and the intrusion of this suspicious stranger into the home of Rachel Brenneman and the life of these good people—people he counted not only as patients but also as dear friends.

One of whom was especially dear...too dear.

Before his thoughts could wander any farther in *that* direction, he forced his professionalism to override his feelings. He even managed to be gentle as he examined the patient's wound, though he suspected that in his present condition, the man would be unaware of any sort of touch, gentle or otherwise.

"You did an excellent job of cleaning the wound, Rachel," he said.

"*Ach,* I did hardly anything. Mamma did most all the work."

David wasn't surprised. Susan Kanagy's cool head and calm hands had prevailed in more than one emergency before he reached the scene.

He glanced up at Susan. "You did well."

She waved off his compliment. "We're just ever so thankful you came as quickly as you did, and on such a bad-weather night as this."

"I'd like to know what he's up to," Gideon said, gesturing toward the injured stranger and then directing a pointed look at the black man. "It's not a night to go tramping around the countryside. Especially with a bullet hole in you."

"Gideon," Susan said, a warning note in her voice.

"I think it might be best for everyone to wait in the other room for now," David said, not looking directly at any one of them. "This man is in very serious condition, and I'm going to do some things you don't need to see."

"You'll need help," said Susan.

David glanced at the black man standing directly across the bed. "You're with him?"

The other nodded.

"Then you can help me if I need an extra pair of hands. Gideon, take your mother and sister to the kitchen now. And Rachel? I'll need starch for the bandages, if you'd be good enough to make some up."

Gideon uncoiled himself from the door frame and put one hand on Rachel's shoulder, the other on his mother's arm. "You heard Doc. Got anything to eat, Rachel?"

After they left the room, David turned back to the black man. "Now, then, while I work why don't you tell me how this happened? And while you're at it, you might explain what you're doing here." He paused and then added, "You should understand that these people live quiet lives. Peaceful lives. They don't need trouble. They've had more than their share of that already."

"Will the captain live?" was all the man said in reply.

"I'll do my part," David said shortly. "The rest is up to God."

"I think perhaps God sent you."

David adjusted his glasses and looked at him more closely. "Well," he said. "We'll see about that, won't we?"

He did the best he could under the circumstances. With the black man—whose name he learned was *Asa*—looking on, David worked by the light of a flickering oil lamp on the bedside table and a lantern hanging from a hook on the ceiling.

He cleaned the wound again, this time with alcohol, and then probed for the bullet and removed it. The tibia was shattered, but he managed to fit most of the pieces of bone back together before suturing the wound closed. He left a small section open to drain. Most likely he'd need to insert a drainage tube later.

The stranger groaned and muttered as David worked. Occasionally he jerked or flailed his arms, and once he leveled an elbow in David's direction, as if he meant to shove him aside. He was a big fellow, but he was also weak, and the man Asa was able to hold him steady so that his movements didn't thwart David's efforts.

Rachel had the starch ready by the time he needed it, and she soaked the bandages for him while he fashioned a splint. Gideon had eased quietly back into the room and stood watching as David bandaged the wound and applied the wooden splint. He made no attempt to dismiss him again, for the boy had peppered him with enough questions in the past to make David aware of a certain fascination with doctoring.

Of course, with the Amish disinclination toward higher learning, it wasn't likely young Gideon would ever be more than an interested observer. Still, David liked the Kanagy lad and actually enjoyed his company. Susan's son had a keen intelligence, a lively curiosity, and a somewhat wry sense of humor that never failed to amuse David.

He'd heard rumors that the boy was wild and ran around with some other high-spirited youths from a neighboring non-Amish farm community. But it seemed that the Amish tolerated a fair amount of this sort of behavior in their young people, the rationale being that after they'd sewn their wild oats, they would come back and settle down within their own community. Meanwhile, they would be able to make their decision with realistic knowledge of what the outside world was like.

From what David knew, most often the Amish youth chose to remain with their own people. David hoped that would be the case with Gideon, for he could only imagine the pain it would bring his mother if he should wander too far afield from the Amish life. Susan was thoroughly and devoutly Plain.

So much so that David had long ago given up any illusions he once might have held that they could ever be more than friends. But they were *good* friends, and he did his best to content himself with that much.

He gave himself another mental shake and checked the tightness of the bandage, reminding himself that the man under his hands was at the mercy of whatever knowledge and skill he possessed. No matter who he was or what he'd done, he deserved better than a doctor who couldn't keep his mind on his work.

After Dr. Sebastian left, the man Asa came into the kitchen and stood waiting until Rachel looked up from the table, where she sat mending an apron.

"Pardon me, missus. I don't like to bother you, but might I ask if you'd mind my staying in the barn—or if you have a shed. I'd like to stay as close to the captain as possible tonight."

Rachel studied him, at first not comprehending what he was getting at. When it dawned on her that he didn't want to presume that he might sleep inside the house, she put her mending down. Truth be, Mamma had raised that very issue before leaving. "He *is* a man of color, Rachel. And a slave. You don't mean to let him stay in the house overnight, do you?"

"A *freed* slave, Mamma. A free man of color. I don't have a problem with him being in the house. Besides, I think Gideon plans to stay the night. I'll be quite safe."

Now she studied the man for a moment more. "If you would feel better staying at the captain's side tonight, you may. So long as you can sleep in a chair."

His expression brightened—with surprise, Rachel thought.

"I would be grateful, missus. And a chair would be all I need. But—you are sure you don't mind?"

Rachel turned back to her sewing. "No, I don't mind. It would be helpful to me if you'd keep watch over him. I'll get you a blanket as soon as I'm finished here."

"Thank you, missus. Thank you very much."

Long before dawn, Rachel awakened with a start. Although lamplight from the stairway shed a soft glow into her bedroom, it took a moment for her eyes to focus.

The night came rushing in on her. The intrusion of the wounded riverboat captain and his companion. Dr. Sebastian's dire warning that the wounded Gant might not survive. The fear and disorientation that had shattered her hard-won peace.

Peace? Could she really call the cloud in which she moved and worked and lived any kind of *peace?*

She glanced over to see that Fannie still slept soundly beside her. Although her mother had left not long after Dr. Sebastian, nothing would appease Gideon but staying the night. Rachel was secretly relieved that he'd insisted, though she made every effort to keep him from sensing her uneasiness.

She got up, quietly dressed, and tiptoed downstairs to the other bedroom. Gideon and the man Asa were asleep in chairs on either side of the bed. The wounded *Englischer*—Gant—appeared to be still unconscious.

She had told Gideon to take the small third bedroom, but she wasn't surprised to find him where he was. No doubt he'd been uncomfortable with the idea of leaving the two strangers alone.

A movement from the foot of the bed startled her, and she jumped back, nearly colliding with the door frame. The big black dog raised its head and gave a low growl but quickly settled at the sight of Rachel. Its eyes caught the glow of the lamplight from the kitchen as it continued to watch Rachel with a steady, but not unfriendly gaze. Its tail thumped against the floor once or twice but not hard enough to cause Gideon or Asa to stir.

Gideon must have taken pity on the animal. He was soft when it came to dogs. Mamma would never have one in the house, so as a boy he'd contented himself with caring for the occasional stray in the barn or the shed. Even now, at nineteen years, he would get a good scolding from their mother if she knew he'd let this big wet creature inside.

For her part Rachel didn't mind. She liked dogs too. Eli had brought his old red hound with him when they married, but the dog had disappeared into the woods one night and never came back. Eli found him two days later, the victim of a hunter's gun—whether an accidental shooting or deliberate, they never knew.

Perhaps more for her sake, Eli had declared it an accident. But Rachel knew it wouldn't have been the first time someone had done a mean, spiteful thing to one of the People. There were those who didn't want the Amish anywhere in the area and weren't past working meanness against them in an effort to drive them away.

In the faint light that filtered through the doorway, she could just make out the outline of the stranger in the bed. Her gaze ran the length of him, and where before she'd had only the sense of a large man, she saw now that although he was tall, his form beneath the bed clothes was anything but stout. His features, too, were lean. Even in his unconscious state, his face wasn't slack but strongly sculpted. He had raven-black hair, and now that it was dry, she could see glints of silver randomly threaded among the thick waves. His mouth was wide and topped with a full, dark mustache.

Rachel wasn't used to seeing men with mustaches. Amish men— married ones, that is—wore full beards but no mustaches. It somehow made him look...raffish. Even dangerous.

Then she remembered the vivid blue eyes she'd caught a glimpse of earlier, when she and the man Asa had tugged him onto the bed, and she chided herself for such fanciful thoughts. Those eyes had held nothing of danger, but only raw pain.

She noted that his breathing was labored, and he was drenched in perspiration. She needed to tend to him, try to cool the fever.

She looked at Gideon and then went to him and put a hand on his shoulder. He jerked and, as he had when he was a child, came instantly awake. "What?"

Rachel put a finger to her lips. "Go lie down in the other bedroom, brother. I'll look in on him."

"I can stay—"

"I'm not sleeping anyway," Rachel insisted. "Go on now. You need better rest than you'll get in that chair, so you can work tomorrow."

Assured that he was awake, she went to the kitchen. The fire had died down, and the house was cold again. She added wood to the stove before drawing some cool water for the pitcher.

It occurred to her that for the first time in two days, she didn't hear the rain on the roof or the wind howling around the windows. A welcome relief, that.

The sight of the pies she'd baked the day before reminded her of Maryann's wedding. What would she do about that now? Of course she should go. Maryann was a neighbor and her family members were friends of the Brennemans and the Kanagys. She wouldn't understand if Rachel were to miss her wedding.

But how could she leave the unconscious *Englischer* for most of the day? What if he died in her bed while she was gone?

Well, he wouldn't be alone. The man Asa would be with him. And Dr. Sebastian said he would stop by. Was there really any need for her to stay away from the wedding?

Guilt stabbed at her. Truth was, she *wanted* to stay away.

What did it say about her that she would choose to stay home to look after a total stranger rather than attend the wedding of a long-time friend?

It says you're a coward, Rachel Brenneman. You're a weak woman who finds the happiness of others too painful to bear because your own joy was so quickly spent…a woman who dreads a future of untold years, living alone in a community that values the love and bond of family above all else.

With her mind fogged by this confrontation with her own weakness, Rachel carried the pitcher of water and some more clean cloths back into the bedroom. Later she would decide what to do about Maryann's wedding.

In the meantime she would pray that God would help her to make the right decision, not necessarily the easiest one.

⇢ 4 ⇠

RESTLESS THOUGHTS

Teach me to feel that Thou art always nigh;
Teach me the struggles of the soul to bear…
GEORGE CROLY

Rachel went through the routine of dressing methodically and quickly, her mind darting back and forth with one question after another. She donned her dark brown clothing and black apron, fastened them with pins, and then brushed her hair, securing it under her *kapp*.

She glanced at Fannie, still sleeping. She would have to send her sister home at first light. Her good clothes for the wedding were there, and Mamma would want to supervise her dressing.

She had a headache before she even started breakfast. Her hands were shaking as she sliced off the bacon and put it in the pan to fry. Before she ever cut out the first biscuit, she spilled flour on the floor and knocked over a cup of milk.

It was still dark when Gideon came ambling into the kitchen, rubbing his eyes and finger-combing his hair. By then Rachel was almost lightheaded with tension and nerves. She never functioned well when her routine was disturbed. She was an orderly person by nature, and when order faltered, so did she.

This need for routine had only grown stronger after Eli's death. Now that he was no longer with her to take her by the shoulders, smile into her eyes, and reassure her that "everything is good now, *ja,*" she often seemed at a loss to maintain her sense of balance.

Now with a stranger in her house who might be dying at any minute, both he and his companion blown in during a two-day rainstorm that had battered her nerves as much as it had the roof of the house, she sensed that her resolve to remain calm and composed was about to crumble.

"Well, you sure made a mess."

Gideon's smirk brought her up short, but for some reason his amusement acted to steady her. Perhaps because her irritation with his teasing took the place of her nervousness.

To her brother's credit, though, even while he seemed intent on aggravating her, he was down on his knees cleaning up the spilled milk and flour.

"Mmm. Soggy biscuits. I can't wait."

Rachel ignored his sarcasm. "Is the black man awake?"

"His name is 'Asa,' Rachel," her brother said, standing.

"I know his name," she bit back. "Is he awake? I'll have breakfast ready in a few minutes. Go call Fannie, why don't you?"

"What's got you so rattled?"

"I'm not rattled. Call Fannie, and if the...if *Asa* isn't awake, you'd best wake him. I don't have time to fix two breakfasts, what with the wedding and all."

"Oh, that's right. I forgot about Maryann's wedding."

Rachel turned from the stove to look at him. "It could have been *your* wedding, if you hadn't been more interested in running around with that *Englisch* girl instead of settling down with Maryann."

He grinned. "Which *Englisch* girl would that be?"

"One of many, no doubt. But I was thinking of that Elizabeth."

"Don't start," he said, his offhand tone belying the warning in his eyes.

"Gideon—"

"I'll go call Fannie."

"Wait."

He turned, his expression guarded as if he expected a lecture.

"Are you going to the wedding?" Rachel asked.

He looked surprised but didn't hesitate. "No."

"Don't you think you should?"

"No," he said again. "We both know Maryann wouldn't want me there."

He was probably right. Rachel loved her brother, but there was no denying that he had hurt Maryann Plank when he broke off their courtship last year to see another girl. An *Englisch* girl. There had been awkward feelings between them ever since. Rachel hadn't missed the way that, even now—though Maryann would marry John Bender today—she avoided making eye contact with Gideon whenever they chanced to meet.

"Besides," he went on, "I have to work today."

Rachel gave a distracted nod while she slid the tray of biscuits into the oven.

"Are you still planning to go? What about him?" He gestured toward the bedroom.

"I don't suppose it would be right to leave, what with the condition he's in."

"You don't really want to go anyway, do you?"

His searching expression made Rachel uncomfortable. Was her younger *bruder* really so sensitive that he would notice she found weddings difficult? Perhaps she sometimes underestimated Gideon because of his bent toward glib humor and the casual exterior he often wore.

She turned away. "It's not important what I want. This is Maryann's special day, and I should be there."

Again Gideon surprised her. "I'm sure she'll understand," he said quietly, touching her hand, "once word gets out as to what's happened here. And we both know word *will* get out. Everyone will know even before the wedding."

Rachel hadn't thought of it, but Gideon was right. Everyone *would* know. There was no keeping a secret among the People. Not only were they a small community, but they were an extremely *close* community as well. An event like this—an intrusion by two outsiders in the middle of the night—would burn through the settlement like wildfire.

Her dismay must have been written all over her face because Gideon cracked a sly smile. "*Ja,* no doubt you'll be getting a visit from a certain deacon once he gets wind of your riverboat captain in there. Old Samuel isn't going to like it one bit, hearing there's a strange man in your bed."

"*Gideon!*"

Clearly he was amused by her discomfort.

Just as the arrival of Gant and his companion, Asa, would be no secret in the community by afternoon, it was also no secret that Samuel Beiler, a deacon and highly regarded Amish farmer, was intent on courting Rachel. He had been sweet on her since before her marriage to Eli, and although he waited a decent time after Eli's death to come around, lately his intentions had become more obvious.

He was a good man, Samuel was, but that's *all* he was to Rachel. And in her deepest heart, she knew that was all he ever *would* be. Some of the women among the People made no secret of the fact that they thought her headstrong and foolish for not warming to the attentions of a handsome spiritual leader and prosperous widower like Samuel Beiler.

Be that as it may, she didn't see Samuel in the same light as many of the others did. In truth she disliked herself for the way she'd begun to view him. Surely she was wrong to feel as she did toward a man so widely respected and esteemed by the entire community, a man who had been her friend—and a friend of her family—for years. Yet there were times when she actually found herself wondering if Samuel might not be somewhat manipulative or, at the least, meddlesome. He did seem bent on insinuating himself into areas of her life where he had no business.

For months now he had hinted that Rachel should seriously consider selling her place to him. She understood his motives—Rachel's property and her mother's rested squarely between Samuel's land and the Troyer farm. Samuel had already acquired Benjamin Troyer's place, so if he could convince Rachel and her mother to sell to him, he would own the largest expanse of property in the Riverhaven area.

Although Gideon and some of Rachel's friends enjoyed teasing her about Samuel's "pursuit," she couldn't help but occasionally wonder whether his real objective was to win her as his wife—or acquire her land.

Of course the moment this poisonous thought crept into her mind, she felt wicked and small-minded. Samuel Beiler wasn't that kind of a man, and she ought to be ashamed of herself for even entertaining such a notion.

"Where's that rambling mind of yours gone to now?" asked Gideon.

Rachel waved him off. "Just thinking about Maryann...and things. That's all."

"You think too much, sister. That's one of your problems."

"I didn't know I had a problem. What would I do without my *bruder* to remind me?" Rachel pointed a finger toward the door. "Are you going to call Fannie or not?"

"I'm going." He made a move toward the stove. "Just let me have a taste of that gravy first."

"You'll have no taste of *anything* if you don't stop acting like such a child." Rachel made as if to smack his hands with the spatula, and he turned quickly to go wake Fannie.

She took a deep breath. And another. *I mustn't inflict the turmoil of my heart on my loved ones, Lord God...please, calm my spirit and help me cling to Your peace.*

From the darkness of the room where he was lying, Gant could see what appeared to be a dimly lighted kitchen where a woman and a man stood talking. Even the faint light hurt his eyes, and he had to keep closing them against the pain. Things looked blurred, as in a dream, and he wondered if that's what this was—a dream. For he recognized nothing, not the bed he was in nor the people in the kitchen.

He'd been drifting in and out of a thick, numbing sleep for what seemed like hours. Every time he thought he was awake, the room would start to sway, and he'd close his eyes against the sick pitching of his stomach and the fire in his leg. The next thing he knew, he'd fallen asleep again.

His gaze settled on the kitchen. An oil lamp flickered on the wooden table. The walls were bare, and so was the floor except for a rag rug at the door. The woman looked young. She was pretty, though clad in a severe dark dress and apron, with a little white cap on her head. The man with her was tall and had longish hair and wide shoulders.

He thought it was nighttime but couldn't be sure. The room was dark. *Everything* looked dark. He caught only a word here and there of the man and woman's conversation. Nothing made sense. He heard "Maryann" and "wedding" and "English." Something about "Gideon." But nothing meant anything to him.

He turned, wincing with the pain. He saw Asa sitting beside the bed and heard something at the foot of the bed—the soft chuffing sound Mac made when he slept. He opened his mouth to call to his dog, but no sound came. Only a strangled gasp.

He closed his heavy eyes, and immediately a blanket of darkness settled over him again.

⇒ 5 ⇐

GANT

The quality of mercy is not strain'd,
It droppeth as the gentle rain from Heaven
Upon the place beneath. It is twice bless'd:
It blesseth him that gives and him that takes.

SHAKESPEARE

Evening came early on the river in November. The outside light was waning and the shadows were drawing in, beginning to crowd the kitchen when Rachel lighted the oil lamp and started supper.

She had already decided to make a large meal, for she had no idea how many she might be feeding. If Dr. Sebastian arrived close to meal-time, naturally she would ask him to stay. Although he hadn't come by yet, he'd promised that he would, and Rachel knew she could count on his word. Gideon might be here as well, if he remembered that Mamma wouldn't be cooking this evening. She and Fannie would still be at the wedding.

Not comfortable with leaving the still dangerously ill *Englischer* for the entire day, Rachel had stayed home. The wounded stranger hadn't yet regained consciousness, although he'd been fitful and rest-less throughout the day, as if he might come to at any moment.

Asa, his companion, was noticeably worried about him and, no doubt, with good reason. Rachel also felt a heavy weight of concern, and she didn't even know the man. His skin was absolutely ashen, his fever still high, and he groaned with nearly every breath he took. There could be no mistaking the graveness of his condition.

"Missus?"

Rachel whipped around at the sound of Asa's voice. She still wasn't used to having someone in the house, and the slightest noise tended to unnerve her. It had occurred to her, though, earlier in the afternoon, that if she had to endure two strangers in her house, this man of color might just be the least intimidating of the two. He appeared to be a quiet, gentle soul, careful with every word he spoke and seemingly eager to be helpful and unobtrusive.

On the other hand, the wounded Gant—even though unconscious and unaware of the dilemma he presented for a widowed Amish woman living alone—somehow emanated a disturbing potential for violence. Perhaps it was because he had been shot. The thought of someone aiming a gun at another human being and pulling the trigger chilled Rachel's blood.

Whatever the reason, the man's very presence seemed to charge the air with a quality of danger. Although Rachel looked in on him at frequent intervals throughout the day and saw to any need she could anticipate, she stayed out of the bedroom as much as possible.

"I'm sorry, missus. I didn't mean to startle you."

Rachel waved away his apology. "No, it's—it's fine. Is there something you need?"

"I was wondering...I don't like to bother you, but with the captain as he is, there is something I need to do. Something I need to ask you about—"

Rachel waited. The man seemed uneasy, even anxious.

"We were supposed to collect...some people, you see. Some people who will be waiting for us."

"What people?"

He pulled a kerchief from his pocket and dabbed his forehead. "May I speak freely—and for only you to hear?"

Rachel nodded, watching him.

"These would be people—like me. People of color. We—Captain Gant and myself—we were supposed to meet them and help them make their way to the North."

Rachel stared at him, understanding finally dawning. "You're talk-ing about slaves. Runaway slaves."

Something like defiance flared in his dark eyes. "Yes, runaway slaves. Are they...here somewhere? I need to get word to them. They're waiting for us to come for them. If we don't—"

As if he sensed Rachel's bewilderment, he stopped.

"You thought there were runaway slaves *here*? There's no one here. No one at all except myself and sometimes my little sister. I don't know what you're talking about."

The man appeared as baffled as Rachel. "We were told they would be here, waiting for us. That there would be a quilt on the line outside the house and a candle in the window. That it would be a place where Amish people live."

Now Rachel was thoroughly confused. "The quilt was on the clothesline because I forgot to bring it in earlier. Later it got soaked from the rain, and so I left it out. As for the candle, I leave a candle in the window every night."

His worried expression deepened still more. "I don't know where they might be or how to find them. I can only hope they wait until I *can* find them. If they get impatient and try to leave on their own, there's a great risk of getting caught."

"Whatever you were told, you're not likely to find them here in Riverhaven." Rachel averted her eyes. "Plain People don't get involved in things like that. We keep to ourselves."

He didn't reply right away, but Rachel could sense him watching her.

"Captain says that some Amish folks have helped in the past," he finally said, his voice low.

Rachel turned to look at him. "Not around here. I'd have heard about it."

His gaze didn't waver. "Most folks who help the slaves—they keep quiet about it. It's safer for everyone that way."

Rachel's mind swarmed with questions about this business of help-ing runaway slaves gain their freedom, but she thought it best to tend to her own affairs. There *was* one question she felt an urgency to ask, however. "You wouldn't leave *now*, would you? With...your captain in the condition he's in?"

The thought of being left alone with a man who might be dying wasn't a possibility she wanted to consider.

He shook his head. But Rachel's relief was short-lived.

"No, of course I wouldn't leave the captain like this. But if—*when*—he regains consciousness and I know he's going to be all right, then I will have to go. It's what he will expect—"

He broke off at a sound from the next room. He and Rachel stared at each other for a split second and then started for the door.

He was awake.

Even in the dimmest of light straying in from the kitchen, his eyes caught the glow as he looked directly at Rachel and then Asa. He moistened his lips as if he would speak, but nothing came.

Asa went to the near side of the bed. After lighting the oil lamp, Rachel went to the opposite side.

He looked so different now that he was conscious. Younger, not so threatening, with those deep blue eyes wide open and fringed with lashes so long and thick they might have belonged to a woman.

He was staring at her, not Asa, studying her so closely Rachel felt relief when he finally turned back to Asa.

"Where—"

The single word seemed all that he could manage, as if the effort had exhausted him and left him empty.

"You're safe, Captain. You were shot, but you're going to be all right. We're in Riverhaven. This lady here is Mrs. Brenneman. This is her house."

Again Gant turned toward Rachel, slowly. Rachel saw him wince, as if the movement caused him pain.

In spite of her resolve to distance herself from this unknown outsider, Rachel felt unexpected sympathy at the sight of him. His skin was gray, his hands almost white, his eyes sunken and shadowed. And sorrowful. Such awful sad eyes he had.

On instinct she touched the back of her hand to his forehead.

The fever had broken. His skin was clammy but cool, almost normal.

He was watching her like a hawk might eye a bobcat, taking her measure, judging what her next move might be.

When she realized she was still touching him, she jerked her hand away. Something glinted in his eyes before he turned back to Asa.

"I'm shot?"

"Yes, Captain. Do you remember?"

Gant seemed to consider that. He looked at Asa with a question in his eyes.

"One of Cottrill's men," Asa said.

To Rachel's amazement, Gant seemed to muster the strength for a grim smile, a smile that quickly fell away. "He's not giving up, is he? He'll not have you back though."

"Thanks to you, Captain. And I do thank you for what you did."

"Am I going to make it?"

Asa leaned slightly forward, putting a hand to Gant's shoulder. "You are. Thanks to these kind people and the mercy of God."

Gant closed his eyes, but only for a moment. When he opened them again, his gaze locked on Rachel.

"You're Amish," he said, his voice so thin Rachel could scarcely make out his words.

"Yes, I am." Even as unfocused and vague as it was, his stare unnerved Rachel. She clenched her hands behind her back.

"Good...people," he murmured and then closed his eyes.

"Captain!" Asa's features froze in alarm.

"He's all right, I think," Rachel said. "He's just sleeping now, not unconscious. No doubt he's too weak to stay awake."

The words were no more off her lips than Gant's eyes flew open.

He reached a hand to Asa's arm. "Where are they? Durham's people. Did you find them?"

Asa bent low. "Not yet, Captain. They're not here. But I'll find them."

"They're not here? What do you mean?"

Asa shook his head. "Missus says no. She doesn't know of any runaways."

Gant's eyes burned as he glanced at Rachel and then reached a hand toward Asa. "You have to find them," he rasped. "You have to find them soon."

"I will, Captain. I'll find them."

"*Now.* Hurry. You have to hurry…they mustn't leave without us… they'll never…"

And then he was gone again, back to the same troubled sleep. Rachel touched his forehead and, finding the fever upon him once more, didn't feel nearly as confident as his friend, Asa, that he was going to be all right.

⇒ 6 ⇐

FRIEND PHOEBE

Let me tonight look back across the span
Twixt dawn and dark, and to my conscience say—
Because of some good act to beast or man—
"The world is better that I lived today."

ELLA WHEELER WILCOX

Rachel didn't know whether she should be relieved or anxious when Dr. Sebastian told her later that evening that Gant would almost certainly survive.

Naturally she was relieved because she wouldn't wish the man to die; but she was also anxious because his good chances of survival meant that Asa would be leaving, at least for a time, to search for the slaves who were waiting to be led to freedom.

If he did leave, just how was she to deal with the wounded *auslander* in her house? Even with Dr. Sebastian's promise to come by every day and knowing she could count on her mother's help, there was more to be reckoned with than the matter of the outsider's care.

She was a widow living alone. How could she take care of a wounded man in her home—an outsider at that—for what the doctor had indicated would be a lengthy recuperation period?

She would surely receive a visit from the bishop soon enough, when that news reached his ears.

And Samuel, too, would no doubt make an appearance, him being a deacon.

Her mouth went dry at the very thought of *that* kind of a visit from Samuel. Several years ago when Eli was still alive, she had suffered one such uncomfortable meeting with him in his deacon's capacity—and with the bishop as well. That occasion had been brought on by Barbara Kurtz, who had come alongside the house one day while Rachel was hanging out clothes. She'd caught Rachel carelessly singing a tune that Gideon had learned from one of his *Englisch* friends and passed on to her, a lighthearted little song with a catchy melody that had worked its way into Rachel's mind and stayed with her for days.

Music had a way of doing that to her. It was as if once she heard a memorable piece of music, she unwittingly allowed it entrance into some deep part of herself. She seldom even realized she was humming or singing it. It simply wove its way into her being and took up residence, only to appear unbidden when she least expected it.

Barbara had chided her for indulging in such a frivolous and worldly activity, and Rachel could hardly defend herself. She knew well enough that singing was to be limited to only songs that were pleasing to the Lord God—in particular hymns from the *Ausbund,* the Amish hymnal.

The lapse in behavior had been wrong, albeit unintentional. Even so, she hadn't once thought that the woman her mother counted as a friend would actually take the matter so seriously as to report her. Eli had been disgruntled for a time over the reprimand, but they both knew that to argue the point would only give the offense more weight than it probably deserved—and at the same time risk provoking yet another rebuke.

Although Mamma at first had seemed impatient with Barbara, she cautioned Rachel that what sometimes seemed like minor offenses could easily turn into more serious ones. "We have to guard our hearts, daughter. I'm sure Barbara's intentions were good. She meant only to protect you."

Rachel managed to bite down the retort that came to mind about Barbara's desire to "protect" her. Afterward she had to ask forgiveness more than once for her resentful thoughts.

The sound of someone stepping onto the porch jarred her back to her surroundings.

Gideon, no doubt. He hadn't shown up for supper, but Rachel was glad he was here now.

The big black dog came to the door of the kitchen and gave a low growl, glancing from Rachel to the back door, but made no move to come any further. Not for the first time, Rachel was struck by the animal's unnerving look of intelligence. Its eyes held an almost human expression of keen insight. Not only that, but in spite of its great size and commanding appearance, it actually seemed to possess a spirit of gentleness. After Rachel opened the door to admit, not Gideon after all, but her best friend, Phoebe Esch, the dog waited only another second or two before returning to the bedroom.

Phoebe was a dear friend to both Rachel and her mother. At forty-five, she was closer in age to Mamma, but over the years she and Rachel had also become close friends and confidants. Especially after Eli's death, Rachel had found herself drawn to Phoebe's compassion and steadying faith—a faith that, to Rachel, seemed more personal, more *practical* than that of some of their other friends.

Unbeknown to some in the community, Phoebe and her husband, Malachi, shared a more intimate relationship with Christ than was common to the Plain People. They regularly studied the Scriptures on their own and prayed so warmly and openly to the Lord God that Rachel always felt as though He was right in the room with them.

As far as Rachel knew, she, Eli, and the Esceh's sons were among the few who were aware of what undoubtedly would be frowned upon as a questionable, even forbidden, faith on the part of Phoebe and Malachi. In fact before Eli died, he had come to share their beliefs, with Rachel warming to them as well. Once she and Eli started studying the Scriptures with the Esches and she began to see for herself what was taught in the Holy Word about salvation being through faith in Christ—and not works as she'd been taught—she had begun to wonder and question on her own.

After Eli's death, though, this part of her life seemed to stop. She still turned to the Bible, and she still prayed—but it wasn't the same. For so long her heart had been a desert, a barren place that no longer sensed the warmth and peace of God's love. She lived in fear and confusion, foundering on dread instead of pursuing devotion and a deeper experience of her faith.

But Phoebe, always sensitive to the slightest shifting or turning in another's emotions, stood quietly by. She allowed Rachel to lean, to grieve, to question, all the while continuing to impart God's love and a rare kind of unconditional friendship for which Rachel would be forever grateful. With unfaltering patience, this dear friend had helped bring Rachel back to the place where she could once again find her way to a closer walk with her Lord and accept His grace.

The sight of her now, standing in her kitchen with that good-natured smile and searching gaze, was a balm to Rachel's frazzled nerves. "Oh, Phoebe, I am so glad to see you!"

Her friend moved to clasp her hands. "What's happening here, then? So many tales I've heard."

"What *have* you heard?"

"Some wild stories about a man dying in your house from a gunshot wound and a man of color standing guard over him." She paused. "Did they really break into your home?"

"Oh, goodness no, they didn't break in! I *let* them in because one was badly wounded and they obviously needed help." She released her hands and motioned Phoebe to the table. "Come, sit. I have coffee and cake left from supper."

But Phoebe shook her head, glancing around the room. "So where are they, these men?"

"In the bedroom."

She thought her friend seemed unusually agitated. But then maybe she was simply reacting to Rachel's own nervousness.

"Who are they? Where did they come from, do you know?"

"Not really. All I know is that the man who was shot is a riverboat man—a captain, his companion calls him. Asa—the other man—is a freed slave."

Phoebe looked at her. "A freed slave?"

Rachel nodded. "Apparently he works for this—Captain Gant—on his boat. But the boat was burned, and the captain was shot. Dr. Sebastian says he'll survive, though."

"But what are they doing *here?*"

"I don't know the whole story. But it seems there are people depending on them, people who need their help. Asa seems insistent on leaving as soon as he knows for certain that Captain Gant is going to be all right. He says he has to find these people as soon as possible."

Phoebe's pale blue eyes, always wide and lively, suddenly took on a look of uneasiness. "Did he say who these people are?"

Rachel shook her head. "Just that he has to find them. And I heard Captain Gant tell him he needs to go now, that he has to hurry." She stopped. "But Asa hasn't left yet. He's still in there, in the bedroom with the captain."

Phoebe had gone positively ashen. "Rachel, this is important. What did they say when they came to your door?"

"What did they *say?*"

"Yes, what exactly did they say?"

Rachel tried to remember. "It all happened so fast...we were in bed, Fannie and I. Gant—the wounded man—was losing consciousness and couldn't talk. The other—Asa—said something about seeing the quilt on the line and the candle in the window. He said his captain was hurt, that they needed help."

"What else?"

"Nothing—at least that I can remember—"

"Are you *sure,* Rachel?"

Puzzled by her friend's intense questioning, Rachel tried her best to remember. "I think he said—though it didn't make any sense—he said something about being 'a friend of friends'."

Phoebe blinked and glanced toward the doorway to the bedroom. After a moment's hesitation, she said, "I need to talk to them, Rachel."

"But—"

"I'll explain. But first I must talk to these men. And, Rachel, you can't tell anyone about this. Not *anyone*."

"But what—"

Phoebe put a hand on Rachel's arm. "Please promise me you won't say a word! Not even to your mother. Susan might not understand—or approve."

Rachel couldn't imagine Phoebe keeping any kind of secret from Mamma. They were so close, had been like sisters for years.

"I could hardly say anything when I don't even know what you're talking about."

Phoebe had already started for the bedroom. "Just—you wait here for now. I won't be long."

Rachel stared after her, her mind racing. Had Phoebe not been acting so strangely, she would have been tempted to follow her. But she hesitated, sensing that, at least for now, anything that could evoke that look of panic in her usually calm, steady-natured friend might be better left unexplored.

So she waited, a part of her fervently longing only for the return of her quiet, uneventful life, while another part of her felt strangely excited, even energized by this unexpected situation into which she'd been thrust.

The thrill that shot through her at the thought of this event—an event that had interrupted the peace of her days—was wrong. It was wrong to allow any form of interference from the outside world to appeal to her baser emotions. It was *verboten*. Forbidden.

Just as forbidden as the way the blood had rushed to her head when the wounded riverboat captain turned the force of his startling blue gaze on her for the first time.

As it turned out, Phoebe's "secret" wouldn't be kept from Rachel's mother. By the time Phoebe returned to the kitchen, Mamma had arrived.

Standing just inside the door, she cast a puzzled frown in her friend's direction as Phoebe came back into the room. "Phoebe? *Was tun sie hier?*"

Phoebe stopped short at the sight of Rachel's mother.

"Phoebe?" Mamma said again.

Rachel watched their friend struggle with the dilemma this presented. Phoebe couldn't lie, of course. The Amish spoke only the truth, no matter the cost.

"So much fuss about the strangers, *ja?*" Phoebe didn't quite look at either Rachel or her mother. "I wanted to see for myself and also make certain Rachel was all right."

That much was true, Rachel knew.

Susan Kanagy studied her friend. "But I told you about the strangers at the wedding, not so? And I explained why Rachel wasn't there."

Clearly flustered, Phoebe looked from Mamma to Rachel and then at the floor. When she lifted her gaze, there was no missing the apprehension that looked out on them. "I hadn't thought to tell a soul what I'm going to tell you. The less you know, the less likely it is to bring trouble to you. But I can see I can't keep this to myself any longer, not from you. Susan…Rachel…please, sit down and I'll explain."

Rachel exchanged worried looks with her mother as they sat down across from each other at the kitchen table. Phoebe seemed to be taking her time, collecting her thoughts before she finally spoke.

"I'm so sorry for your trouble, Rachel. It seems that these men you've taken in…mistook your house for ours." She stopped, pulled out a chair, and sat down.

"What do you mean? Our house is nothing like yours—"

Phoebe lifted a hand as if to indicate she would explain. "They were looking for a house with a candle burning in the window and a quilt on the line outside. They thought they'd found our place. You said you also had a candle in the window, Rachel, and a quilt—"

Rachel nodded. She leaned forward, intent now on hearing this story that was sounding more and more like a mystery. "But why would they be looking for *your* house?"

"Of all things to happen," Phoebe said, shaking her head. "I can hardly believe such a mix-up. It makes me wonder if it isn't God's will, this mistake they made."

"But who *are* they, these men?" Mamma pressed. "And as Rachel said, why would they be looking for *your* house? For that matter, why would they be looking for *any* house here among the Plain People?"

Again their friend indicated that they should wait while she went on. "This Captain Gant," she said, "and the man, Asa, belong to a group of people who help runaway slaves make their way to safe settlements where they can live free."

Rachel glanced at her mother, whose expression told her that Mamma was as bewildered as she.

"But what does that have to do with you? Or our people?" her mother said.

Phoebe pressed her lips together and met Mamma's gaze straight on. "I'm a part of that group, Susan. So are Malachi and Reuben."

Reuben was Phoebe's only boy still living at home. Their other two sons were married with young families.

"What do you mean?" Mamma pressed. "What kind of a group is this—surely not Plain folk?"

"No." Phoebe seemed to be considering how to explain. "There are people, not just here in Ohio, but in other states as well, who help to hide the runaway slaves until their guides can come and take them to the next safe place. It's like a—a kind of railroad. Some even call it an 'underground railroad.' Houses like ours are 'stations' along the way. People like this Captain Gant and his friend, Asa, are 'conductors' on that railroad."

She paused. "The people they came looking for—these people have been staying at our house, waiting for someone to take them on their way. They were waiting," she said, glancing from Rachel to her mother, "for this Captain Gant and his man, Asa."

7

EXTENDING GRACE

*Inasmuch ye have done it unto one of the
least of these my brethren, ye have done it unto me.*

MATTHEW 25:40

Rachel's mind fumbled to take in Phoebe's words. Mamma, however, seemed to grasp their significance in an instant. With her hands splayed so hard against the tabletop that her knuckles turned white, she leaned forward, staring at their friend.

"Phoebe, you know we're not to traffic with *auslanders*. We're to have nothing to do with outsiders and their world. This could get you in terrible trouble with the People. And with the *Englisch* law as well. You could be fined. You could go to *jail!*"

Incredibly, Phoebe gave a faint smile. "I daresay that's true, *ja*."

Mamma stared at her and then slumped back in her chair. "Why, then, would you do such a careless, foolish thing?"

Phoebe's gaze remained steady. "It's not a careless or foolish thing, dear friend. It's a work of the Lord God."

Mamma gasped and cautioned, "Careful what you say, Phoebe!"

"No man or woman was meant to be owned by another human being, Susan. No law can justify such a terrible thing. All God's people are meant to live in freedom, no matter the color of their skin." She paused. "I know you believe that too."

Rachel's mother spoke in a low tone. "What I believe is that you are doing a wrong thing, Phoebe. Against the law, is what it is. And against the *Ordnung* as well. You're bringing the things of the world into our community. You could face the *meidung* for this! Does Malachi know?"

Phoebe looked at her friend with a strange softening of her expression. "Susan—dear friend—better I should be shunned than go against the Lord God's will. And of course Malachi knows. I would never deceive my husband. We decided together that this is something our Lord would have us do."

Was it fear that glinted in Mamma's eyes now? "How do you *know*, Phoebe? How can you be so sure this is God's will? How can something so dangerous—something that goes against the rules by which we live—be approved by God?"

"Oh, Susan! Do you have any idea what these poor slaves must endure? The beatings, the torture, the humiliation they suffer? Working inhuman hours under conditions that sometimes kill them? Children torn from the arms of their parents, wives sold away from their husbands, women used and savaged by tyrants who treat them like animals—"

She stopped, reaching to grasp Mamma's hands in hers. "Think, Susan—think! The Plain People have undergone all manner of cruelty at the hands of others. Even now, here in America, we're not altogether free of ill treatment. Yet it's *nothing* compared to what the slave endures. What if it were us? Can you imagine what it would be like to live in such a way, to see our children live such a life? *Can* you?"

Rachel's mother looked down at her friend's hands clasping her own "I'm not saying it's a right thing, that people—any people—should have to suffer so." She raised her head to look at her friend. "But to live with secrets, Phoebe, secrets from our own people? That can't be right either, sure. And how, pray tell, have you managed to keep such a secret from the People? Aren't you frightened of being found out?"

When Phoebe finally spoke again, Rachel could almost hear the pain behind her words. Clearly this wasn't the first time their friend had wrestled with the question of right and wrong in her actions.

"Of course I'm frightened. I'm *always* frightened. We know there's every likelihood that we might be discovered at any time. Truth is, this is only the third time we've ventured our help. But even at the risk of discovery, we believe we *must* do this. Besides, you know our land. We're at the outer edge of the community and the woods nearby work to hide our house and the barn. Most everything is done at night, while our neighbors are asleep. So long as we stay very quiet..." She stopped and then went on, her voice low and not altogether steady. "Susan, this isn't an easy thing for me. I pray every day that I'm doing the Lord God's will. What I know is this: Many of these poor people will either die or live in torment if they're returned to their owners. They have no hope of ever knowing what it is to be free from such evil unless those of us who are already free are willing to help them."

She paused only a second or two. When she continued, her voice was stronger, her words firm. "I have to believe we're doing God's will, dear friend. But if you can't in good conscience keep our secret, I'll understand. You do what you must do."

Rachel could scarcely draw a breath as she watched her mother. Mamma seemed to be searching the very soul of her old friend.

Phoebe was the one to finally break the tension between them. She released Mamma's hands with a gentle pat and stood, saying, "Captain Gant's friend, Asa, and I must go now. He's going to take the people who have been hiding at my house on their way."

Rachel also stood, but it seemed to take Mamma forever to get to her feet.

Only when Phoebe came back from the bedroom and stood at the door with Asa and the large dark dog did Mamma finally speak again.

"Phoebe—"

The other turned. Rachel went very still, waiting.

"Your secret will travel no farther than this room."

Phoebe smiled and closed her eyes for an instant and then opened them. "You're a wonderful-*gut* friend, Susan."

Mamma shook her head. "Just…be careful. Please. Be very careful."

Clutching his cap in his hand, Asa looked from Rachel to her mother and dipped his head as if to apologize. "I wouldn't leave Captain Gant like this if I didn't have to. But he knows—we both know—that I must do this. I must help these people. It's why we came here."

"We'll take care of him." Surprised by her own words, Rachel stopped, looked at her mother and then pressed her lips together.

Mamma studied her long and hard before turning back to Asa and Phoebe. "*Ja*. He'll be safe here with us."

After they left, Rachel turned to her mother. "I'm sorry, Mamma."

Her mother gave her a quizzical look. "Sorry for what, daughter?"

"For all this," Rachel lifted her hands in a gesture of frustration. "For letting these strangers into my house, for drawing you into such trouble. For…everything."

"Well, it's done now," her mother said in her practical, let's-get-on-with-it tone of voice. "What's left to us is to work things out, to take care of this man as best we can. And to take care, as well, that we don't let slip our Phoebe's secret."

"I can't think what to do, though, Mamma. How can I keep a man—an outsider—here in my house, and me a widow?"

The look in her mother's eyes was a clear indication that she was already working on a solution to the problem. "We'll figure that out later. We need first to see to this—Captain Gant. Dr. Sebastian said he'll require a close watch and special care."

"I confess I don't quite know where to begin."

Her mother lifted an eyebrow. "We begin by giving him a bath. That man stinks of the river and—who knows what else?"

Rachel stared at her. "A *bath*? But, Mamma—"

"Yes, a bath. And don't look so shocked, daughter. You're not *maidal*. You were married. You know about men."

"But he's a stranger—an *auslander*."

Mamma was already rolling up her sleeves. "An outsider in bad need of a bath. Truth is, I'd hoped we could put Gideon in charge of this, but who knows where that boy is tonight?" She gave a shrug of annoyance. "Out with some of his *Englisch* friends, no doubt. Well, let's get to it. We're going to need plenty of hot water and soap. Did you keep any of Eli's clothes?"

"I—" Unwilling to part with the few items of her husband's clothing she still had, Rachel stumbled over her words. "This man…is too big for Eli's clothes. They wouldn't fit him."

She felt herself grow warm under her mother's studying gaze. "A nightshirt, Rachel," Mamma said, her words gentle. "That's all we need. A nightshirt would surely fit."

Rachel almost refused. She wanted to refuse. But a sense of her own pettiness struck her, and she finally nodded. "I'll find something," she said, hurrying from the room.

→ ←

A good hour later, Rachel stood on the opposite side of the bed, watching as Mamma turned Gant on his side, keeping the sheet pulled discreetly above his waist.

Suddenly her mother gasped, staring at the wounded stranger's back with an expression akin to horror.

"Mamma? *Was ist letz?*"

"*Komm!*" Her mother beckoned for her to come and look.

Rachel crossed to the other side of the bed, watching Mamma and then turning her gaze to Gant, who stirred but didn't wake.

Mamma clasped Rachel's hand in hers as they stood staring at the riverboat captain's bare back. A map of deep, angry scars crisscrossed his skin, seared for all time against his flesh and bone.

Rachel blanched. "What—would have caused this?"

"This man has been whipped," Mamma said tightly, still clutching Rachel's hand. "Whipped like a beast, he was."

"Who would have done such a thing?" Rachel whispered.

Mamma shook her head. "Only the Lord God knows."

"I'll get some salve—"

"There's no point," her mother said. "Those are old scars, already healed."

She expelled a breath, saying, "Let's finish his bathing and give him some peace. He's getting restless."

As if in reply, the stranger groaned, arched his back, and then let out a sharp cry as if the movement had been too much for him.

Painful as it was to see, Rachel could scarcely take her eyes off the scars. She couldn't imagine what pain this man must have endured with each lash of the whip that had sliced his skin.

When they were finished, she smoothed a quilt around the sleeping man's shoulders, trying not to mind too much that her dear Eli's nightshirt now clad another man's body. Clothing was meant to be worn, after all, not packed away. And Rachel had a certain sense that Eli would have approved of the disposition of his nightshirt.

Now that the ordeal was over, she actually felt a small satisfaction at the difference their attentions had made. The stranger did look more comfortable—and there was no denying that he smelled considerably better.

Her satisfaction was quickly replaced, however, by a disconcerting awareness that in spite of the scars they'd discovered, their efforts had also served to reveal an unexpectedly handsome man in his prime. Long-limbed and hard-muscled, this was a man who, even in his weakness, gave off an unmistakable power. His raven hair, though randomly laced with silver, was glossy and thick, his features rugged but strong-boned and well-set. And that heavy mustache—forbidden to Amish men—gave him a strange appeal that Rachel found difficult to ignore.

The entire time she was helping to bathe him, she had been uneasily mindful of how long it had been since she had touched, or been touched by, a man. Truth was she'd missed the warmth of Eli's touch, the comfort of his arms, ever so much—had missed him to the point of weakness at times. The intimate act of caring for the riverboat captain had evoked old, all but forgotten feelings and the same aching, sick emptiness she had felt during the first months after Eli's death. More than once she had to clench her jaw and deliberately will those feelings of longing and loneliness away.

But almost as troubling as those forbidden emotions was the unexpected wave of something near to pity that came washing over her at the sight of a man who must have once been able-bodied and fit. He now lay weak and helpless as a babe—badly scarred by a vicious whip—and nearly destroyed by a bullet meant for another.

Greater love hath no man than this...

Her mother's voice jerked her back to their surroundings. "It's fortunate he slept through most of his bath." Mamma's tone was wry. "Big as he is, he could have given us a scuffle."

Rachel nodded. Gant *had* attempted a feeble protest at first, but so weak was he that he lapsed almost immediately into the same deep sleep from which their efforts had first roused him.

"From what you told me," her mother said, "the man was nearly dead when he showed up at your door. This sleep is the body's way of closing his mind to the pain so healing can take place. David—Dr. Sebastian—says it's a healing sleep now, not a dying kind."

Rachel didn't miss her mother's use of Dr. Sebastian's given name. But then that shouldn't surprise her. Titles such as "Mr." and "Mrs." weren't used among the People. Given names, even nicknames, were common.

Besides, the doctor and her mother had known each other for years. He had long ago begun calling Mamma by her first name, and it was probably a natural thing that she would call him by his. Even so, was there a chance her mother might return, even unknowingly, the interest Dr. Sebastian so obviously felt toward her?

She hoped not, though she wished things might have been different. As it was, however, a shared affection could mean only heartache for both of them. Rachel deeply admired and trusted Dr. David Sebastian, but a Plain woman and an *Englisch* man had no hope of a future together. Even a friendship between the two could mean trouble, and a romantic relationship could bring shunning upon an Amish woman. She could never bear to see her mother hurt in such a terrible way

"Rachel? Did you hear me?"

Her mother's voice snapped her out of her troubled thoughts. "I'm sorry, Mamma."

"I said we'd best empty the man's suitcase." She pointed to the big leather bag on the floor near the chair. "Whatever belongings he may have in there will probably be soaked—perhaps already ruined. Why don't you set everything out to dry? We'll salvage what we can for him. You do that while I clean up here and put away his bath things."

Rachel took Gant's valise to the extra room Eli had built onto the back of the house, the room she thought of as her "workshop," where she made her birdhouses and kept her supplies. Carefully she took the articles from the bag, placing them one by one on the work table. There wasn't much to retrieve. A small pouch with a clasp that held some bills and coin. Apparently the pouch had protected the money to some extent, for it was damp but not ruined.

A sodden envelope revealed a sheaf of wet papers, on which the ink had run and smeared so badly she feared they were beyond saving. Still Rachel pressed them out on the table to let them dry. The discovery of a small Bible heartened her, though it appeared to be nearly ruined by water damage. Still, it might be an indiction that the wounded stranger was a Christian man—reassuring since they would be much together in the days to come.

There were two shirts and a pair of trousers, all soaked through, as were the few other small articles of clothing. But these she could launder, and they'd probably be good as new.

At the bottom was something that felt hard. It seemed to take up a lot of room, and Rachel had to tug at it before she finally pulled it free. It was a case—a case with a strange shape. She opened it, and when she saw what it was, she gasped in surprise.

A fiddle! Gideon's *Englisch* friend, Orson Newley had one of these. It made music. Rachel had come upon her brother and Orson in Mamma's barn once, drawn by the wailing, rasping noise. Under Orson's hands, it sounded more like a screech owl than music, but every once in a while he managed to coax some pleasant sounds from it.

Had the water damaged this one beyond repair, or had the case kept it dry enough to protect it from ruin? She ran her hands over it and found that, although it felt damp, when she turned it over to let any water drain out of the opening, nothing spilled out on the table. Carefully she shook it, turned it over, and then again, shook it several times. Then she took a dry towel to it, just for good measure. Perhaps it would be all right after all.

For some reason she found it hard to imagine the big, hard-looking man having a liking for music. But then how was she to know what he liked or didn't like? He was a stranger, after all.

The only other item was an oval tin, smaller than the palm of her hand. Running her index finger over it, she found a small clasp that, when unlatched, opened onto a photograph.

Rachel stared at the image, trying not to be fascinated by it. Photographs were forbidden to the Plain People, not only because of Scripture's admonition against graven images, but because they also violated their desire for privacy and humility. But the loveliness of the face so captured her interest that she couldn't resist studying it, *verboten* though it was. The young woman, who looked out at her with just a hint of a smile, appeared worldly and somewhat exotic, so dark were her eyes and the heavy mane of hair that partly hid one side of her face.

Rachel stood staring at the photograph for a long time. Was this the riverboat captain's wife? His sweetheart? She must be very special to him, that he carried her likeness on his journeys. And she was ever so beautiful…

An unpleasant and unidentifiable sensation stung Rachel and then flitted away. As if the tintype had suddenly turned hot in her hand, she dropped it on the table. But after a second or two, she picked it up again and dried it off on her apron as best she could before laying it down among the other things.

Everything should be dry by tomorrow, except perhaps for the Bible, the wet papers, and the envelope. She would put the money and the photograph away in a chest of drawers, where they would be safe for the time being.

When she returned to the bedroom, her mother had already cleared away the bath items and gone to the kitchen. As Rachel's gaze lighted on the sleeping stranger, her mind again went to the tintype she'd found in his belongings. After another moment though, she shook off the dark-eyed image in the photograph and turned to leave the room, her thoughts crowded with unsettling questions and a sense of impatience with herself for caring enough to wonder about this stranger, this Jeremiah Gant.

8

FAMILY BLESSINGS

*A home by love and family blessed
is peace on earth and joy expressed.*

ANONYMOUS

By the time Mamma left for home that evening, she and Rachel had worked out a tentative plan they hoped would forestall—at least temporarily—any fuss from the bishop and Samuel.

In order that Rachel would seldom be alone with the wounded stranger, Gideon and Fannie would take turns staying nights at her house, with Fannie spending a large part of the days there as well. Mamma would also maintain a frequent presence until Gant was well enough to be on his way.

During this time Rachel would take over the part of Fannie's lessons that Mamma usually supervised. Like many of the other Plain children, Fannie was schooled at home. While some Amish families did allow their *kinner* to attend the *Englisch* school in town, most parents preferred to teach their children at home. They believed it lessened the danger of worldly influences and the possibility of turning their minds and hearts away from their Plain upbringing.

The People considered it a fundamental right to raise and educate their children in their own culture, according to their customs and beliefs. They hoped some day to have their own school, but in the meantime, those who were unwilling to avail themselves of the nearby *Englisch* school made do with home instruction.

There had been talk, however, of problems with government interference. Rachel hoped there wouldn't be trouble. And so far, perhaps because Riverhaven was such a small, somewhat isolated community, no attempts had been made to force public education on them.

Rachel wondered just how cooperative Gideon would be about spending nights at his sister's house. He was used to staying out late—sometimes, Mamma fretted, until the wee hours of the morning. When Rachel voiced her doubts to her mother though, Mamma simply pressed her lips together and said that in this instance her *bruder* would have to consider the needs of his family before his own. His *rumspringa* goings-on could wait.

Easier said than done, perhaps...

Fannie spent the night. By the time she got up the next morning, Rachel had already milked the two cows, Ginger and Rosie, and started breakfast. As soon as they finished eating, she sent Fannie home to collect her lesson books and other things she might need. "When you come back, you can feed the chickens and gather the eggs."

"I'll hurry, Rachel! Promise you won't do it while I'm gone?"

"I'll wait for you. But you take time to do anything Mamma might need help with. And stay and talk with her a few minutes. Mamma gets lonely if she's by herself too long, you know."

Fannie nodded. "It's my job to keep you both company as best as I can," Fannie said, not prideful, but serious as could be. "I won't shirk Mamma. You needn't worry."

Rachel smiled. "I know you won't. And see that Gideon comes over right away, before he goes to work."

Her brother was employed by the *Englischer* Karl Webber at his carpenter shop in Riverhaven. To give him his due, Gideon was a hard worker. When he wasn't at the shop, he worked the family farm and helped Rachel at her place too. He had also agreed to stop by mornings and nights to help the outsider with his personal tasks. Truth was, Rachel didn't know what she would do without Gideon, especially now.

She watched Fannie cross the quarter-mile field that lay between her own house and Mamma's. Back inside, she went to pull the curtain away just enough to peek in on Gant and make sure he was all right.

He was still sleeping, but restlessly, it seemed. He kept turning his head from side to side, making a low rasping sound in his throat as he did. She tiptoed into the room and cautiously put a hand to his forehead. He was still cool. The fever had stayed down through the night.

And then without warning, his eyes shot open. Rachel gasped and jerked her hand away. Even in the gloom of early morning, his look was startled—wild and almost panicky.

He tried to raise himself partway, but the very effort caused him to go white and fall back onto the pillows. His eyes closed for an instant and then opened again. Then, as if he suddenly remembered where he was and what had happened, his gaze cleared.

He made Rachel think of a hawk. Those searching eyes, looking out over a prominently bridged nose, put the bluest of blue to shame, yet held a dark and piercing aspect.

"Asa…" he finally said.

"He left last night. He and your dog. They went with Phoebe."

A questioning look crossed his face and then faded. "Your friend. Her house—that was where we were *supposed* to go."

"That's right. Do you remember Phoebe being here and talking with you and Asa last night?"

He attempted a nod with what seemed a great effort.

"I'm sure Phoebe will stop by again sometime today. You can talk to her then. And Gideon, my *bruder*. He's going to help you—" She broke off. "Dr. Sebastian will be here later too. He'll be glad to see you're awake."

It occurred to Rachel that she was rambling. Talking too much, she was. He watched her as she spoke, and the way his gaze went over her face made her uncomfortable. Immediately she glanced away.

"What's your name?" His voice was thin, little more than a whisper.

She looked back at him. "I'm Rachel. Eli Rachel."

He frowned. Probably her use of Eli's name with her own had confused him. An *Englischer* wouldn't understand that. Because so many of the Plain People had the same first name, women often combined their husband's first name with their own. As for the men, they were frequently identified by such names as "Young Jacob" or "Old Jacob" or even by a kind of nickname name related to appearance or trade— "Tall Noah" or "Carpenter John."

"Rachel Brenneman," she clarified.

"Rachel…" He stopped, as if trying to catch a breath. "Thank you."

Rachel waved off his thanks. The Amish had no use for words such as "thank you." Helping one's fellow man was simply expected. Besides, what did he think, that she would turn him away with him near to death?

But in her fear, hadn't that been her first thought—to turn him away?

"So, then, who might Eli be?"

"What?"

He was smiling a little. Not a taunting smile, but an open, curious one.

"Eli is—was—my husband. He's gone now. Eli is…dead."

"I'm sorry," he said, looking as if he meant it. "That's a hard thing for you, Rachel Brenneman."

The man had a strange lilt to his speech, a rhythmic way of talking that was completely strange to Rachel, like music spilling off his tongue.

"I—I'll go and make you some breakfast," she said, hurrying from the room before he could say anything more.

→ ←

As soon as she reached the kitchen, Rachel realized she had no idea what to feed the *Englischer*. She wished she'd thought to ask Dr. Sebastian the day before what he might have.

Well, he had to eat *something*. She set about heating water for tea and decided to cook some thin oatmeal.

She drew a sigh of relief when Gideon showed up. Rachel immediately hustled him off to the bedroom to see to Gant's needs. In the meantime, she added a spoonful of molasses to the oatmeal and sliced off a small piece of bread. She set the oatmeal and bread on the wooden tray Eli had made for her and waited for the tea.

A few minutes later, her brother walked into the kitchen. "You can go in now," he said, starting for the door. "I have to go. Mamma has a list of things she wants done before I leave for work. I'll be back tonight, though."

When Rachel carried the food into the bedroom, she found that Gideon had elevated Gant's head slightly with another pillow. He still looked awfully pale, but brighter-eyed than earlier.

He cast a dubious look at the food Rachel placed beside him on the bed.

"I don't know if I'm…ready for that just yet," he said.

Rachel saw that his hands were trembling. Peculiar, it seemed, to see such a big man in such a weak state.

"You have to eat, Captain Gant."

She tried her best to sound matter-of-fact like her mother when she was being kind but meant to tolerate no opposition. "I'll help you."

Without meeting his eyes—though she felt his gaze hard upon her—Rachel tucked a freshly laundered napkin about his neck and then sat down on the side of the bed to feed him. "So you met my brother, *ja?*"

"Gideon, aye. He seems a good lad."

Rachel had to steel herself to keep her own hands from shaking as she spooned the oatmeal to his mouth and helped him with the tea.

"Oh, Gideon will be fine, once he gets his running-around foolishness out of his system and settles down to be responsible."

"Running around?"

Rachel nodded but didn't explain about the *rumspringa*. This *Eng-lisch* stranger would have no interest in the Plain way of doing things. Besides, she wasn't all that comfortable carrying on a conversation with him. She knew little of his kind and their worldly ways and had no desire to encourage contact with him beyond aiding in his recovery. The sooner he recuperated, the sooner he would be out of her house. And her life.

She almost sighed in anticipation of returning to normal, to the life she had known that was quiet and content and safe.

"I expect I've caused a bit of trouble for you." Gant's words snapped Rachel out of her musing. She looked at him, uncertain as to how to reply.

"I don't know much about Amish ways," he said, "but I do know you like to keep to yourselves, that you have little use for the outside world. Or its people."

Making no reply, Rachel lifted another spoon of oatmeal toward him, but he shook his head. "No more, " he said. His voice had weakened and turned hoarse. "Another sip of tea, though, if you would.

"That's fine tea," he said after swallowing. "In any case, Rachel Brenneman, I apologize for the intrusion."

"I suppose—it couldn't be helped," Rachel said, awkward in the face of both the compliment and the apology.

She offered him another drink of tea, but he lifted a hand in a limp gesture and then closed his eyes.

Rachel could see him fading. In another moment he was asleep. She stood, carefully removing the napkin from about his neck and taking the wooden tray with his dishes from the room.

Just as she reached the kitchen, Fannie opened the door, came bounding in, and plopped her books and papers on the table. Rachel put a finger to her lips to warn her to be quiet and then went to close the curtain between them and the bedroom.

"Is the *Englischer* still alive?" Fannie whispered.

"Yes, but he's very weak. He's sleeping now, so we'll have to work quietly on your lessons. Keep your coat, though. I'll get mine, and we'll go feed the chickens and gather the eggs before we start with your books."

Rachel didn't share her little sister's sense of fun when it came to taking care of the chickens. Truth was, if she didn't use so many eggs for cooking and baking, she would have been only too happy to get rid of the smelly, noisy creatures. The chicken house never failed to make her sneeze, and their squawking and cackling always made her think of demanding, quarrelsome old women.

She had kept only the two cows and a few hens after Eli died. Mamma insisted—and it was so—that the family farm provided far more in the way of produce and crops than they needed, and so they freely shared with her. Because Rachel had no great love for farming— and because the leaders of their community frowned upon women doing men's work—she managed just fine by keeping a modest garden, a few chickens, and the two cows. She also garnered a small income by selling her baked goods and cheese to the Riverhaven Market.

In addition, Rachel's custom-made birdhouses had sparked a real enthusiasm in Denley Snider, the proprietor of a general store in Marietta. He and Rachel had an arrangement whereby she agreed to furnish him at least four houses a month. Apparently a number of the ladies in town were the main buyers.

Rachel thoroughly enjoyed making the birdhouses, giving each one at least a slightly different design. Not only did she relish the process itself, but it helped her to maintain a kind of closeness with Eli. He was the one who had taught her how to build the birdhouses in the first place. She used the tools that had belonged to him, followed the instructions as he had directed, and all but felt his guiding touch on her arm as she worked.

Of course not everyone was as enthusiastic about her handiwork as Mr. Snider. Bishop Graber and Samuel, too, had discussed the matter with her as soon as they got wind of her growing business. But Rachel stood her ground, insisting that it was only right for her to make *some* contribution to the family income, given how much her mother and Gideon did for her. Finally, with Gideon agreeing to take her birdhouses into Marietta each month, thus sparing Rachel any unseemly contact with a worldly male businessman, the bishop had relented, and Samuel grudgingly followed suit.

Only Rachel and her mother knew that Gideon had been the one responsible for the birdhouses coming to Mr. Snider's attention in the first place. Her brother had coaxed Rachel into giving him one of the little houses to give to a girl—an *Englisch* girl—he'd been seeing at the time. The girl happened to be Mr. Snider's niece, and after seeing this example of Rachel's workmanship, he'd driven out to talk with her, placing his first "order" that same day.

Watching Fannie laugh as the chickens scattered and chased after their breakfast, Rachel smiled a little at the thought that her brother's foray into the outside world had actually brought a blessing her way. At least it seemed a blessing to *her*.

Far more important than the payment she received for the birdhouses or even the enjoyment of the craft was the way it helped to keep Eli's memory close. He had been a master craftsman, Eli had. She turned and glanced back at the house, her heart warming even as it ached at the sight of the home her husband had built for them before their marriage, with help from the other men in the community.

And it was a fine house too. Rachel was careful to avoid forbidden pride, but there was no denying the stamp of excellence on any work from Eli's hand. Their home was no exception. He had built it with love and careful attention to detail.

"My gift to you, my Rachel," he had whispered to her when she praised his efforts upon completion.

After Eli's death, Rachel had been urged by her friends and her mother, as well, to sell the house and move back to the family home. Mamma, especially, didn't like her living alone and saw no reason for it. But Rachel couldn't bring herself to leave the place where she had found the deepest happiness of her life. She would never leave her home, not unless the Lord God Himself beckoned her away.

She drew a shaky breath, fighting to hold back the familiar pall of loneliness and heart pain that sometimes accompanied her memories. Leaving Fannie to gather the eggs, she went back inside.

An hour or so later, Fannie, who had been standing at the kitchen window while waiting for Rachel to check her arithmetic lesson, turned around. "Someone's coming, Rachel! I think it's Deacon Samuel."

Rachel looked up, pressing the tip of the pencil on the paper hard enough that it broke. "Are you sure?"

"Uh-huh. That's who it is, all right. Deacon Samuel. Want me to go and sit with the *Englischer* while you visit?"

"No!" Rachel hadn't meant to snap, but the last thing she wanted was to be alone with Samuel right now. She was going to be chastised, for sure and for certain. She'd known it was coming but had hoped to avoid it as long as possible.

"Captain Gant is still asleep, Fannie. You can stay right here in the kitchen with us. I'm sure Samuel won't be staying long at this time of day."

Fannie came to stand beside her at the table, her brown eyes watchful. "Do you like him a lot, Deacon Samuel?"

Rachel stood and walked to the window, avoiding Fannie's scrutinizing gaze. Sometimes her little sister seemed too old for her nine years. "Of course, I…like him. He's an old friend."

"But do you like him *more* than as a friend? Like he does you?"

Rachel whipped around. "What?"

"Are you going to marry him?"

"*Marry* him? Samuel? No! Why would you even ask such a thing?"

Fannie shrugged. "Everyone thinks you're going to. Even Mamma says you might. Some day."

"I don't know who 'everyone' is, sister, but they don't know what they're talking about. I'm not thinking of marrying *anyone.*" Rachel paused. "Mamma said that? That I might marry Samuel?"

"I heard her tell friend Phoebe."

"It's rude to listen in on other people's conversations, Fannie." Rachel waited another second and then added, "What exactly did Mamma tell Phoebe?"

Again her sister gave a little shrug. "Just that Deacon Samuel would like to court you, but you weren't ready to let him yet. But maybe some day he'd win you over and you'd get married. Will you?"

"Not likely," Rachel said, irritated. "And I wish folks wouldn't go speculating about what I might or might not do."

"Mamma didn't mean anything. She just worries about you being alone."

Rachel sighed, regretting her sharpness. "I know she does. But she needn't. I'm fine."

At the knock on the door, Rachel secured her *kapp* a little more snugly on her head, only too aware that today she would be facing *Deacon* Samuel rather than her old friend Samuel.

A Deacon Comes Calling

A sick man helped by thee shall make thee strong;
Thou shalt be served thyself by every sense
Of service which thou renderest.

Elizabeth Barrett Browning

Rachel held her breath as she opened the door, trying for a pleasant expression, even though she sensed this would be no friendly social call.

"Samuel. This is an early visit for you."

He stood straight, his gaze studying, his broad-brimmed hat framing his sand-colored hair and strongly molded features. At first glance his expression was stern. But when Rachel offered a smile of greeting, he seemed to soften and finally met her smile with one of his own.

"You have time for a visit, then, do you, Rachel?"

"Of course. Come in out of the cold." Rachel stepped aside so he could enter. "Here, I'll hang up your coat."

But Samuel went to hang it up himself, hitching it on the wall peg beside the door before removing his hat and hooking it over his coat.

He then nodded at Fannie, who sat at the table watching him and Rachel with interest.

"Would you like a cup of tea, Samuel?"

Samuel disliked coffee, but like the *Englischer*, seemed partial to Rachel's tea.

He shook his head, standing in the middle of the kitchen, looking big and awkward as though he wasn't sure why he'd come. But after another second or two, his expression cleared and returned to the sober, dignified set he'd been wearing when Rachel first opened the door.

Deacon Beiler had returned.

In that instant Rachel changed her mind about having Fannie stay in the room. "Sister, why don't you go up to the bedroom and work on your lessons? I'll help you with them later."

Fannie stuck out her lower lip in the beginning of a pout but did as she was told.

Rachel waited until her sister had left the room and then indicated that Samuel should sit down.

Instead, he remained standing. "Where is he—the *Englischer*?" he said, looking around the room. He spoke to her in the *Deitsch* of the People, as he almost always did.

Rachel glanced toward the closed curtain. "In there," she said softly.

"In your bedroom, Rachel?"

Rachel felt the heat sear her face but refused to wither under his probing gaze. "My *extra* bedroom."

"I want to see him."

"He's sleeping, Samuel. He sleeps almost all the time."

He studied her. "What have you done, Rachel?"

The rebuke in his gaze and his voice could not have been clearer. Rachel suddenly felt like a disobedient child, but she refused to be quelled by Samuel's disapproval.

"What have I done?" she echoed. "I took in a dying stranger and gave him shelter and what medical care I could, Samuel. What would *you* have done?"

He blinked, and a small muscle beside one eye twitched, as if Rachel's reply had surprised him.

But Samuel, being Samuel, recovered quickly. "From what I've been told, the man will live, not die."

"That would seem to be true, thanks to Mamma and Dr. Sebastian."

Some rebellious strain in Rachel made her refuse to speak the

Deitsch with him. To her shame, she realized her stubbornness was partly due to the fact that it would put Samuel at a disadvantage. Even though the Plain People learned English in their childhood, his command of their language wasn't as good as hers.

Rachel had deliberately studied the English language until she became fluent in it. From childhood she had wanted the ability to communicate with those outside the Amish community as well as with her own people and had taken the necessary steps to become as comfortable with their second language as the *Deitsch.*

Samuel looked annoyed but did his best to match her English with his own. "You had the doctor for him?"

"Well, of course, we had the doctor. The man had been shot. He was unconscious. Dying, we thought. Mamma and I did everything we knew to do, but there wasn't much we *could* do. The *Englischer* would almost certainly have died if Dr. Sebastian hadn't seen to him."

His mouth hardened still more. "So you let two worldly outsiders into your home, and you a woman alone."

"Dr. Sebastian has been doctoring our people for years, Samuel. He's delivered our babies and watched over the dying. You know him as well as you know your neighbors." She paused. "And there were three men, not two."

Rachel was just impatient enough with him by now to be reckless. "You seem to know everything else that's happened. Didn't you also hear that Captain Gant was accompanied by his friend—a man of color?"

His mouth thinned still more, and he lapsed back into the language of their people. "Oh, I heard, Rachel. Hard as it is for me to believe you would be so foolish, I see now that what I heard was true."

"What should I have done, Samuel? Let a man die on my doorstep? Keep him and his companion standing out in the middle of the night in a rainstorm?"

"You could have sent for help."

"I *did* send for help! Fannie went for Gideon and Mamma right away, and we also sent for Dr. Sebastian. But I couldn't leave a wounded man outside my front door to die before the doctor even got here, could I?"

For a moment he seemed confused, uncertain as to how to respond. But Samuel was never without words for long. "No, I suppose not. You have a good and kindly heart, Rachel. But now what? Now that these men have brought the world into your home, how do you plan to manage? You're a woman alone—a widow with no husband to protect you, no children, no one to help with this outsider's care—"

He broke off but only for an instant. "And do you even know how—or why—this man was shot, Rachel? He may be a criminal, a deceitful man. You've put yourself at great risk, perhaps endangered your friends and neighbors as well."

The silence in the room hung heavy between them. Rachel felt anger flame up in her. Anger because Samuel had so little regard for her common sense and ability to manage and assumed he had the right to rebuke her for doing the only thing she'd known to do, the only thing that seemed right at the time.

And yet, he *did* have the right to question her actions. He was one of the leaders of their community. He was also a friend, and in spite of all the little things about Samuel that tended to annoy her, Rachel didn't begin to doubt his concern for her well-being and safety. Besides, the anger that had risen toward him was wrong, and she already regretted allowing it any place in her emotions.

If only he would sit down at the table and talk to her as a friend instead of a deacon—or an adversary. But even if he did, how could she hope to convince him that the wounded stranger in her house wasn't putting her at risk? She had to believe Gant *wasn't* a threat. Would a dangerous man—a bad man—endanger himself by helping slaves escape to freedom? And would such a man pose a threat to a harmless woman? She had to believe that turning him away would have been the real sin, not the breaking of a rule or an ordinance.

Yet the only way she could hope to convince Samuel of this would require that she reveal Gant's efforts to help the slaves and, at the same time, expose her friend Phoebe's secret activities. She couldn't do that. Mamma had promised Phoebe that her secret would be safe with them. Not for anything would Rachel go against her mother's pledge to their mutual friend.

It seemed she would have to let Samuel think what he pleased. She turned away from him and went to the sink to pump water for rinsing the dishes she'd washed earlier.

As she worked she spoke, thinking it better not to face him with her impatience and irritation. "You needn't worry about my being alone here with the stranger, Samuel. Gideon and Fannie are going to take turns staying the night as long as necessary, and Fannie will be spending most of her days with me as well. Mamma will also be helping out with his care."

He waited to reply. "It's not seemly that you should be caring for him at all. A woman's care should be all for her husband."

Rachel couldn't help herself. She whirled around, splashing water down her front and onto the floor from the dishcloth. "I *have* no husband to care for! And I'm not a blushing *maedal* who knows nothing of men. I'm a widow woman fully capable of looking to the needs of a wounded man who has no one else to depend on."

She tried to steady herself, but she was so angry—*too* angry. "If you're so concerned about any impropriety, Samuel, why don't *you* take in Captain Gant? I'm sure we can arrange to have him moved to your home by this evening. And I can give you Dr. Sebastian's instructions for taking care of the wound. You can take a few days out of the fields and your other business doings, can't you? Or if you don't want the extra work and can't find the time necessary to tend to a wounded stranger night and day, perhaps the bishop would take him in. Or what about one of the other families—perhaps the Glicks or the Lambrights?"

She should stop. She was going too far. But she wasn't finished yet. She would say her piece, never mind the consequences. "You can tell the bishop or anyone else who's bothered by my tending to a wounded man in my home that I can have his few belongings packed in a matter of minutes—sooner than they can have a bed made ready for him in *their* home! I'd be only too glad to be relieved of the responsibility!"

Her outburst had clearly shocked him. His eyes widened, and the brackets around his mouth tightened. "Rachel—"

"Samuel, I'm sorry, but the day's getting on, and I have to help Fannie with her lessons. I think it would be best if you'd leave now."

She didn't trust herself to say anything more.

"I didn't intend to upset you, Rachel."

"Nevertheless, you have."

He started toward her, but Rachel was firm. "I don't want to argue with you, Samuel. I know you mean only what's best for me. But I'm a grown woman, and *I* have to be the one who decides what that is.

He crossed his arms over his chest. "Eli was too lenient with you, I think. We all knew he was giving you too much free rein."

For an instant—a sharp, stinging instant—Rachel had a wicked urge to throw the sopping wet dishcloth at him. So shocked was she at her own impulse that her anger died in a heartbeat, and she managed to answer him in an even tone of voice. "Eli was good to me, gentle and kind, if that's what you mean."

What kind of husband had Samuel *been?*

His wife, Martha, had died giving birth to their third son a few years past, even before Eli's death. Martha Beiler had always seemed the perfect Amish wife—quiet, agreeable, respectful, and quick to serve others. Had she been happy with Samuel? Had he tried to *make* her happy?

Not for the first time, Rachel recognized the truth about herself: Even if she could eventually grow to love Samuel, she could never be the kind of wife he'd want her to be, the kind of wife he would no doubt *expect* her to be. She wasn't like Martha Beiler, yet she suspected Samuel would try to *make* her more like Martha.

"*Ja,* Eli was a good man, and good to you. But you have a way about you, Rachel. You're headstrong, stubborn, and full of opinions. And apparently Eli did little to correct these faults."

Again Rachel lifted a hand to silence him. "Samuel, I'll not listen to you speak against Eli in his own house."

"*Your* house, Rachel. Eli is gone. And this latest—situation—only proves what I've suggested to you before, that you need to seriously consider marrying again. It's not good for a woman to be alone. You need the protection and guidance of a husband."

Rachel clamped her teeth together but managed to smile, weak though it was. "As I said, Samuel, I think you should leave now. I have much work to do yet today, and I'm sure you do as well."

Rachel figured the long breath he pulled in was exaggerated for her benefit. He studied her for another moment, then lifted his hands in a gesture of resignation. "All right, then, I'll go. But you haven't heard the end of this. And I'll be stopping by often to see that you're all right."

Rachel didn't doubt him for a minute. She was quite sure she *hadn't* heard the end of this, and she was just as certain that Samuel would be stopping by often.

She drew a long breath of her own and saw him to the door.

Gant wished he were stronger. A great deal stronger. Strong enough to leave this bed and face that stiff-necked Amishman.

What kind of a man talked to a woman so? Especially a woman who seemed as gentle-natured as this Rachel Brenneman.

Though he had to hand it to her, she'd stood up to him well enough.

From what he could tell, which wasn't all that much since they'd been speaking in that foreign tongue of theirs part of the time, the man was some kind of an important fellow in the Amish community, a deacon in the church or some such. Even so, he ought to keep a civil tongue in his head and not take on as though the woman had committed some sort of black-hearted sin.

Is this how the Amish treated their women? Giving them what-to for helping a body in need? Talking down to her as though she hadn't all her wits about her, as if she were some sort of a troublesome wee child?

In truth she *did* seem little more than a girl, though she'd said she was a widow. That being the case, she must be older than she looked.

He'd been tempted to give a shout to the man from his bed and shame him where he stood. But he sensed the woman wouldn't thank him for interfering. And when it came right down to it, it *wasn't* any of his business, not a bit of it. What was it the Amishman had called him? An "outsider"? Well, there was no denying that's what he was.

Besides, he hadn't the grit just now for a match with anyone. He was as weak as a cat that just crawled up on the riverbank.

He almost smiled at the thought. Wasn't that exactly what he'd done—crawled up on the riverbank? And even that had required Asa's help.

He ground his teeth in frustration. What a fix this was! His boat gone. His leg shattered. People waiting on him hand and foot. Asa left to manage by himself. Completely useless, that's what he was. No good for anything or to anyone. Nothing but trouble for the young Amish widow and her family.

He'd never been in such a state before, had never had to depend on anyone but himself. Now he needed tending like a helpless babe. His insides burned with humiliation.

Meanwhile, Asa was off on his own, jeopardizing himself without anyone to watch his back. They worked as a pair, and they'd done well. So far they hadn't lost a single "passenger." Not a one of them.

He should have known their luck wouldn't hold forever.

Luck? His conscience prodded him. Hardly luck, given some of the scrapes they'd gotten in and out of. Nothing or no one but the Almighty could have saved their necks as many times as they'd needed saving. Ah, no, he doubted that luck had anything to do with it.

He would talk to that doctor next time he came round. He had to know just how long he'd be laid up like this—and what he could do to hurry things up. He'd lose his mind if this went on too long.

No doubt the pretty widow shared his frustration. This had to be a hard thing for an Amish woman, having a stranger in her house with no man but a brother to help out.

He'd spent a couple of days near another Amish settlement last year, up in Pennsylvania. There hadn't been time to get to know the people all that well, but there was no mistaking their eagerness to see him gone. They'd been godly folks and given him the supplies he needed willingly enough. But they'd made it clear he wasn't welcome. They made him feel as if they feared his very presence might taint them.

His last thought before drifting back to sleep again was that this Rachel Brenneman seemed skittish around him all right, but at least she didn't treat him like he was some kind of a devil.

Though perhaps to her and her kind that's exactly what he seemed to be.

ASA

Watch not the ashes of the dying ember.
Kindle thy hope. Put all thy fears away—
Live day by day.

JULIA HARRIS MAY

*I*t wasn't like he hadn't worked alone before. He had taken other runaways to the North twice before without the captain. But those other
times, there had been one or two men among the passengers. Had he
known that this time he would be transporting only two women and three
little girls, he would have been even more worried than he was.

The abolitionist doctor at Marietta, who provided the wagon and
a draft horse, had sent them on their way with blankets, enough
food for several days, and a stern warning about what they might
face. "You're going to be traveling through woods filled with wild
animals—including wolves and bobcats. But your worst enemies will
be the bounty hunters. They're thick in this area, hoping to collect the
reward for runaways. Have you used this route before?"

"No, sir. But the captain has. I have a map, and he gave me good
instruction as to what to expect."

"Yes, well, don't get careless. There are always surprises."

What Asa didn't say was that the doctor was one of the biggest
surprises of all. He'd come across all manner of folks on other routes.
Some were kind, others stern and harried, though helpful. But the
doctor was a different sort from all the others.

A number of the people who helped them in various places were
clearly nervous, even frightened. Some seemed so fearful it was a

wonder they were willing to help at all. But the good doctor, if he had any misgivings about what he was doing, kept his doubts to himself. There was a steadiness about the man—it calmed Asa, and the runaways had responded to it too.

Now that they had been on their way for a time, though, Asa could tell by the barrage of harsh whispers and stirrings in the back of the wagon that their fears had returned in full force.

By midnight the fog was so thick it covered the wagon like a shroud. Asa's head felt as if it would split from the tension of straining to see and, at the same time, stay alert to the sounds all around them. Even Mac, riding the bench beside him, seemed on edge. The big dog pricked his ears at every small sound that came out of the fog, occasionally making a low but warning growl.

What bothered Asa most, though, was the *lack* of sounds. Other than the occasional snap of fallen tree limbs or the sound of small animals tossing eerie calls upon the night, there was nothing to be heard.

He supposed he ought to give thanks that it wasn't raining. He'd had enough of cold rainy nights to last him a good long while.

They were still close to the river, and the dank night air smelled of fish mingled with wood smoke from a nearby farmhouse. The pungent aroma of the smoke made him think how nice it had been inside the Amish widow woman's house, where he could walk to the kitchen and warm his hands by the stove. And the missus had provided him with a good warm quilt to cover himself while dozing in the chair beside the captain's bed.

He shook off the memory. Who could say how long it would be before he again would sit close to a fire or tuck a warm blanket around himself? The blanket he'd thrown around his shoulders before leaving was anything but warm.

The women and children rode in back of the wagon, under the canvas cover. If their whisperings grew much louder, he would have to hush them for fear of discovery. But for now he would let them take their comfort as they could.

There would be little enough in the way of comfort this night, and only the good Lord knew for how many other nights to come.

II

WHEN THE PAST DIVIDES

*So here is my desert
and here am I
in the midst of it alone…*

THOMAS MACDONAGH

After David Sebastian finished his examination of Gant's wound and applied a fresh dressing, he stood, stretched his arms out in front of him, and eased his back.

He was pleased with Gant's progress. It had been five days since the riverboat captain showed up near to dying on Rachel Brenneman's doorstep, and today, for the first time, David no longer feared for the man's life. Not only did the wound look to be in the initial stages of healing, but Gant's color had improved, and there'd been no fever for two days now.

He was also more alert than he'd been since the injury, having stayed awake most of the entire time David tended to him.

Awake, but not exactly communicative, merely mumbling a short response to anything David asked him. Those responses, however, were enough to identify something of his origins.

"You're Irish," David said, meaning to learn something more about his wintry-eyed patient.

"And you're British." The words were edged with acid.

David lifted his eyebrows. "I suppose you think that makes us natural adversaries."

Gant made no reply, but his hard-eyed stare never wavered.

In an attempt to bridge the divide, David ventured what he thought would be a safe topic of conversation. "How long have you been in the States?"

Gant seemed to consider whether he would reply or not. "Ten, eleven years or so," was the curt reply.

He looked to be in his mid to late thirties. A big, raw-boned, rangy fellow. Probably strong as an ox before he was shot. Square-jawed, deeply bronzed and weathered skin, and the kind of piercing eyes that could peel away several layers of another man's defense in scarcely no time.

He wouldn't be an easy man to know. Even in his weakened state, he kept a stony barrier in place. Yet there was a certain *substance* and keen-eyed intelligence about him that David couldn't help but find intriguing. "So what's your story, Captain Gant?"

"What story would that be?"

David met and held the unreadable blue gaze. "The story that found you washed up on the riverbank with your leg shattered and your companion suddenly gone missing."

Something glinted in the other's eyes before the shutters closed on all expression. "Nothing all that interesting, Doc."

"Even so, *I'm* interested. As it happens, I expect I already know most of it, so you needn't dissemble with me."

One heavy eyebrow lifted, and the hard stare turned defiant.

"You're a 'conductor,' I imagine. Isn't that what you call yourselves, you fellows who help the runaway slaves make their way to the North?"

A look of surprise scurried across the rugged features.

"It must have complicated things considerably when you lost your boat."

Gant frowned, and David went on. "Rachel told me what your man Asa related to her. About your taking a bullet for him, the burning of your boat—and the rest of it."

The other moistened his lips. "And would that be all the lady told you, then?"

David feigned a look of innocence. "Oh, so there *is* more, then? I thought there might be."

Gant struggled to haul himself up a little against the pillows, pulling a face at the obvious effort it took. "You've my gratitude for doctoring me. And I'll see you're paid for your time and your effort. But the less you know of anything else, the better you are for it."

Suddenly impatient with him, David said, "I don't doubt that for a moment. And I'd ask you to take that same tack with Rachel and her family."

Gant frowned, and David went on. "Don't bring any trouble down on these people. Things haven't been easy for them as it is. If you're who I think you are—if you're up to what I suspect—for the sake of all that's decent, keep your secrets to yourself. Don't draw these good people into anything that will cause them harm."

The other's probing gaze unsettled David, but this man knew nothing of the sorrows Rachel and her family—and too many of the other Riverhaven families—had seen. Gant was a stranger, a total outsider who almost certainly wouldn't care what the consequences of his intrusion into their lives might be.

But David cared.

Still, the Irishman's tone sounded almost apologetic with his next words. "It wasn't my intention to barge in on them as I did," Gant said, his voice low. "I had no wits about me whatsoever at the time, and Asa mistook this place for—for another. My word on it. I have no intention of causing them trouble. None at all."

"What you intend and what you could actually bring down on them might not be the same thing," David snapped.

He glanced away, disliking himself for speaking as he had, especially to a patient. But he had to consider Rachel.

And Susan.

"You don't look Amish, Doc."

David turned back to him. "I'm *not* Amish."

"Then what, you're their guardian angel or something of the kind?"

David drew a long breath. "I've taken care of these people as their doctor for years. I've many friends among them. Naturally I care what happens to them."

Gant raked him with a long, measuring look. "Do you own slaves, Doc?"

"What? No, I don't own slaves. Ohio's a free state, man. And I expect you already knew that."

Gant shrugged and gave a faint smile that didn't reach his eyes. "Just wondered, is all. Would you have any idea what the life of a slave is like?"

"No more than any other white man would know, I expect."

It was on the tip of David's tongue to suggest that Gant most likely knew something more about slavery than he, judging from the looks of the scars he'd seen on Gant's back during his initial examination. But he had no wish to humiliate the man or pry into his past, though there was no denying he was curious about the unmistakable signs of a beating.

Gant's eyes bored into him, but he said nothing.

David could see that he was tiring, and so he moved to end the exchange. "Well, then, I'll be back in a few days. In the meantime don't try to get out of bed. You mustn't put any weight on that leg yet."

Gant nodded. "As you say, Doc. And I do thank you for your assistance."

David could almost feel that icy gaze on his back as he left the room.

The British and the Irish. A case of old wounds that continued to fester, with hope of healing almost beyond imagining. What would it take to end that ancient, bitter enmity?

Gant didn't want to like the man. He was a Brit, after all.

On the other hand, would he be alive today if the British doctor hadn't treated him?

He had to admit it was doubtful. The man might well have saved his life.

Apparently, though, a good measure of credit was also due to the lovely young Amish widow. And she *was* lovely, this Rachel Brenneman. Lovely indeed. The more he saw of her, the more he looked forward to the times she came into the room, though she spoke only when she seemed to find it necessary. In truth, she turned pink every time she got close to him or caught him watching her. And he did like to watch her.

Her face was enough to make a strong man whimper. She might be Amish, but there was an almost exotic, Mediterranean look about her. Eyes so dark they were almost black, the blush of apricots on her creamy skin, and a wee band of freckles that neatly marched across her nose. Her hair was mostly concealed, of course, under that pert little white cap she wore. Even so, he could see enough to know it was a rich, glossy chestnut. She was slender, like a young willow, and she moved easily and lightly, like a dancer.

He smiled at his own fanciful image. No doubt the Amish Rachel Brenneman wouldn't take kindly to being thought of as a dancer.

It wasn't likely she'd take kindly to his thinking about her at *all*.

But she was fine. Fine, indeed. And when she smiled...Ah, when she smiled, it was a good thing he wasn't yet able to stand, or surely his knees would have buckled under him.

He glanced at the window, saw that the light of evening would soon be gone entirely. Good. That meant Rachel Brenneman would be coming in with his supper.

The days were long and the times when he was actually awake were dull and boring as dust. The best parts of the day were mealtimes, not so much because he was ever hungry—he had no appetite as yet. But because mealtime meant a few far-too-brief moments with Rachel.

How long might it be, he wondered, that he could keep her believing he was still too weak to feed himself?

FOR THE LONELY

God pity all the lonely folk
With griefs they do not tell,
Women walking in the night
And men dissembling well.

LOUISE DRISCOLL

D avid deliberated between stopping by Susan's place or going on to the farm. He was finished with his calls for the day and had closed up the office earlier that afternoon, so there was no reason he should hurry home.

On the other hand, he had no reason to stop at Susan's, other than the obvious one—he wanted to see her. The wiser course would be *not* to stop. But with Fannie at Rachel's and Gideon no doubt still at work, Susan would be by herself. They might have a rare opportunity to talk without anyone else around.

The temptation was too great. He pulled up in front of the Kanagy house, making an effort to smooth his hair before getting out of the buggy. After tethering Chester, his mahogany Morgan horse, he walked quickly up the steps of the front porch.

When Susan opened the door, she was wiping her hands on her apron and there was a smudge of flour on her cheek. The sight of her, her tentative but welcoming smile, sent a dizzying happiness through him.

"David! Is something wrong?"

"No, no, not at all. I just left Rachel's and thought I'd stop and say hello. Is this is a bad time?"

"Of course not," she said, standing aside and motioning him in. "*Kumm re.* Come in. I was just starting supper. Gideon's always late these days, seems like. I never quite know when to look for him. Do you have time for a cup of tea? Or coffee? I have both. My boy always wants coffee when he gets home from work. Here, let me take your coat."

"No I can't stay long, Susan. I thought I'd just stop by for a moment and…see how you're doing," he said, following her to the kitchen.

The quizzical look she gave him over her shoulder might have had something to do with the fact that he'd just talked with her two days before, at Rachel's house. Admittedly it was doubtful that much had changed in two days.

"Smells wonderful in here," he said. The kitchen was as plain as all Amish kitchens, with nothing but a long plank table and benches, a black woodstove, and dark blinds at the uncurtained windows. No ornaments decorated the walls, and the cupboard was for food storage only—no trinkets here. But the room was warm and richly scented with supper in the making. It was a friendly, inviting room that made one want to stay.

"You're welcome to stay for supper, David."

He laughed a little. "I wasn't hinting—honestly. I'll take you up on it another time when you know to expect me."

"Oh, I always make too much as it is. Seems I still can't get used to cooking for only the three of us—and now with Fannie at Rachel's, it's even harder to judge how much to fix for just Gideon and myself."

She talked him into a cup of coffee, but he remained standing as he drank it. He supposed it was foolish, but somehow it seemed less *intimate* than sitting down at the table with her. He'd learned to guard against excessive closeness, not merely for his own sake but mostly for hers.

Even after all these years of friendship with Susan and her late husband, Amos, and finally gaining the acceptance of the Riverhaven Amish as their physician and friend, David was still keenly aware of the strict code of conduct for an *Englischer* and an Amish woman. Especially an Amish woman alone. It had taken him a long time to win the respect of the Plain People; he had no intention of doing anything that might cause him to lose it.

He was especially careful to do nothing that might place his friendship with Susan at risk. He stood at the far end of the long wooden counter that ran nearly the length of one side of the kitchen, while she stayed midway, near the sink.

"So, then, how is your patient, Captain Gant, coming along?" Susan asked.

"He's doing well. I'm actually surprised at how well. If infection doesn't set in, I believe he'll heal nicely."

"Good. Perhaps he won't need to stay so long, then."

"It will be some time before he's able to leave here, Susan," David cautioned. "A few weeks, at least."

She drew a long breath. "This is a bad situation for Rachel, you know that."

David nodded. "I hope your church leadership will be patient. There's simply no way the man will be able to leave soon. Not in his condition."

"Surely there's somewhere else he could go to recuperate."

"I can't think where it would be. He certainly can't take care of himself. He's going to need medical attention for quite some time."

"What about the hospital?"

"The hospital wouldn't keep him for any length of time, now that I've done the surgery and he seems to be recovering." He studied her. "I know you're troubled about this, for Rachel's sake, but there's really nothing else in it except for Gant to stay put until he's well enough to be on his way."

She gave a slow nod, but there was no mistaking her unease. "I was concerned about Rachel even before this happened, you know."

"Because of her being alone?"

"That, and she's been so sad. It's been three years, and I would have thought by now..." her voice trailed.

"Yes, I know, Susan," he said gently. "But have you considered that having someone to look after might actually help her? It can't hurt to keep busy, to keep from dwelling on her loss too much."

Susan looked at him, and the pain that lined her features tugged at David's heart. He didn't know exactly how old she was, but she'd always looked almost as youthful as a girl. But at this moment, she appeared drawn and tense. She looked, as was only natural, like a worried mother.

He ached to touch her, to reassure her—and immediately dismissed the thought. "Rachel is a strong young woman. She'll be all right. But it would help if your bishop doesn't make things difficult for her. She doesn't need to be badgered about this situation."

Her eyes widened in a look of rebuke. "Bishop Graber would never badger Rachel. Or anyone else. He has a kind heart, David."

David knew the bishop and had even treated him, once for a broken wrist and another time for phlebitis. Susan might be right about the man's kind heart, but he'd always struck David as a stern, patriarchal sort.

"Susan, you're afraid Rachel might be disciplined for taking in an outsider, aren't you?"

She hesitated, glancing away for an instant. When she turned back to him, her eyes were dark with sadness. "How is it that you always seem to know what I'm thinking, David?"

The doctor laughed. "I daresay no man can read a woman's mind."

She gave him a rueful smile. "I don't know but what you might not be the exception." She paused. "Yes, I'm worried that Rachel might face disciplining. She's a young widow with no children, and this… riverboat captain, who is a worldly man we know nothing about, is staying in her house."

"But I'm sure you're in and out often. And Fannie is there most of the time."

"That's true, but it's still a treacherous situation for Rachel. You must know that."

"Of course I do." And he did. David had moved and worked among the Amish enough years to be familiar with the *Ordnung,* the unwritten but uncompromising rules by which they lived. He didn't have to agree with all their regulations—and he didn't—to understand that these people truly lived in a world of their own making, as far removed from his own world as possible. They were required to honor the code they'd set for themselves, or else they were disciplined, sometimes severely, for disobedience.

It occurred to him that Susan was regarding him with an uncharacteristically open, curious expression. More often she was careful not to look directly at him and seldom, if ever, made eye contact with him.

"It sometimes puzzles me, David, that you would be so...accepting of our ways," she said. "You never seem to judge us or condescend to us, like some among the *Englisch* do. Why is that, I wonder?"

Taken off guard by her observation, David made an awkward shrug and even laughed a little. "Perhaps I'd make a good Amishman myself."

Her gaze locked with his for another instant before she glanced away. "Perhaps you would at that," she said, her voice soft.

"I do live a fairly simple life, you know, Susan. I'm probably not as 'worldly' as the Plain People might believe. I tend to my patients, my garden, and my house plants. I read, I go for walks, and I enjoy simple food—meat and potatoes are my style. What's so worldly about that?"

She turned teasing now. "Ah, but think of all your fine education! No doubt you find our disregard for higher learning right peculiar, to say the least. We must seem dreadfully boring to you."

"I could never find anything about you 'boring,' Susan."

The words escaped David's lips without his taking time to think. He quickly moved to fill the ragged silence that hung between them. "Well...I expect I should be getting home and let you tend to your supper."

She hesitated before making a reply. "I'm glad you stopped," she finally said, no longer looking directly at him. "It's always good to see you."

He set his cup on the counter. "Well," he said again, feeling awkward, "thank you, Susan. You take care now. And give Gideon my best."

She hadn't wanted him to go. That was her feeling all too often of late. A forbidden feeling that should have wracked her with guilt. Yet it always seemed so...right, being with David.

How could she have let such a thing happen? Why hadn't she realized where her feelings were going and reined them in before things ever reached such a point?

And what about David? Did she only imagine what she saw in his eyes sometimes? What she *thought* she saw?

Surely she was wrong. He knew as well as she that the barrier between their worlds was impassable. Even the thought of anything more than friendship between them could never be more than a ridiculous, futile imagining.

She shook her head as if to cast off her girlish foolishness. How could she begin to believe that a man like David Sebastian might care for her...*that* way? She was a simple, middle-aged Amish matron, not well-educated, with no fancy manners. Her hands were rough and red from laundry soap and gardening. She was short in stature, a bit too plump in figure, and her face was beginning to line from worry over her children.

David was a professional man, a scholarly man of refinement and gentility. *Englisch* women would find him attractive—a highly eligible bachelor, for sure and for certain.

There also remained the fact that he was an *Englisch* man. In the eyes of her church, he was as much an *auslander* as that wounded riverboat captain he was treating.

Well, perhaps not *quite* so much the outsider as that man Gant, for the Plain People considered David a friend as well as their physician.

But he was still of the world, and any kind of romantic feelings between them, even if such a thing should ever happen, would never be tolerated.

Forbidden, that's what it was, and that was what it would always be.

So why was she standing here, daydreaming like a young girl in love? She had supper to get and evening chores to do. Best empty her head of such nonsense and get to work before her son caught her at her folly.

As he entered his home, a sprawling old farmhouse he'd restored and redecorated some years back, David stood in the entryway, listening to the oppressive silence.

When Aaron had still been a boy and living at home, there had always been some sort of noise about. Even after Lydia's death, when David had sometimes felt as though he would choke on the loneliness, there had been the sounds of welcome when he came home: Aaron's boyish eagerness, the dog's playful yelping, the sound of Mrs. Cunningham working in the kitchen.

Now Aaron was a man grown, practicing medicine in Baltimore. Abner, the dog, was dead. Mrs. Cunningham, no longer needed, had moved on to another family. So every day David came home to an empty house.

Some days it was all he could do to face the quiet. In his medical practice, he dealt with families. Young families with small children, middle-aged couples helping to tend to their grandchildren, and aging husbands and wives who were still part of their families' lives. Amish households were almost always large and busy, with lots of children and grandparents, nieces and nephews, and aunts and uncles involved in the lives of their loved ones. Not only did David feel set apart because of being an outsider to the Plain People, but also—perhaps more so—because he was so alone while they almost never were. He spent his days in the company of families joined not only by blood, but by love and laughter and the common cause of taking care of each other.

And then, at the end of the day, he left it all behind and came home to a cold, empty house with shadowed rooms that held only furnishings no longer used and hollow echoes of the past.

Sometimes he thought he would die of loneliness long before old age or a wasting disease brought his life to an end. When he caught himself lapsing into such morbid thoughts, he tried halfheartedly, then more rigorously, to drag himself up and out of the mire of self-pity, only to plunge into a flood of overwork that ultimately led to an unhealthy avoidance of reality.

In truth there was a hole in his heart, a dank void that nothing—not work, not busyness, not things or all manner of pursuits—could ever fill. From time to time he considered selling the farm and going to live nearer his son, Aaron, and his family in Baltimore. But they had their own life, and it was a different kind of life from what David had ever wanted for himself.

Besides, he couldn't imagine leaving Riverhaven and his Amish families. He had grown to be genuinely fond of the lovely countryside and these good people with their simple, decent lives. The thought of separating himself from them—*and from Susan*—stabbed at his heart with a vengeance.

So he continued to make do. Most times he even managed to be thankful for what he had rather than regretting what he lacked.

But, oh, how bitter the loneliness could be on a cold winter's night after leaving the welcome and cozy comfort of Susan's home.

And how empty his own house felt without the sweet warmth of her presence. Sometimes, in a rare idle moment when he let his guard down, he would allow himself to wonder what it would be like to come home to Susan. She seemed to bring a steady sense of peace into any room she entered with the light of her smile, the grace of her goodness.

To all appearances, he himself had a fine home, a good life, an existence some men might envy. Only he knew it was nothing more than a facade.

Until he'd been forced to face the bleak emptiness of his spacious, rambling rooms, he'd never stopped to think about what it actually meant to be *alone*, truly alone.

Once he realized—once he understood the constant battle that had to be waged against gradually falling into a kind of meaningless existence—he valued all the more the ties of family and friends and faith that helped to keep his heart from becoming as cold and empty as the house in which he lived.

✣ 13 ✣

A GOD-FEARING MAN

By mercy and truth iniquity is purged:
and by the fear of the LORD
men depart from evil.

PROVERBS 16:6

A nother three days passed before Gant asked about his belongings.

"I had a suitcase," he said to Rachel, "about yea big." He spread out his hands to show her. "There were some things in it—money, for one, which I'll need to pay the doctor, and a couple of changes of clothes—"

"—And a fiddle," Rachel finished for him. She said nothing about the photograph of the pretty lady. "There was a Bible, but I'm afraid it's ruined."

He twisted his mouth. "The fiddle—I expect it's ruined too."

"I laundered your clothes—they were soaked—and emptied everything else out on a table in the other room. The money's there." She pointed to the chest of drawers. "I think the fiddle might be all right. It seems to have dried out just fine, though I'm not sure about the strings."

He expelled a long breath. "Thank you, ma'am. You've gone to a lot of trouble for me."

Rachel bit back a smile. No one had ever called her "ma'am" except Mr. Snider. It made her feel as old as a *grossmutter*. Not that her grandmother in Indiana had ever seemed old to her. Last spring when Mammi Hannah had come to visit, she'd helped can and bake and plant flowers like a woman half her age.

Gant was sitting up in bed today and looking much better. Gideon had come and seen to the captain's personal needs and even given him a shave. Gant appeared more lively and seemed more given to conversation now than at any time since he'd first arrived.

"Dr. Sebastian will be by later this afternoon to change your dressing," she told him.

"Who is this Dr. Sebastian anyway? What's the connection between him and your people?"

"No connection, except that he's doctored most of us for several years now. He's a good friend to us."

"That's a bit unusual, isn't it? I'd have thought you folks would have one of your own kind tending to your medical needs."

"No," Rachel said. "It takes too much education to be a doctor, and the Amish don't go to school so long. Dr. Sebastian has lots of schooling. We're blessed to have him."

"I have to wonder how a Brit ended up in a place like this."

Rachel frowned. "A Brit?"

"An Englishman."

"Oh. Yes, he's *Englisch,* but also a friend. It's difficult to think of him as an outsider anymore."

"No, I mean he's *really* English. Not like the *Englisch* you call outsiders, such as myself."

Rachel stared at him.

"He comes from England," Gant said.

"Oh—*ja,* I know. That's right," she said, smiling, "the doctor is *Englisch,* and he's English."

He was watching her with a peculiar expression, a look that put Rachel on edge. "I wish you'd sit down and talk for a bit," he said, motioning to the chair beside the bed. "You scurry in and out of here like you're scared to death of me. Frankly, I could use the company, if you can spare the time. The days are what you might call deadly dull."

Truth be known, Rachel could almost imagine how long the days probably seemed to him. She suspected he was a man given to lots of activity. It must be terribly hard not to be able to do anything but lie in bed.

She could almost feel guilty because she hadn't made an effort to be friendlier and help him pass the time. On the other hand, *she* was too busy to sit and talk much.

Besides, while she wasn't exactly afraid of the *auslander,* she *was* uncomfortable with him. He was so straightforward, so blunt in his way of speaking. And his eyes were bold. Too bold. She found it almost impossible to meet that deep blue gaze directly. Something about the way he watched her made her feel as if she amused him.

No doubt, like most outsiders, he found her and the rest of the Amish to be oddities, peculiar in their dress and customs and their plain way of living.

Ja, vell, he could think what he liked. *She* wasn't the one propped up in bed with a bullet hole in the leg. Still, after a brief hesitation, Rachel sat down.

"Where's your little girl this morning?" he asked.

"Oh, Fannie isn't my daughter. She's my sister. She's studying her lessons in the kitchen."

"She doesn't go to school?"

"No. Lots of Amish families teach their children at home instead of sending them to the *Englisch* school. We like to know what they're being taught, to make sure their values remain Christian."

Gant made no reply, merely looked at her as if she were a puzzle he couldn't quite figure out.

Was he a Christian man, she wondered?

She decided to ask. After all, she was providing him shelter. Didn't she have a right to know what kind of man was beneath her roof?

Her question brought a look of surprise, then a quirking at the corner of his mouth. "Are you thinking an Irishman isn't likely to be a Christian, Miss Rachel?"

Rachel sensed he was deliberately trying to goad her. Well, she didn't embarrass all that easily. And even if she did, she wasn't about to let him see it.

"Truth is, I don't know anything about Irishmen at all. I'm just curious, as I should think you would understand, about the kind of person I've given shelter in my home." She paused. "And you needn't call me 'Miss.' I'm just Rachel."

"I expect you're right to be concerned about your sister's education," he said, the small, cynical smile still in place. "And even more to care about what kind of man you've taken into your home. Be easy... *Rachel*. Sure, and I'm no saint, but I'm not a devil either. You might say I'm a God-fearing man."

He seemed always to be making light of things. Even things that were meant to be taken seriously. Rachel didn't know what to make of him. But she was relieved to hear that he feared God. Hopefully, that meant she needn't fear *him*.

"Where is your home, Captain Gant?"

"Mostly on my boat. Until it burned up."

"You don't live in a house?"

He shrugged. "I have a house. But it's precious little time I spend there."

"Well—where *is* your house?"

"In Virginia, ma'am. *Rachel*."

"Dr. Sebastian says you came here—to America—from Ireland."

"Aye, some years ago now. I settled in New York—Brooklyn—when I first came across. But later, when most of my trade started coming from the South, I moved to Virginia."

Rachel was hesitant to ask her next question, but she *was* curious. Thinking of the woman in the photo, she said, "And your wife and family, then? They live in Virginia?"

"There's no wife or family," he said.

"Oh, I'm sorry. I didn't mean to pry—"

He waved off her apology. "No need to be sorry. The simple fact is, no woman is ever going to put up with the way I live, what with my being gone most all the time."

Rachel didn't know what to say, and so she said nothing at all. With the knowledge that he wasn't married, though, the question remained about the identity of the pretty young woman in the photo he carried with him.

Just then Fannie appeared at the door. "Rachel—" she stopped, apparently remembering her manners as she glanced toward Gant. "Hello, Captain Gant."

He nodded and smiled at her. "And good morning to you, young miss."

Fannie giggled. But her expression quickly sobered. "Rachel, Bishop Graber and Deacon Samuel are coming. They're getting out of their buggy now."

Rachel stood. She had to make a concentrated effort not to groan in front of Gant and Fannie. She had known it would come to this. Even so, she wasn't at all sure she was ready for it.

Gant reached to touch her lightly on the arm. "I'm sorry for the trouble I've brought on you."

Rachel stood. "Any trouble here is only what I've brought on myself. Besides, Bishop Graber is a kind man. Though he and Samuel will probably want to see you as well."

Gant shrugged. "Fine by me."

Maybe not so fine for me, though, Rachel thought as she headed for the kitchen.

"Come, Fannie. I imagine the bishop will want to speak with me alone. Say your hellos and then take your lessons to your bedroom."

"Are we in trouble, Rachel?"

Trying to ignore the weariness creeping over her, Rachel managed a smile for her little sister. "*You* are in no trouble at all," she said, giving Fannie's slender shoulder a pat. "I'm sure there's nothing to worry about. Everything will be just fine."

Rachel wished she'd had time to change from her choring dress before welcoming the bishop. But no doubt he was used to women greeting him in their work dresses when he came calling. Besides, Bishop Graber wouldn't be concerned about her appearance. He was calling for one reason, and that was because a stranger—an outsider— had found shelter under her roof.

Rachel knew the bishop and some others in the community faulted her as being less submissive than the other Plain women. She had been reprimanded more than once for her outspokenness and for "dabbling" in the *Englisch* world with her birdhouse business.

She had no illusions but what she was about to receive yet another talking-to for providing aid and refuge to an *auslander*.

Patting her hair and securing her *kapp*, she started for the door. She might just as well get this over with.

Rachel's assurance that everything would be all right didn't fool Gant. The taut set of her delicate features and the frown that creased her brow told him otherwise. She was dreading this meeting with her bishop.

He hated the trouble he'd made for her and wished there was something he could do to smooth things over a bit. He rubbed his fingers over the sleeve of her dead husband's nightshirt, thinking.

It struck him then that perhaps there *was* something—a small thing, but it might help.

Turning, he dipped his hand into the bowl of water beside the bed and splashed his face and hair. He lowered the pillow and rolled onto his back, pulling the bed clothes snug around him except for his head.

Then he shut his eyes and waited.

14

FOR THE GOOD OF RACHEL

...her eyes deep wells that might
cover a brooding soul...
JOHN BOYLE O'REILLY

"*Guder mariye,*" Rachel said, holding the door open for the bishop and Samuel to enter.

"Good morning to you, Rachel. And to you, Fannie." As was usually his way, the bishop spoke in the *Deitsch* of their people.

His greeting was cheerful enough, but his smile seemed mostly for Fannie, not for Rachel. As for Samuel, he was as solemn as if he were about to preach a funeral sermon. At Rachel's invitation, each man took a chair at the kitchen table.

As soon as Fannie excused herself and went to the bedroom, the bishop turned to Rachel, his expression grave. "Deacon Samuel and others have made me aware of the outsider you've taken in, Rachel. I understand the stranger had been shot and needed help...but why did he come here, to your home?"

With his white, flowing beard and considerable girth, Isaac Graber might have presented a formidable figure. But his manner was mild, his voice quiet, and he spoke to Rachel with the same kindness he'd often shown her throughout the years.

She had nothing but respect for the man who had served as their bishop for as many years as she could remember. Even so, she knew the probing gaze and stern reproach of which he was capable and

shrank inwardly at the thought that she might be about to experience it.

No doubt Samuel had given the bishop an earful about Captain
Gant, but it was obvious the older man expected a full accounting
from her. So after both men declined her offer of refreshment, she
proceeded to explain the events that had brought the badly wounded
Gant and Asa to her door.

Bishop Graber listened without interrupting until she had finished.
"And this other man who accompanied him—the man of color—he
is no longer here?"

"No, Bishop. The man called Asa went away on…some business
for Captain Gant."

"So you are here alone with this man—this riverboat captain?"

The tone of his voice gave every indication that he not only dis-
approved but was troubled as well. Then there was Samuel, who sat
watching her with a hard, accusatory stare.

"It's not like that, Bishop. Not really. You see—"

But he didn't give her time to explain.

"Rachel, I do not want to embarrass you," the bishop continued,
"but there are things I need to ask. Who tends to this man's…personal
needs?"

Rachel felt the anger rise, but despite her discomfort, she would *not*
be humiliated by these intrusive questions. When she hesitated, she saw
Samuel lean forward slightly, his large hands knotted on the table.

"Gideon comes every morning," she said. "And he stops again in
the evening after work. And Dr. Sebastian, of course. He comes by to
change the dressing on his wound and examine him. Mamma comes
often too, and Fannie is staying here for now, day and night."

The bishop nodded slowly, and Rachel thought her reply had satisfied him.

Silent up until now, Samuel finally spoke up. "What do you know
about this man, Rachel? Do you have any idea how he was shot—or
why? Where does he come from—and why did he come to *your* house?
What's he doing in Riverhaven in the first place?"

Rachel fumbled for answers to his questions, but annoyance with Samuel for his red-faced diatribe clouded her mind, and it took her a moment to formulate a reasonably coherent reply. "He was shot by mistake. He stepped in front of his friend to save his life. The bullet was meant for Asa—the man who accompanied him here. As to where he comes from, his home is in Virginia, though he spends much of his time on his boat. I've already told you, he's a riverboat captain."

Samuel twisted his mouth in an expression of distaste. "A man with no roots, living on a boat. An undependable sort."

The bishop held up a hand to silence Samuel. "It's not up to us to judge, Samuel. We know nothing about this man, except that he allowed himself to be shot to save his friend. That would seem to be a mark in his favor."

"If it's true," Samuel said, his tone grudging.

The bishop went on. "Even though this man may be a good person, Rachel, he is still a stranger to you, to all of us. And his being here puts you in a difficult situation. You know that no Plain woman is to be alone with an *Englisch* man. Not under any circumstances. Not only that, but the longer he's here, the more you're exposed to his worldly nature."

"And at risk that he might try to take advantage of her in some way," Samuel put in. "Rachel is naturally unaware of the dangers an outsider holds for our people."

Rachel shot a look at him, amazed that he could say such a thing. A flush of crimson stained his face, indicating that he knew he'd misspoke.

Bishop Graber frowned. He, too, seemed to find the remark out of place.

Rachel drew a long, steadying breath. "I would hope that my faith is strong enough to resist a stranger's worldly influence. And I am not so easily taken advantage of, Samuel."

He drew back a little, as if restraining himself from saying more.

"Please take me to this man now, Rachel," said the bishop. "I would like to meet him."

Rachel hesitated and then stood to comply.

The two men followed her into the bedroom where she stopped short just inside the doorway. She stood staring at Gant. *What in the world…*

He had nearly buried himself beneath the quilts, with only a portion of his face exposed. His eyes were closed, his hair and his face damp, as if he were perspiring heavily. He moaned, thrusting his head from side to side without opening his eyes.

Rachel's surprised gaze went from Gant to the washbowl on the table next to him. Beside her now, the bishop said in a voice little more than a whisper, "I can see that the man is in much pain. What does Dr. Sebastian say about his condition?"

She looked back at Gant. Still distracted by this unexpected change in his appearance—but with understanding beginning to dawn—she nodded. "He's made…some progress, but he's still very ill," she said carefully. "I thought perhaps you'd spoken with Dr. Sebastian and knew the seriousness of his condition. I should have prepared you—"

"No, I haven't seen the doctor for several days," Bishop Graber said, still whispering. He inclined his head toward the door. "We won't disturb him. We'll stop by another day soon."

Back in the kitchen, a silence hovered between them. The bishop finally broke it, saying, "You seem to have worked things out that allow you to be cautious, Rachel. And it's clear this man presents no threat in his present condition. But once he grows stronger and is able to move about, we'll need to help you make other arrangements in order to protect yourself and make sure he has the proper care to recover. We can't let him suffer simply because he's not one of us." He paused, studying her. "In the meantime, you will be vigilant and keep yourself well-removed from this man."

Rachel glanced down at the floor. "Yes, Bishop."

She felt Samuel's gaze hard on her, but she refused to meet his eyes, even though he turned back to look at her when they stepped outside the door.

✦✦

After the bishop and Samuel left, Rachel took a moment to collect herself before going back to the bedroom, where she found Gant again propped up against a pillow and dabbing the moisture from his face with his sleeve.

He stopped when she entered the room, watching her with an unreadable glint in his eye.

Rachel stood staring at him, her hands clasped tightly at her waist. "I can't believe you did that."

"Did what?" he said easily, continuing to dry his face and hair.

"You—made them think you're in worse condition than you are."

"Well, now, it seems to me I'm not in such great shape as all that."

"No, of course not," Rachel stammered. "I didn't mean to imply that you are. But you made yourself out to be…at death's door!"

"Did it work?"

"Did it—what do you mean?"

"You know what I mean. It seemed to me it might go a bit easier for you if they thought I was next to useless."

"Yes, it probably did help. All the same, you shouldn't have done it. It was the same as *lying*."

He lowered his arm. "I didn't open my mouth, Rachel, so that's hardly lying. Now tell me the truth—was what I did such a terrible sin in your eyes?"

"Only God's eyes matter, Mr. Gant, not mine."

"Gant."

"What?"

"Stop calling me *Mister*. It's *Gant*. Or even *Jeremiah,* if you must. But drop the *Mister*."

She stared at him. This man confused her, made her mind uncertain of itself. "*Ja, vell.* I suppose you meant to help me, and so you did."

He regarded her with a curious look. "How do you put up with all this, Rachel? *Why* do you put up with it?"

"Put up with what?" she asked, genuinely confused.

He gestured toward the door. "You might have been speaking in German or whatever your language is, but I know the tone of a scolding when I hear it. You're a grown woman. Why would you allow yourself to be talked to that way?"

She frowned. "The bishop wasn't scolding me."

He lifted his eyebrows in a skeptical look.

"Well, maybe Samuel was, in his way. Samuel is just…Samuel. You'd have to know him. But the bishop is simply protecting me. That's a part of his responsibility as bishop. I'm a widow, and he wants to make certain I'm safe, physically and spiritually." She paused. "A woman alone can be…vulnerable."

He was studying her intently. "I have a hard time imagining a woman as strong as yourself being vulnerable, Rachel Brenneman."

The look in his eyes startled her. She wanted to look away, but this time there was something more than the usual bold glint of amusement in his look, something that seemed to hint of approval and… admiration as well. For one long breathless moment she felt caught in his gaze.

And then Fannie stuck her head through the doorway and said, "Rachel?"

Rachel whipped around as if she'd been struck.

"I'm hungry," her sister said, grinning at Gant. "Can we make lunch yet?"

The lock on Rachel's mind snapped open, and she virtually swept across the room. "A fine idea," she said to Fannie. "*Ja*, we'll make lunch right now!"

15

ASA

And before I'd be a slave
I'd be buried in my grave
And go home to my Lord and be free.

FROM "OH, FREEDOM," A SONG OF THE UNDERGROUND RAILROAD

About two miles out of Stafford, Asa heard the distant sound of a gunshot, followed by the baying of hounds. One of the women in the back of the wagon let out a yelp, while next to him Mac gave a low growl. Asa hushed the dog, then turned and warned the women to be still.

"What you're hearing is over east—nowhere close to us. But everybody hush now, in case they're headed this way."

A child wailed, but her mamma's harsh whisper quieted her. Asa slapped the reins and urged the big draft horse on.

They should be nearly to the Patterson farm by now. He prayed he was right about the distance of the gunshot and the hounds.

It seemed they'd encountered one hindrance after another ever since leaving Riverhaven. During their second night on the road, they met up with three runaway slaves trying to make their way to the North on their own. The older of the group explained that there had been five of them originally, but they'd encountered a bounty hunter who managed to capture two of them. The three who escaped were convinced that the same bounty hunter was still hot on their trail.

With the sound of gunfire and dogs barking in the distance and a blanket of fog making it nearly impossible to see anything more than a few feet away, Asa felt desperate to get to a safe place as quickly as possible.

A gun meant that bounty hunters might be in the area. These were ruthless men who would do most anything to claim the reward on a runaway. A professional slave hunter could turn a highly lucrative profit capturing or recapturing fugitive slaves—from several hundred dollars up to a thousand for a prime male. A bounty hunter was willing to go anywhere, no matter how far, to make that kind of money. There were tales of slave hunters who had tracked runaways as far north as New England for years, hauling them away from as much as a decade of living in freedom and returning them to their former captivity.

Asa knew only too well that no escaped slave was ever truly free, ever entirely safe, no matter how long he might have lived in freedom, unless he disappeared into Canada. There was even a law now that made it illegal for anyone to hinder a slave catcher or assist or harbor a fugitive slave. Fines and jail sentences were being handed down that made it more dangerous—and costly—for folks to help runaway slaves in their efforts to make their way to freedom.

But there were still some good people who believed strongly enough in liberty for *all,* no matter their skin color, and were willing to risk their own freedom to help the runaway slave find *his.* Captain Gant was such a man.

Apparently the folks at the next station were among these people. He knew nothing about Arthur Patterson and his wife, other than what he and the captain had been told—that the Pattersons were a kindhearted couple who always stood ready to help a fugitive slave gain safe passage to freedom.

Safe passage was what Asa prayed for this night. And the faint light glowing in the window of a farmhouse in the distance gave him hope that his prayers had been answered.

But the sound of dogs was closing in on them, and the horse that had been loaned to them was a stodgy one with no apparent inclination to increase his gait.

Even so, Asa jiggled the reins again and gave "Calvin" a shout of encouragement.

From the back of the wagon came a moan, most likely from the younger woman who was with child. Asa hated to cause her even more discomfort, but for her and her baby's sake—for the sake of them all—they needed to stay well ahead of those dogs.

→ ←

By the time they drove up the lane to the farmhouse, the hair on the back of Asa's neck was standing up. His mind told him it wasn't so, but the fear pushing at him made him feel as though a pack of demon dogs was slavering and snapping at the wheels of the wagon.

From the sound of it, they were still a good length away, but as he jumped down from the bench and hauled up to the side door, he was praying with every heartbeat that he'd reached the right place, the Patterson farm. When a fair-haired man—a younger man than Asa had expected—appeared in the doorway holding a lantern, he pulled in a ragged breath and blurted out the greeting before the man even asked.

"I'm a friend of friends, sir. Would you be Mr. Patterson?"

The man held the lantern a little higher, studying Asa and then looking out across the yard to the wagon. Now he trained the lantern directly on Asa's face and regarded him for another moment before replying.

"I'm Arthur Patterson. How many are you?"

"Two women, three children, and myself, sir." He paused. "And a dog."

Patterson looked down the yard and toward the road, plainly listening to the barking dogs.

"My wife will take your people to the root cellar for now. Pull the wagon in the barn. Quickly!"

Patterson's wife, a slender young woman with a blue shawl around her shoulders, took charge of the women and children, while Patterson met Asa in the barn to close and bar the door after the wagon was pulled out of sight. Then Asa gladly followed him to the root cellar, which was cold but still warmer than the raw night air.

"Once we make sure those dogs and whoever is with them aren't headed this way, we'll see that you folks are fed," Patterson told them. "We'll have to get you hid well before daylight. For now, you stay here until I come to get you."

After Patterson left, Asa motioned the women to a bench at the far end of the cellar. With a bench and the couple of blankets stacked on top of it, he figured this storage room must be used as a hiding place sometimes.

He hadn't taken the time before now to study his "passengers." They'd exchanged a few words whenever necessary, but most of Asa's time was spent on the driver's bench. When they stopped to rest, he had to care for the horse, study the map, and make sure everyone got fed from the box of food they carried with them—which by now was almost gone.

He watched as the two women, the young one cumbersome with child, sat down wearily on the bench. The woman in the family way— Mattie was her name—looked to be little more than a child herself. Her mother, Dinah, also appeared to be fairly young to have a daughter grown. He wasn't sure who the three little girls belonged to, but they were scarcely more than babies. The smallest one might have been three years old, but not much more, while the other two were probably both under six.

Not for the first time, Asa wished at least one other man had accompanied them on this journey.

The mother held the youngest child, who soon fell asleep, in her arms, while the other two little ones sat close together on the bench, holding hands.

Asa walked over to them. "Would the two of you be sisters?" he asked the two with their hands linked together.

The one who appeared to be the oldest looked at him from eyes that seemed too sad to belong to a child. "Yessuh," she said. "I be Sissy, and my sister be Charlotte."

"Well, those are pretty names," said Asa. "We will all have to be real quiet, until Mr. Patterson comes to get us, and then we'll have something to eat."

The child nodded solemnly, and her sister followed suit.

Asa glanced over to find the older woman watching him as if she were taking his measure. "They seem to be good children," he said. "Are all three yours?"

Her eyes warmed a little. "Those two are," she said, nodding toward Sissy and Charlotte. She glanced down at the sleeping child in her arms. "This one here is my grandchild. She belongs to Mattie."

"Where are your men?"

Her gaze clouded. "My man was killed early in the fall takin' a tree down for Mr. Jackson. Mattie—she ain't got no man. Lucy here belongs to Mr. Jackson, and so does the one she's carryin'." She paused. "Mr. Jackson, he gonna kill us both if he catches us."

The bitter taste of anger burned Asa's mouth. "Then we have to make sure he doesn't catch you."

"He'll have the bounty hunter after us."

"He won't catch us," Asa said, meaning it as a promise he hoped he could keep.

"When Luther and his family run, they caught 'em all and brought 'em back. They were beat almost to death."

"That's not going to happen to you."

Lord, help me keep my word.

He knew the Lord was with him. But he surely did wish Captain Gant was here as well.

Asa froze and shot a warning glance at the women. He put a finger to his lips when the sound of voices came filtering in from outside.

One of the sleeping little girls stirred, but Mattie stroked her hair and soothed her back to sleep.

Asa pressed his ear against the wall of the cellar and listened.

"I was with Wyman when his dogs tracked a runway from over in Wood County tonight. Henry's holding him until he can get him to the judge at the courthouse. But the way those hounds were carrying on even after they caught the one, I'm not so sure that boy was the only runaway in the area. You hear anything about any others, Arthur?"

"Just your pounding on the door, Thomas. You can see I'm in my night clothes. You know how late it is?"

"Well, I'm sorry to waken you, Arthur, but I'd just as soon beat the bounty hunters to the draw and claim some reward money for myself. A good strong boy'll bring a goodly amount. I could use the extra cash, you know."

"I do know," replied Patterson. "But I'm afraid I can't help you with any information. The wife says I sleep like the dead once I'm out."

For a moment their voices dropped too low for Asa to tell what they were saying. Then he heard a horse whinny, and someone tell Patterson goodnight.

"You send word, hear, if you catch sight of any runaways. If you help me, we'll split the money."

"Sure thing, Thomas. You be careful going home, now."

Finally Asa drew a long breath but kept his ear to the wall until he heard the sound of the horse clopping away. Only then did he relax—and only a little.

Nearly half an hour later, Arthur Patterson came to take them inside the house. "I took my horse out and around for quite a ways, and I didn't hear anything more from those dogs. Henry Wyman has probably taken them home by now along with his runaway." His tone was harsh, his eyes hard. "You folks have some food, and then I'll show you where you can stay. We want to get you hid before daylight."

Usually when there was at least one man along on a trip, they separated and hid in different places. That way there was a chance that not everyone would be found if one was discovered. Asa didn't see how they could do that this time, though. He should stay with the women and children for fear something went wrong.

After they wolfed down big plates of sausage and eggs and potatoes, Patterson agreed with Asa about keeping the women and children together. "We have a good place for you here. Another cellar right under the house. Nobody even knows it's there except us. There's a couple of mattresses and some blankets. You'll be safe there for the day. I'll be working around the place, so everything will look normal to anyone nosing around."

"We can't thank you enough, sir." On impulse Asa extended his hand and then dropped it. White men didn't take to shaking hands with blacks.

But Arthur Patterson reached out his hand and waited until Asa took it. "My wife and I will be praying for you throughout the day. You get some rest."

Asa knew only too well what kind of rest he would get. On one of these trips, a man needed to sleep with his eyes open and his ears alert. The danger of discovery was everywhere, and the danger was not only for the runaways he was guiding to freedom.

If Ainsley Cottrill ever caught up to him, he would be a slave again for the rest of his life.

No. He needn't fear being enslaved again. If Cottrill ever found him, he'd simply be dead.

16

LIVING BY THE RULES

Saviour, teach me, day by day,
Love's sweet lesson, to obey…

JANE ELIZA LEESON

"Hear my warning, those who are in danger of being corrupted by the world and its allurements."

Bishop Graber looked toward the women's side of the congregation and, finding Rachel, captured her gaze as he neared the end of his Sunday sermon, the final sermon of the day.

She had to steel herself not to squirm under his piercing gaze and the harsh words of his admonition, spoken in German as were all the preaching service messages. The singsong rhythm of the bishop's words had lulled her into a kind of peaceful haze up until this point. She had listened, but in a vague and contented way, as if she were wrapped in a cocoon and slightly removed from her surroundings.

But now she felt herself singled out, appointed for rebuke, and she struggled to keep her expression passive.

"*…know ye not that the friendship of the world is enmity with God? Whosoever therefore will be a friend of the world is the enemy of God.*"

Resentment stirred in her. Why should she be reproached for administering aid to an injured man? A man who had taken a bullet for a friend and possibly saved his life by doing so. A man who had made a mission of helping the enslaved escape their chains and make their way to freedom.

And yet the bishop was only pointing out a rule by which Rachel had lived her entire life, a rule that was a fundamental part of the Amish faith and the *Ordnung.* They lived separately from the world. Not because they saw the world or the *Englisch* as evil, but because to involve themselves in the things of the world would more than likely draw them away from their own community and their faith.

Community and faith meant everything to the Plain People. In the way they dressed and earned their livelihood, in their manner of worship and recreation—in all of life itself—they followed the Plain way first established by their ancestors.

There was no denying that by allowing an outsider to stay in her house, Rachel was flirting with disobedience to the rules by which she and her people lived. According to the church, then, the bishop had every right to admonish her, to remind her of the treacherous path she was following. She was in very real danger of facing the consequences that could come from breaking her vows to God and the church—vows that were meant to be valid for a lifetime.

Resentment suddenly gave way to a chilling sense of dread. She knew herself to be Amish in every way. She was thoroughly and uncompromisingly Plain. To go against the *Ordnung* would mean not only to go against everything she believed, but it could even put her at risk of the terrible *Meidung*—the shunning.

The very word stirred fear in her. She would rather die than be cut off, expelled from her family, her friends, from the only way of life she had ever known.

As she walked out of the spacious home of Eben Mast, where the worshippers had met for today's preaching service, Rachel had to stop and shield her eyes from the bright sun and chill of the day. Three hours of sitting on a wooden bench and listening to three different sermons would have normally left her contemplative and comforted, if somewhat stiff from the inactivity.

Today, though, she felt raw and bruised. She couldn't bring herself to face the meal and fellowship that followed services. Truth be known, she had sensed the stares of a number of her friends, including Samuel, whose gaze seemed to follow every move she made throughout the morning. Did she only imagine that once friendly eyes now looked upon her with disapproval or even censure?

Defiance heated her blood, but she managed to keep her gaze straight ahead as she stepped down off the porch. In the side yard, she told her mother and Fannie to stay, that she would walk home. "I have a headache. I think the fresh air might be good for me."

She really *did* have a headache, but that wasn't her only reason for wanting to be alone. Mamma studied her for a long moment before answering. "*Ja,* you go on then. I'll bring Fannie to you later, after the meal."

Rachel started to walk away and then turned back when her mother spoke her name.

"It won't be much longer, daughter."

Rachel nodded, understanding Mamma's meaning.

She started walking toward the road. Mamma was right. Gant wouldn't be needing to stay much longer. He was able to stand and put his weight on the injured leg for several minutes at a time now. Dr. Sebastian said he was doing remarkably well.

Once he was gone, her problems with the church leadership would also go away. Why, then, did she feel no relief at the thought of his leaving?

She found him sitting in the rocking chair, staring out the window of the bedroom. He'd propped up his leg on a footstool Gideon had fashioned out of an old toolbox. He still looked pale and drawn. He also looked thoughtful and perhaps a little sad.

He seemed surprised when she walked in, as if his mind had been far away and he hadn't realized she was in the house.

Now that he could get dressed and sit upright, Rachel was more aware of his *presence,* of the way he seemed to fill a room just by being in it, as though there were no surroundings, only him. Though he was tall, he was lean—not a heavyset man at all—and yet he seemed to occupy so much space.

She stood just inside the room, suddenly feeling awkward and at a loss for words.

"You folks have long church services," he said. The way he was watching her made her feel more uncomfortable than ever.

Rachel hesitated, then walked the rest of the way into the room. He smiled at her as if he knew she was feeling ill at ease. That was foolishness, of course. There was no way the man could know how she was feeling or what she was thinking.

"Our preaching services are probably different from yours." She stopped. "Or...do you go to church?"

Still smiling, he shrugged. "When I'm near a church, I go. But it's not always possible when a man is on the river."

"No, I suppose not."

"I'm no heathen, Rachel. I told you, I'm a God-fearing man."

She reminded herself that he couldn't know what she was thinking, and she was glad of it, for the thought that crossed her mind was an unkind one: Jeremiah Gant might not be a heathen, but there was a worldly, mocking air about him that didn't seem to mark him as a godly man either.

But now she was judging, and he still a stranger. Stung by guilt, she attempted to change the subject. "I hope you ate the lunch I left for you, Mr. Gant."

He sighed. "Ah, we're back to 'Mr. Gant' again, are we?"

Flustered, Rachel didn't respond to his smile. "It feels—rude to simply call you by your last name. And you don't seem to like your given name."

"I have nothing against my given name, Rachel, other than the fact that it doesn't suit me. Not only is it a mouthful to be saying, but I don't feel comfortable wearing the name of an Old Testament prophet. 'Jeremiah' is surely meant for a visionary or a saint. 'Tis too big a name for me by far. Clearly my mother's hopes for me exceeded my character. And yes, ma'am, I ate my lunch—it was delicious, thank you very much."

Rachel studied him. Unlike herself, he seemed to find amusement in being scrutinized. "I wonder...do you ever take anything seriously—Gant?"

He grinned. "If 'Gant' makes you choke, Rachel, you may call me 'Jeremiah.' And, yes, to answer your question. I take many things seriously."

He paused, and the glint of humor in his eyes died. "I take *you* seriously, Rachel Brenneman. I take you *very* seriously."

Rachel had no idea what he meant, nor did she want to know. Without saying another word, she turned and quickly left the room.

As she hurried to the kitchen, she could almost feel that probing blue gaze following her all the way.

Gant gripped the arms of the rocking chair so tightly his wrists cramped. Only when she was completely out of sight did he relax his grasp.

The woman was making him crazy. No question about it, he was daft entirely. For days now he could scarcely think of anything but her. When she entered a room, he was immediately aware of the difference her presence made. And when she left, all the warmth and light of day seemed to follow her.

Madness.

For one thing, he hardly knew her. Moreover, he'd warrant she was little more than a girl. Never mind that she was a widow. She was a *young* widow. He knew a little about the Amish, and one thing he knew was that they often married young.

And then there was the way she sometimes looked at him, as if she feared he might come after her with an axe.

But worst of all—the one thing that made the situation unthinkable and altogether impossible—she was *Amish*. Oh, aye, Rachel was *very* Amish.

She lived by *rules*. Rules not of her own making but rules set down and enforced by her church. And a fierce set of rules at that, no doubt. Young Gideon had given him to understand what a fix Gant had placed her in just by showing up on her doorstep and staying on. From what he'd learned from the lad, these people were strict to the extreme. Sounded to him as if there were a lot more "don'ts" to their faith than "do's," but then he didn't know everything there was to know about these people.

As for Rachel—rules or not—she seemed content with things as they were. At least most of the time. Once in awhile when she didn't see him watching her, she took on a look of great sorrow. He expected she was thinking about her dead husband during those times. But more often than not, she appeared at peace with her world, with herself.

Though it rubbed him raw to admit it, he was all too aware that the smartest thing he could do for himself—and the kindest thing he could do for Rachel—would be to leave as soon as possible. Only then could she get on with her normal life, back to the ways that were acceptable to her church and her family. Then she would be free from the trouble he'd brought upon her just by being here.

He was interfering with her life, making things difficult for her, though unintentionally. He had done that once before another time, though with the best of intentions. By interfering he had meant to "save" a woman. Instead, he had prompted her to run away.

He wouldn't make that mistake again. When the day came that he was fit to leave, he would go.

But every time he thought of that day—which most certainly would come soon—his heart felt to be squeezed in a vise, and he pushed the thought out of his mind to block the pain.

He knew little enough about the Amish and their ways but enough to know that Rachel would most likely be horrified to learn that he had feelings for her. A word to her of the sort, and she would either laugh in his face or run screaming from the house.

Even so he still couldn't quite bring himself to consider leaving her. Not yet. Besides, didn't he have a legitimate excuse to stay in

Riverhaven for a time? He could hardly leave until Asa returned, after all. The two of them would then leave together, make their way to Cincinnati, to his other boat. He had only part of a crew there. He needed Asa before taking on more cargo and heading south again.

But he couldn't wait here, in her house. Not much longer.

He would have to find another place to stay. Somewhere in the vicinity and close enough that Asa would have no difficulty finding him when he returned. But far enough away that he'd make no more trouble for Rachel.

The thought of staying nearby, close enough to see her now and then, made the idea of leaving a bit more tolerable.

17

FIRESTORM

*Oh! What shall come of
this lonely dreaming?*

THOMAS CAULFIELD IRWIN

I t started with a fire.

The following week, just two farms down the road from Phoebe and Malachi Esch's place, Abe Gingerich's barn burned in the middle of the night. Before enough neighbors and the Riverhaven fire wagon could be rallied to help, the structure burned to the ground. Nothing could be saved except the two draft horses that were rescued from the flames by Abe and his oldest son.

Losing a barn was a grievous occurrence for an Amish family. Not only was a barn built by the Plain People a fine work of craftsmanship, but it often housed their work and buggy horses, sometimes the buggy itself, farm implements, tools, and other items needed for their daily tasks.

Rachel was explaining all this to Gant the day after the fire. "It's a terrible thing," she said, "but what keeps it from being even more of a disaster than it might be is that the men in the community will rebuild it quickly. Probably within the next week, if the weather holds out. When something like this happens to one of us, then everyone pitches in to raise a new barn as soon as possible."

They were sitting at the kitchen table after lunch while Gant helped Fannie draw a map of the routes leading from Riverhaven to Marietta, one of her lesson assignments.

"How do you know these roads so well, Captain Gant?" Fannie asked.

"Oh, I've been in the area before, lass. Now and again."

Intrigued not only by his obvious facility with drawing, but also the rapport he'd developed with Fannie, Rachel watched them work as she let the hem out of one of Fannie's dresses. "You're growing up too fast, sister," she said, feigning a stern tone of voice. "Seems that every time I turn around you're needing another hem eased."

Fannie looked up from her paper and grinned. "I'm going to be taller than you and Mamma, don't you think, Rachel?"

"No doubt about it, at the rate you're going. Maybe I'll put a brick on your head to slow you down."

"Huh-uh. I don't care if I grow up to be as tall as Gideon."

"You do that and you'll have a hard time getting yourself a sweetheart," Rachel teased. "There aren't that many tall fellows to go around."

"I'll just have to find one like Captain Gant. He's taller yet than Gideon."

"Well, now, Miss Fannie, might be I could arrange to stay the age I am now, and you won't have to look any further than myself."

Fannie smiled as if she liked that idea, but then her face fell. "That won't work, Captain Gant. You're not Amish."

"There's that," he said with a sigh. "So it seems you'll either need to slow down a bit or else we'll have to find you a giant when the time comes."

"Or maybe you could join the church and wait for me."

Rachel nearly pricked herself with the needle. She avoided Gant's gaze, but irrational as the thought might be, she wondered how he'd respond to Fannie's remark.

"I doubt that they'd have me, Miss Fannie. But I'm flattered by your interest."

"Fannie, take this up to the bedroom now and try it on. I don't want to iron it until I see if I've let it out enough."

An awkward silence hung over the room when Fannie left. Finally

Gant broke it with a question. "Do they have any thought as to what caused the fire?"

"They think it was arson," Rachel said tightly. "Phoebe said there's no other explanation. Abe's sure no lanterns were left burning. And he doesn't smoke, so there would have been no ash or sparks to ignite anything."

"Why would anyone set one of your barns on fire?" Gant said, frowning.

"Perhaps for the same reason they've done it before."

"This has happened before?"

"Three years ago." The words were hard coming for Rachel. "Before it stopped, three barns and a tool shed burned down. Malachi and Phoebe's barn was one of the ones destroyed."

"And did they find who was responsible?"

Rachel shook her head. "No. It just—stopped. All of a sudden. Until now."

"Surely there were suspects?"

"Not that we ever heard," said Rachel.

Gant leaned back against the chair, and Rachel noticed that he winced with the movement. "Captain Gant, you've been up long enough for now, I think. You'd best lie down for a while."

He scowled at her, probably because she'd called him "Captain Gant" again. Well, too bad if he didn't like it. She simply couldn't bring herself to call him "Gant" or "Jeremiah." It was too…personal. It seemed to bring him too close.

Somehow she knew she dared not close the distance between her and the man sitting across from her, regarding her with an openly curious expression.

"I feel fine," he said. "I'll not coddle myself any longer. So, these fires, then—did anyone come up with a reason for them? A motive?"

"It wasn't only the fires." Rachel spoke before she thought and instantly regretted it. She glanced away but felt him watching her.

"What do you mean?"

She looked at him but didn't answer.

He leaned forward to hold her gaze. "Rachel?" he said softly. "What else happened besides the fires?"

And then Fannie came tripping down the steps and sailed into the kitchen. "Look, Rachel, it's still not long enough! I really am growing fast!"

Rachel exhaled a breath of relief for the interruption and managed a smile for her sister. "You're right. I'll have to start over and let the full hem out this time."

As soon as Fannie left the room again Rachel got up to follow her. "I think I need to measure the dress on her this time," she said, starting for the door before Gant could question her further.

But she had seen the questions in his eyes, and he had the look of a man who wouldn't be satisfied until he had the answers to those questions. Still, if she could put him off until the time came for him to leave, then surely she could avoid telling him anything more than he needed to know.

Gant got up, settled himself on his crutches, and then walked around the kitchen and the bedroom for a few minutes. He had it in his head that if he walked enough, moved about enough, the healing would go faster. Not that the doctor had advised any such thing. It was just something he *felt*.

The need to heal, to get back to normal, seemed to accelerate every day. Even though he was pretty much stuck in this place, nearly at his wits' end with nothing to do until Asa got back, he needed to at least *feel* ready to get on with life. And now something about the news of last night's fire had added even more pressure to his resolve to quicken his recovery.

Maybe it was just Irish superstition trying to crowd its way into his usually practical nature, but he couldn't shake the feeling—especially after hearing what Rachel had to say—that last night's fire might be the harbinger of more trouble ahead for this Amish community. True, he didn't know enough about the folks in the settlement to genuinely have a care or concern for their well-being, but he *did* care about Rachel and Fannie. And Rachel's mother as well. From what he'd seen of Susan Kanagy, she was a lady worth a heap of respect.

Whatever was working on him, he didn't like it. He felt—pressured. Frustrated. Oppressed by his own haste to heal.

Moonstruck, is what he was.

By a woman with heartache in her eyes and the blush of peaches on her skin and a smile that set the stars to shame.

All that he was feeling—all that he was wanting—was wrapped up in a girl-woman he hardly knew. A woman who considered him forbidden, perhaps even an abomination.

Suddenly exhausted, he dragged himself on his crutches to the bedroom and sank down in the rocking chair by the window. He sat staring outside at a barren skeleton of a maple tree that appeared as storm-battered as his heart.

18

TWO MEN ON THE SAME ROAD

Drive the demon of Bigotry home to his den...

WILLIAM DRENNAN

David Sebastian closed his instrument case and bent over the crib for a final look at Peter and Rebecca Schrock's baby boy. Nearly two months early, the tiny fellow had weighed in at only a little over three pounds at birth. Now, five weeks later, he seemed to be thriving, thanks to God and Rebecca, clearly a successful partnership as seen by all four of the Schrock children.

Rebecca had never carried a baby full-term. David had tried everything he knew with all four pregnancies, but in spite of everything, each time she delivered a few weeks early. Tiny Ben here, as the community was already calling him, had come earliest of all, and David had been seriously concerned about his condition. From the looks of things so far, however, he was getting along just fine.

He checked the hot water bottles that lined the baby bed to keep the infant warm and as always found them just the right temperature. These drafty farmhouses in the winter could work against an infant. It took continual diligence to keep a baby—especially an early baby—warm enough. But Rebecca Schrock was conscientious to a fault when it came to her children. Although each newborn presented its own special challenges at birth and sometimes for months and even years afterward, David doubted that there were any healthier children in the Amish community.

Before leaving he allowed himself the indulgence of a generous piece of apple pie. Had he ever left after a call at the Schrock farm without having a piece of pie or cake pressed upon him? Not likely. Certainly not that he could remember.

Nor could he recall sitting at the kitchen table without an audience of little Schrocks. Today was no different. Two-year-old Anna of the dimpled cheeks and turned-up nose stood right beside him, watching his every move. The shy, quiet four-year-old Leah stood at his other side, but not quite so close. At the end of the table Moses, a very wise and wiry seven-year-old, stood studying David as if he'd never seen him before.

Rebecca tried to shoo them out of the room, but David just laughed. "Let them be. I enjoy their company."

"I'll send them home with you for a day, and we'll see how well their company wears. You should have a house full of your own *kinner,* Doctor, a good man like yourself."

"I do have a son, you know."

Rebecca did know, but she would still make her point. "*Ja,* but he's all grown up now and you hardly ever see him. You're still a young man. We need to find you a good wife so you can have another family."

For as long as he could remember, one Amish wife or the other had been trying to marry David off. The Riverhaven folks were so oriented to big families and ever expanding households that they were convinced it was the only way to live.

David wasn't so sure but that they were right.

On the other hand, if he were to openly agree with them, they'd never let up. As Rachel Brenneman sometimes teased, they'd do their best to "Amishize" him.

What he never admitted to his Amish friends—or to anyone else, for that matter—was how much he would *like* to have a "second family," even if that family included only a wife. But not just any wife. Only one….

He'd planned to drop by and check on Gant yet today, so with some reluctance, he left the congenial Schrock fireside and started off for another good-natured confrontation with the Irishman. In truth their meetings these days *were* good-natured. Ironic as it was—and almost in spite of themselves—he and Gant seemed to be on their way to becoming friends. They'd gone long past the national disdain typically reserved by an Englishman for an Irishman and conversely. They actually got along quite well.

And wasn't *that* something?

These days Gant found himself looking forward to the doctor's visits. He enjoyed the physician's dry sense of humor and flair for irony. Plus the man's intelligence seemed to favor curiosity as much as book learning. Lately they'd had some good talks, not to mention a few rousing, though not rancorous, arguments about politics and world events. In truth Dr. Sebastian wasn't a bad sort at all.

For a Brit.

The thought flared in his mind like a wayward spark blown away from the fire before it could be put out. Yet the reality was that he had grown weary of the old Irish-British enmity. Seen from the perspective of distance—he'd been away from the chokehold of Ireland's poverty and the all-encompassing atmosphere of hatred for several years now—the hostility of the one nation toward the other seemed a deadlock from which neither country would ever be extricated.

As his Uncle Bran had put it, "England writes the music for Ireland's misery, while the Irish are only too glad to furnish the lyrics. Trouble is, neither one of them knows how to sing."

Of course Gant had never been sure what exactly his somewhat unhinged uncle had been talking about most of the time, but he did have a way with words.

Not that hatred for the Irish was limited to the British. His years in New York had taught him that. Americans aplenty made no secret of the fact that they'd like to round up all the Irish immigrants and send them packing back where they came from.

That is, until they came up against a job with which they disdained to dirty their hands. Then let's hear it for the Irish.

David found his patient impatient.

A good sign. Clearly Gant was frustrated with his inactivity and bored with being housebound. He was eager to be fully recovered and back to doing whatever it was he did when he wasn't on the river. Apparently that included breaking the law to help runaway slaves.

In any case the Irishman's desire to return to a normal life should help to fuel his strength and hasten his recuperation.

"I also need a place to stay," Gant was saying. "Rachel hasn't said as much, but I've no doubt her church folks are giving her a hard time. And now that I'm up and about and no longer as helpless as a sick cat, things are sure to get worse for her the longer I'm about."

"There's no argument to be had there," said David. "I'm surprised Samuel Beiler hasn't given you a shove out the door himself." He stopped. "Though of course he wouldn't resort to such, being Amish."

Gant scowled and nodded. "The deacon who's sweet on Rachel."

"You've noticed."

"Well, from what she says, it's also a part of his and the bishop's *responsibility* to protect her," Gant said, his tone dripping with sarcasm.

David leveled a look on him. "And that's the way it should be. Rachel is young and on her own. No father, no husband, no children."

"What happened to her husband?"

Gant's tone was blunt. David was on the verge of telling him that what happened to Eli Brenneman was none of his business, but he saw something in the other's eyes that made him soften his reply. If he wasn't badly mistaken, he'd worn that same look himself more than once.

"It's really not for me to say. That needs to come from Rachel."

His reply seemed to exasperate the other.

"Is it true, then, what I've heard—the Amish don't believe in any sort of violence, even when it comes to self-defense?"

"That's right. Their way is to turn the other cheek."

Gant scowled again. "Then if the good deacon Beiler and the rest of them feel so duty-bound to protect Rachel, just how would they go about it?"

Gant wasn't the first person to raise this particular question, and David didn't have a particularly good answer. "I suppose what they do is try to keep themselves and others out of harm's way."

Gant grunted his disapproval.

"There are other ways to protect oneself and loved ones besides violence," David added, cringing inwardly at the sanctimonious tone of his words.

But Gant seemed not to notice. He was ready with another question. "You've heard about the fire, I expect?" Gant said.

Surprised by this abrupt change of subject, David nodded.

"I understand there were fires before. A few years ago."

Again David gave a nod. "Several. We can only hope this isn't the beginning of another wave of harassment."

"That's what it was, then? Harassment?"

"It was that...and more."

Gant was clearly waiting for an explanation, but David was loath to bring up that awful year. It still brought a sick feeling every time he thought of it. Moreover, he almost felt as though it might be a kind of betrayal of trust to the Amish community to discuss what had happened with an "outsider."

And yet he sensed that the man wasn't simply curious or intent on prying. One didn't have to look too closely to see that Gant had a genuine interest in Rachel and that it was that interest—and concern—prompting his questions.

Even so, he didn't feel it was his place to go into detail. "It was the sort of thing that's happened in other Amish communities. There's no explaining, is there, why some take a dislike to a particular group? Sometimes it's due to race. Other times it focuses on differences in religion or a way of life. It was a bad time for the Riverhaven Amish— a very bad time."

"Is that when Rachel's husband died? During that time?"

David hesitated and glanced away. "Well...yes. A little before then, actually." He turned and pointed to the footstool. "Let's have a look at your leg."

Gant stayed in the chair, hoisted his leg up, and watched as David examined the wound.

"Well," he said after a moment, "it looks very good. *Very* good. It's as I told you the other day, you're doing quite well." He straightened. "So—you mentioned wanting a place to stay. It shouldn't be all that long, you know, before you can travel again. But it's still too soon to tell."

"Well, in the meantime I need to find a place around here—some-where nearby—to stay until Asa gets back, and I have no way of knowing how long that might be. As I told you, I don't want to make any more problems for Rachel."

"You must have some idea of how long you'll be needing a place. Where did he go?"

The shutters closed on Gant's expression. "He's doing some busi-ness for me."

David twisted his mouth. "No doubt."

He waved off Gant's attempt to interrupt. "Never mind. I don't need to know. Let me think for a moment."

He knew a place all right, but that wasn't what he needed to think about. What he questioned was just how much he trusted this man. He had blown in from out of nowhere, gunshot and half-dead, offer-ing next to no information about himself and where he'd come from. The little information David knew had been gleaned from what the man Asa—a former slave—had revealed to Rachel and Susan.

Gant was Irish. Not that that mattered to him—he'd seen enough in his lifetime to hold no man's race or nationality above another's. But he was clearly a loner, a solitary sort, and apparently without roots. A loner and a wounded stranger who stepped out of the night and into a community that wanted nothing to do with him. Jeremiah Gant was about as welcome among the Riverhaven Amish as a wounded wolf.

Maybe even less so.

Yet some instinct about the riverboat captain had told David for some time now that he could trust the man.

There was also the fact that his idea might help to put his own mind a little more at ease about Rachel. And Susan. He'd simply feel better if there were a man besides Gideon—who was gone more than he was at home—in reasonable proximity to both women.

Especially in light of last night's fire. Just in case the old trouble was starting up again.

He didn't want to think that way, mustn't think that way, at least not unless something else happened. But there was no putting out of his memory what had happened before.

At the time he'd been convinced that Rachel and her family had been targets of the harassment. *Harassment?* No, it was as he'd told Gant—it had been more than harassment. Much more. And even though other families besides Rachel's had been victims of what some had called the *persecution,* he'd believed then and believed now that the other incidents had been random, perhaps designed to distract the authorities from the real intent.

Moreover, he still wasn't convinced it had been a *religious* persecution rather than something more personal.

In any event a man like Gant on the premises—or at least nearby—injured though he was, well, it couldn't hurt.

He sat down at the foot of the bed and studied Gant, seated only a few feet away from him in the rocking chair. At first glance the man had the look of a rogue. Somewhat rough in appearance with a hard edge about him, his bearing hinted at what might have been a dark past. Certainly there was no real "refinement" to him. Yet his intelligence, his self-deprecating sense of humor, and the way he had of meeting another man's gaze straight on served to reassure David that there was nothing furtive about him.

"You really have no idea how long you'll be needing a place?" he asked him.

"I don't, no. But I'm hoping that by the time Asa gets back, I'll be well enough to leave."

Was there a hint of reluctance in his tone? Somehow David got the sense that Gant might not be quite so eager to get away as he would have been if he'd not had these past few weeks with Rachel.

David's mind made a few more turns before he finally reached a decision. "I own a small house just down the road, close to Riverhaven. It's outside the Amish settlement but nearby. I use it sometimes in winter if I have a bad patient or a mother about to deliver—I have several patients in Riverhaven as well as here among the Amish. Especially in bad weather, I don't always want to go all the way back to the farm. It's furnished, though it's nothing fancy. If you think you're ready to be on your own, you can use it for the time being."

Gant's eyes brightened. "That would be grand. That way I can stay close enough to—to know when Asa gets back."

Almost had a slip of the tongue, there, didn't you, man?

David was almost tempted to warn him not to set his feelings on Rachel Brenneman. He knew all too well, from his own experience, how utterly futile—and painful—it could be to lose one's heart to an Amish woman. But that would be poor form entirely. Gant's heart was none of his business, other than his professional duty to keep it beating.

He'd done that and wasn't responsible for anything more.

Still, he couldn't help but feel a measure of empathy for the man, enough that he hoped Gant didn't let his emotions go wandering down the same dead-end road as his own.

19

SAMUEL PLEADS HIS CASE

The hope, the fear, the jealous care,
The exalted portion of the pain
And power of love, I cannot share,
But wear the chain.

LORD BYRON

A week later Rachel was still trying to get used to being alone
again.

After Gant moved into Dr. Sebastian's house at the crossroads,
Fannie had returned home, Gideon no longer dropped by except for
a hurried cup of coffee, and of course the doctor wasn't stopping in
on a regular basis to check on Gant. So other than an occasional visit
from Mamma, she had her house to herself again.

She had thought she would welcome the peace and quiet after all
the distractions of the past few weeks. Instead, she found herself at
loose ends. No matter how busy she kept, she missed the more harried pace, the lack of a predictable routine, the flurry of folks coming
in and out.

She missed Gant.

The realization shook her so badly she almost dropped the basket
of eggs she'd just collected. She half expected to see him perched on
a chair at the kitchen table, looking up at her with that crooked smile
as he helped Fannie with some aspect of her schoolwork.

But of course the kitchen was empty. No Gant. No Fannie.

No laughter or noise. No sound at all.

She set the egg basket on the counter by the sink and then went to look out the window. From here she could see down the road quite a ways, but the small white frame house, where he was staying, was still out of view.

What did he do with his days now? How did a man with an injured leg, alone in a house with no real work to do, spend his time?

He had stopped by only once. He'd come by the day after he moved out to pick up the clothes she'd laundered for him. At the same time, he'd tried again to pay "for his keep." Rachel hadn't taken his money the first time he'd offered, and she refused the second time as well.

She tried to explain that the Amish didn't do for others with any expectation of payment. They helped because it was what the Lord God would *want* them to do, what He would expect them to do.

Gant had seemed frustrated with her refusal. She sensed that he was a man who was used to paying his way for everything and didn't quite know how to respond when he couldn't.

His confusion had almost been amusing.

She hadn't seen him since. Nor should she *want* to see him. Her life was considerably easier with him out from under her roof. She had less work to do, fewer worried looks from her mother, and surely by now tongues had stopped wagging among the People about the outsider she'd taken in during the middle of the night.

She was still standing at the window when she saw Samuel Beiler coming up the road. As he drew closer, pulled up to the house, and stepped out of the buggy, she saw that he wasn't wearing his work clothes but was instead dressed more formally in his best clothes and hat. Church-going clothes.

She gripped the edge of the counter.

Now what?

→ ←

"*Guder mariye,*" Samuel said when Rachel opened the door.

"Samuel. Good morning to you also."

He entered without being invited, as he once had before the tension over Gant had developed between them. Rachel hoped this was an indication that his visit was a casual one, but given the way he was dressed, she wondered.

Once inside he did wait until she'd invited him to sit down before hanging up his coat and hat. He sat at the kitchen table, watching her while she fixed him a cup of tea. Rachel smiled as she sat down at the table across from him. She needed this to be a friendly visit, not a rancorous one. She had little energy these days for confrontation.

Besides, with Gant now out of the house, Samuel shouldn't have any reason to be making a visit in his capacity as a deacon of the church. At least none that she could think of.

"You make the best tea of anyone I know, Rachel," he said, speaking in the *Deitsch.*

"I think you're not so particular about your tea, Samuel."

"But I am. And yours is the best."

She had set a tin of molasses cookies she'd baked yesterday on the table with his tea, and he helped himself to one now.

"I have a terrible sweet tooth, as you know," he said.

Samuel almost always took his time easing into a conversation, but Rachel had little use for small talk and deliberately tried to keep him focused. "So, Samuel, what brings you out for a visit so early?"

He finished his cookie and took another sip of tea before replying. "Truth is, Rachel, I've been wanting to talk with you about this for some time now, but you've been…busy, so I decided to wait."

His mood seemed to have turned so solemn that Rachel felt a clench of apprehension in her chest. Even his tone of voice deepened.

Samuel clasped his hands on top of the table, looking directly at her. "Rachel, it's surely no secret that I'm very fond of you and have been for a long time."

Rachel froze. This wasn't the first time Samuel had spoken of his feelings. She thought she had put this to rest once before. That had been over a year ago. Apparently he meant to try again. And this time he seemed prepared to be more direct.

"Samuel—" She hoped to stop him before he could start.

"No. Let me speak, Rachel. You must know I...have strong feelings for you, have had these feelings for a long time. I continue to hope that eventually you might return those feelings. In any case I think it's fair to say that we *are* good friends and good companions. Surely you know me well enough by now to believe that I would make you a good husband. And I believe I know *you* well enough to know you don't really enjoy being alone."

Again Rachel tried to protest. And again he stopped her.

"Wait. We both know that many couples marry without a strong romantic love on both sides. Sometimes they marry as friends and the love comes later, after they're together for a time. I believe that could be the way for us too, Rachel, if you would just allow yourself to try. We *are* friends, are we not?"

"Of course we are, Samuel, but—"

"And you do care for me on some level, do you not?"

"I care for you," Rachel said, choosing her words with caution, "but not the way you want me to. Samuel, you mean much to me as an old and dear friend but only in that way. I thought I'd made this clear to you before."

He seemed not to hear her words or, at least, dismissed them. "Many good marriages begin between good friends, Rachel. Right here among the People, it's a common thing. Not so unusual at all."

He was right, of course. Rachel knew more than one couple who had married for reasons that had more to do with friendship and companionship than romantic love. But it could never be that way for her. Not after the love she had shared with Eli. She could *never* live as husband and wife with a man she didn't love.

Clearly, though, Samuel had no intention of giving up. "Rachel, it's because we *are* good friends that I believe a marriage between us would work. I—need you, Rachel. I need a mother for my three sons, and I've seen how you are with Fannie. My boys love you and would welcome you into our home. You would be a wonderful mother. And, Rachel, I'm not an old man. Thirty-eight is all. We could have more children, babies. We'd be happy together, good for each other." He stopped but only for an instant. "I—have much affection for you, Rachel. And I believe your feelings for me would deepen in time. Can't you trust me to know what's best for you?"

It was all too much. It had to end. Rachel stood, moved behind her chair, and placed both hands on the back of it. "Samuel, even *I* don't know what's best for me. I don't think we can assume that *you* do. Please, don't let's have this discussion again. I've told you how I feel. I'm not comfortable with our talking together like this. I want to *keep* our friendship as it's always been, but to do that, you *must* accept the fact that there's never going to be anything else between us."

"There could be, if you would allow it," he said, his tone stern. "Rachel, Rachel—you can be so stubborn..."

"This has nothing to do with my being stubborn!" Rachel blurted out, exasperated with him. "If anyone is being headstrong, it's you. Samuel, why can't you understand? I can't *force* myself to feel something that isn't there. You have to accept this."

He stood, suddenly seeming taller and thinner than usual. His eyes were hard, his mouth tight. "It's that man, Gant, isn't it? His worldliness has distracted you. He's enticed you with his outsider ways. I *warned* you he would be trouble, Rachel. He's even turned you away from your friends."

"Gant turned me away from *nothing*, Samuel! And besides, he's gone now. Why must you keep bringing him up?"

He uttered a low sound of frustration. "He's not gone, not really. I don't understand Dr. Sebastian opening his house to him and giving him a place to stay nearby."

Rachel studied him, puzzled at what appeared to be a mean-spiritedness she had never seen in him before. "I don't understand why you're acting like this. He needs to stay close by until he's completely healed and until his friend Asa returns. Then he'll leave. Why does he bother you so, when you don't even know him?"

"Because I *don't* know him, that's why! And neither do you. The man is an outsider, Rachel. He doesn't belong here. If you have no caution for yourself, I'd think you would at least be concerned for your mother's and Fannie's welfare."

By now Rachel was fighting to keep her patience from snapping altogether. "Gant is no threat to anyone. Not to Mamma or myself, and certainly not to Fannie. To the contrary, they get on very well together."

"Because he's playing up to *you,* can't you see that?" He thumped his hand on the table so hard Rachel jerked.

She tightened her grip on the back of the chair, struggling to keep her self-control. This was wrong, so wrong. His being upset as he was, the way she was speaking to him, the way she was *feeling* toward him. He was her friend, her deacon. A man she'd known most of her life and trusted for as long. It was a bitter thing, a bad thing, to be angry with someone who was such an important part of her life.

She was also angry with herself, for her reluctance to admit that Samuel might be right about one thing. She wasn't so certain but what Gant *hadn't* distracted her. If truth be told, even in the short time he'd stayed here, she had felt a reluctant attraction for him, almost a fascination for him. He flustered her with his crooked smile, his roguish mustache, his piercing stare that of late seemed to soften when it rested on her, his rhythmic Irish words—even the way he said her name.

It shamed her that the first man who had sparked any feeling at all in her since Eli's death was an outsider, a forbidden stranger. Why indeed, couldn't it be Samuel who drew such attention from her?

The silence between them gave way as Samuel said, "I'll go now, Rachel. I see that you're not ready to talk more in depth about us just yet. I'm a patient man, you know. I'll wait."

She looked at him, trying to hide her relief that, at least for the time being, he wasn't going to continue pleading his case.

Although "pleading" was never the right word to use when Samuel meant to persuade.

He retrieved his coat and hat from the wall hook before she could get them for him. Just before he opened the door, he turned, and said, "Will you at least think about these things, Rachel?"

Rachel followed him to the door but kept a discreet distance. She didn't quite know how to answer him. No doubt she *would* think about what he'd said because his words and attitude troubled her deeply—in part because she wished she could respond to him as he so obviously wanted her to. "Yes, Samuel, I'll...think about these things."

His smile was faint and fleeting, but at least he didn't seem so agitated as before.

"It will all work out in God's will and in His time, Rachel. You'll see."

After he left Rachel pressed her back against the door and breathed deeply from relief and weariness. She found herself praying that God *would* work things out, that He would bring Samuel the love he wanted and seemed so desperately to need...but would never find with *her*.

❖ 20 ❖

ASA

I looked for Him in holy halls,
In great cathedrals fair,
But in a child's bright eyes of hope,
I looked and found Him there.

ANONYMOUS

After leaving Mt. Ephraim, which according to the captain's map was the last big hill on their trip for quite a distance, the journey became less grueling. The weather was decent, and they were finally making good time. They passed through Barnesville, where a Quaker family sheltered them for two days and nights, fed them well, and replenished their food supply with enough to last them for several days on the road.

Before they reached Freeport, however, they ran into a hard storm of rain and sleet, with a sky that threatened snow before morning. The wagon skidded and bumped all over the place because of the mud slicks and ruts in the road. Asa shivered under the blanket wrapped around him, while the icy rain pelted the canvas of the wagon with a vengeance. He knew the women and children in back were probably miserable, but they still had a ways to go yet before reaching any hope of shelter.

There couldn't have been a worse time to hear the announcement Dinah brought as she crawled forward and parted the canvas flap between them.

"We got to stop."

Asa called over his shoulder to her, "We can't stop now, woman. There's no sign of town yet and no place to pull off. " Beside him, Mac chuffed as if to agree.

"Town or no town," she said, clutching his sleeve, "Mattie is going to have this baby. We got to stop, I tell you!"

"The baby's coming?" He again shot his words over his shoulder, trying at the same time to watch the road. "Are you sure?"

"Sure as can be. You need to find us a place to stop *now*."

"But there *is* no place. We should be close to Freeport—we *are* close—our next station is just this side of the town. We'll have to wait until we get there."

"How much longer will that be?"

"I'm not sure, but according to the map, we're almost there."

"Well, Mister—" she stopped. "You got a last name?"

He shook his head. "Just Asa."

"Well, Asa—this baby don't care nothing about your map. I'll do what I can, but you need to find us a place and find it right soon."

And with that, she crawled back under the canvas. Mac gave a short bark, as if to add his own sense of urgency.

When another half hour passed with still no sight of Freeport, desperation gripped Asa. The groans and cries coming from the back of the wagon told him that Dinah hadn't exaggerated. Mattie's baby was meaning to be born.

"Lord, Lord, what a bitter night for a new little life to arrive. Surely You don't want a helpless baby to be born in the middle of nowhere, without so much as a roof over its head. And in such a storm, Lord…"

Mac put a heavy paw on Asa's arm. That dog was something. He even seemed to understand when his people needed reassurance.

Asa continued to search ahead and look around, from one side of the road to another, as he went on praying.

"Come to think of it, Lord, You didn't have it any better the night You were born, did You? You didn't have a roof over Your head either, and that stable was most likely in a nowhere kind of place. But at least it was dry, wasn't it? Our situation being what it is, we really need to find a place soon. Real soon. Those poor folks in the back of the wagon have already been through a lot. Why, that young girl who's about to give birth is hardly more than a child herself, and here she is, without any help in sight, and myself without a single thought of what to do. I need You to show me where to go so she can have this baby in a safe place. And, the thing is, I need You to show me now..."

Ahead of him, the road gradually took on a wideness, and as the wagon rounded a curve, he caught sight of a faint light set back maybe thirty or forty feet from the road. A narrow dirt lane branched off the main road, and Asa slowed to a near stop. He could see other lights in the distance now, only a few, but enough to indicate a town ahead.

Mac watched him as he studied the house, which looked to be small and surrounded by a primly painted fence and a large area of lawn. It didn't appear to be a farm, but simply a residence.

A residence at the edge of a town.

That town would be Freeport. And that light in the window would be a candle. And off to the side, thoroughly soaked by the rain and sleet, hung a quilt.

He hesitated only a moment more before turning off the main road and onto the lane leading up to the house.

"The Lord is good, a stronghold in the day of trouble...Blessed be the Lord...

The woman, holding a lantern, opened the door only a crack to peek out. She was small and elderly, with white hair and a white nightcap on her head. *Frail* was the first word that came into Asa's mind.

"Missus? I'm Asa, a friend of friends. We need help."

She raised the lantern a little higher and studied him and then looked past him to the wagon.

"You are Mrs. Scott?" said Asa, praying she was.

After a long moment, she nodded. "I am Mary Scott. Bring your people around back," she said, her voice little more than a whisper. "Quickly."

Asa left the others in the wagon while he spoke with her at the back door, explaining he had a woman in the family way about to give birth. "If you have a barn or a tool shed, we'll make do. I'll carry water and fetch whatever they need. We'll not put you to any trouble."

She looked fragile enough to break in two if she were to move suddenly. "You will bring your passengers inside. A woman about to deliver a baby needs a warm bed, and I have plenty of room."

Greatly relieved, Asa nodded. "Your kindness is much appreciated, missus. But—we have a dog too."

"A *dog?*"

As if he knew he was being discussed, Mac barked from his place on the wagon bench. "Well, all right," she said, the reluctance in her tone all too evident." He needs to stay quiet, though. I suppose he can stay in the wash house for now. Folks around here know I don't have a dog. But we need to hurry and get you hid. We've had a slave hunter in the area for two days, and there are some who are amenable to him."

Asa hesitated. "If you're alone, Mrs. Scott, I don't want to bring any trouble to you. We'll move on if you'd rather."

"You will not," she said sharply. "Bring your people inside now. And then hide your wagon in the copse of trees behind the well in back."

Her tone left no room for argument. Besides, they *did* need her help and needed it badly. What choice did he have? Asa hurried the women indoors, he and Dinah supporting Mattie, with the children following behind them.

Mary Scott led them down a hallway, the lantern she carried their only light, to a flight of steps leading off the kitchen. The room below the house looked as if at one time it might have been a man's workshop.

A neat row of hand tools hung above a long table flanking the right wall, but on the other side of the room was a full-size bed and a large rocking chair.

As they started across the room, Mattie cried out, grabbing her abdomen. Mrs. Scott took Asa's place at her side, murmuring as she might have to a small child. "You poor dear. You must be terribly uncomfortable. We'll get you to bed right away."

She took another lantern from the wall, lighted it, and hung it from a hook near the bed. With little more than a glance at Asa, she said, "Are you the father to these girls?"

He gave a vigorous shake of his head. "No, missus. I'm just a conductor."

"Well, you help the little mother onto the bed—I keep it fresh and clean for new visitors—and then take those children up to the kitchen," she instructed him. "You'll find some bread and jam on the sideboard and a sugar cream pie. Help yourself and feed the children."

She looked at Dinah. "Are you this girl's mother?"

"Yes'm, I am. That there's Mattie. And I'm Dinah."

"Well, Dinah, you help me get your daughter settled in bed. From the looks of her, you'll have to wait a spell for your supper. Right now we need to get things ready for the baby. Are the little girls yours as well?"

"The oldest two are. The youngest is Mattie's child."

"My. And she looks so young."

"She's seventeen." Dinah's tone held a trace of bitterness.

As Asa lifted Mattie onto the bed, Mary Scott studied the girl, her face lined with kindness. Then she turned to Asa. "You go on now," she told him. "This is no place for a man. You go take care of those children."

Feeling awkward at the position he'd been thrust into—he knew next to nothing about children—Asa herded the little girls upstairs and down the hall in search of the kitchen, the older two clinging to his hands while the little one clutched at his pants legs.

He reckoned Mrs. Mary Scott to be a fine woman with a big heart, but he thought she might also have a sharp tongue on her if folks didn't do as she said. In any event, the woman was obviously not nearly as frail as she looked.

Nearly an hour later, Asa had settled Mac in the wash house and hid the wagon where Mrs. Clark had said. The children had eaten their fill and quizzed him to the point of distraction about everything from having babies to what kind of shoes horses wore.

Mrs. Scott came to the kitchen just then, long enough to order the girls upstairs and to bed.

At first Asa attempted to protest. "These children are none too clean, Mrs. Scott. We've been on the road for a long time, in the dust and mud and rain. You don't want them mussing up your nice things."

"Then clean them up," she said shortly. "Just wash their faces and hands and have them take off their shoes. That will have to do for tonight. They're clearly exhausted. You'll find towels and washcloths in the upstairs closet at the end of the hall. Put them in the room right across from that closet. Go on now, so they can have a good rest. Dinah and I will see to things down here. We'll do just fine by Mattie."

Asa had no doubt about that. He had a sense that Mrs. Mary Scott could take care of just about anything.

As it turned out the two older girls pretty much took care of themselves and the youngest one—Lucy—as well. Mostly, all Asa had to do was listen to their prayers.

"Mamma says don't never go to sleep till we thank Jesus for our blessings and say a prayer for one another," Sissy told him. "Tonight we'll thank Jesus for you, Mr. Asa. And for Mrs. Scott too. I think she's one of the Lord's holy angels, just like you."

"Child, I'm no angel," Asa said, dismayed that this little one would even think of him as such. "But I surely would covet your prayers for me, all the same."

After taking some food out to the wash house for Mac—with Mrs. Scott's permission of course—Asa had gone back to the kitchen. He was dozing in a chair by the stove when he heard a loud shriek, followed by an infant's thin wail. He jumped up and went to the top of the steps to listen.

The crying continued amidst women's hushed voices and an occasional soft laugh. Finally he left the landing and began to pace. It was another fifteen minutes or more before Mrs. Scott came upstairs to give him the news.

"It's a baby boy. He's a tiny thing, but he appears to be healthy, and I'd say his lungs are excellent."

Asa smiled. He couldn't seem to *stop* smiling. "Well, isn't that fine?" he said. And then said it again.

Much shorter than he, Mary Scott looked up and regarded him with a raised eyebrow. "Indeed it is fine," she said dryly. "And aren't you fortunate that you get to go traveling north in the middle of winter with three children and a newborn? Of course you can't leave right away. You'll have to stay here until Mattie and that baby are strong enough to travel."

The significance of her words struck Asa hard. "We can't do that, missus! The longer we're here, the more danger we'll be caught—and bring trouble down on you as well. No, we'll be leaving tomorrow."

Mary Scott seemed to stretch herself up on tiptoes, for she suddenly appeared a good deal taller than before. "It's *already* tomorrow, and you most certainly won't be leaving yet. You must wait here at least two more days—longer, if need be. And if there's any danger, we'll just have to trust the Lord to handle it."

She moved toward the stairway and then turned, saying, "In the meantime and after breakfast tomorrow, I wouldn't mind if you'd busy yourself fixing a few things around here that have needed doing ever since my husband passed away. Indoors, of course. We can't take a chance on having you seen outside."

Asa stared at her, already resigned to the reality that he was no match for this small woman's iron will.

"First thing in the morning, missus, you just point me to whatever needs doing," he said, "and I'll tend to it. And Mrs. Scott?"

She looked at him.

"I can't thank you enough for what you've done—what you're doing for us. God bless you, missus."

"God has blessed us all, Asa." She gave a quick little nod toward the steps. "Did you remember that today is Christmas Eve? Why don't you come with me now and see the gift the Lord has given."

CHRISTMAS DAY

And bless the door that opens wide
To stranger as to kin...

ARTHUR GUITERMAN

It snowed on Christmas Eve. When Rachel got up on Christmas morning and looked out her window, she could see nothing but pleated folds of white with a gray sky overhead, from which snow was still falling.

She wished she could feel some of the excitement that a snow-covered Christmas morning had evoked in her as a child or even as a young woman, when she and Eli were first married. Instead, the same heavy grayness of the sky seemed to color her emotions.

Before Eli died she had loved the winter season—the beauty, the quiet, and the peace of it. He had often laughed at her "little girl excitement" about snow, but the look in his eyes had always been tender.

Back then her heart had been that of a bride, a butterfly heart that floated and soared and danced over the snow.

Today her heart seemed weighted with lead.

Holidays had been hard since Eli's death. Christmas, especially, was almost unbearable without him. Today, though, she would do her best, as she did on every special occasion, to put a smile on her face for her family's sake. No reason to take away from their Christmas happiness with her heart-heavy memories.

She would have Christmas dinner at Mamma's house with her

mother, Fannie, and Gideon. She would help prepare the meal, help clean up afterward, play a game or two with Fannie, and then come home. Alone.

What was Gant doing this Christmas Day?

Here she was, feeling sorry for herself and almost dreading the day to come, when just down the road, a man still on crutches, a man without friends or family anywhere nearby, would almost certainly be spending this special day by himself. If she felt this lonely today, even though she would be surrounded by her loved ones, what must it be like for Gant, who had no one?

How was he making do by himself? She and Mamma had sent food by Gideon every day or so since he moved out. But was he eating? And could he get around all right on his crutches? What if he happened to fall while he was alone, with no one to know? Dr. Sebastian had taken the train last week to spend Christmas with his son and family in Maryland and wasn't due back until tomorrow. Had he checked Gant's wound before he left?

She wished she dared suggest to Mamma that they invite Gant to share their meal today, but she knew what the answer would be. He was an *auslander*. It just wasn't done.

Or was it? Mamma didn't always hold to tradition or the "rules"— at least not in every instance. Last year when she'd learned that Dr. Sebastian would be staying in the area for Christmas and would be alone, she invited him to Christmas dinner, and he'd accepted. Of course the rules didn't seem to apply to the doctor anymore. He was like family, almost like one of the People himself.

But her mother did seem to like Gant. Rachel had seen it in the way she treated him, the way she laughed so quickly at his friendly, easy sense of humor. Could she be persuaded? Should she at least ask?

A blast of wind howled outside the bedroom window just then, jarring her out of her thoughts and reminding her that she had other things to do besides stand and daydream.

→ ←

As soon as Fannie heard Rachel and Mamma discussing whether to invite Captain Gant for Christmas dinner, she knew it was the right thing to do. But Mamma still sounded doubtful, so Fannie decided to take it upon herself to convince her.

The three of them were working in Mamma's kitchen, preparing the food. Fannie was chopping giblets for the turkey dressing. Mamma had apple pies ready to bake, with the apples she'd dried from the orchard back in October, and Rachel was peeling potatoes. The kitchen already smelled wonderful-*gut,* and it was only a little after ten.

When there was finally a lull in the conversation, Fannie saw her chance and broke in. "I think we should do it, Mamma. We should invite Captain Gant for dinner. It would be awful to spend Christmas Day all by yourself in a house that's not your own, without any family or friends. Why, it wouldn't seem like Christmas at all!"

She saw her mother look at Rachel and Rachel look back.

"Please, Mamma," Fannie coaxed. "It isn't right *not* to ask him, is it? It's not like he's a *real* outsider. We've known him a long time now, and he's oh so nice. "

Her mother turned to give her a long look.

"He helped me with my lessons and made me a paper house. And he's funny too. Besides, wouldn't Jesus say we ought to invite him, that we're supposed to feed the hungry?"

"Careful what you say, daughter," warned her mother. "We don't use Scripture to justify our own wants."

"Oh, come on, Mamm," said Gideon, sauntering into the kitchen and palming a piece of giblet out from under Fannie's knife. She was in a really good mood today and just grinned at him instead of smacking his hand.

"What's the harm in having the captain in for a meal?" he said. "He's a good enough guy."

Mamma wiped her hands on her apron. She paused. Then looking from face to face, she said, "Oh, all right! But he can't walk up that road in the snow on crutches. You'll have to take the buggy and fetch him, Gideon."

"Sure, I will. But hadn't we better ask him first if he wants to come?"

"He'll want to—I know he will," Fannie put in. "I'll go ask him right now! I want to make some snowballs anyway."

"Fannie, it's too cold," her mother said.

"Mamm—let her go. She'll be fine."

Bless Gideon's big-*bruder* heart! When he used his grown-up tone of voice like that, Mamma almost always did what he said.

Fannie knew Mamma worried about her because she'd had pneumonia two winters straight, and it kind of dragged her down. But Dr. Sebastian said she would probably get stronger as she got older. And besides, he was keeping a really close eye on her this year so it wouldn't happen again.

"I'll bundle up real good, Mamma," she promised. "And I won't stay out long. I'll go to Captain Gant's first and invite him to dinner, and then I'll just play outside for a few minutes. Honest."

"Rachel, you go and make *sure* she wraps up plenty good," Mamma said. "That wind is raw today."

By the time Rachel helped her with her boots and her coat, her cap and gloves, Fannie felt as stuffed as that old turkey in the roasting pan. But it was worth it. She would get to see Captain Gant again today—and she was going to play in the snow!

"I'm so glad Captain Gant is coming for dinner, aren't you, Rachel?"

"We don't know that he *is* coming, Fannie. We haven't even asked him yet. Now you go there first and then come right back here to make your snowballs." She gave her coat collar another tug to make sure it was good and tight. "Why do you want to make snowballs anyway?"

"For our snowball fight later on."

"*Whose* snowball fight?"

"Ours. Yours and mine and Gideon's."

"Oh, we're having a snowball fight, are we?"

Rachel was trying to look stern, but she wasn't a bit cross. Fannie could tell. She knew because Rachel was smiling.

Fannie wanted to look just like her big sister when she grew up. Rachel was so pretty, especially when she smiled. Trouble was she didn't smile a lot anymore.

"Don't expect too much," Rachel warned. "You know Gideon won't stay around long after dinner. He'll be off with some girlfriend or other, soon as we eat."

Fannie pulled a face. "Probably that *Englisch* girl he likes. The one with the pointy nose and thick lips."

"Fannie Kanagy!"

"Well, have you seen her?"

Rachel admitted that she hadn't.

"*I* did one day when we went to town. I don't understand why Gideon likes her at all. She's not nearly as pretty or as nice as Emma Knepp. And Emma likes Gideon a lot. She'd be his sweetheart if he wanted her to."

"And just how do you know that?"

"I can tell by the way she looks at him at preaching service, and how she gets all tongue-tied if he tries to talk to her."

"And I think sometimes *you* talk too much, little sister. You go on now. And remember—tell Captain Gant that dinner's at four o'clock and that Gideon will come get him in the buggy. And, Fannie—"

"I know, I know," Fannie chanted as she went out the door. "Don't stay out too long, don't get too wet, and keep my coat buttoned all the way to the top."

"And don't sass," Rachel shot back.

Fannie gave a wave without turning around, but she could tell by Rachel's voice that she was still smiling.

~ 22 ~

UNFRIENDLY SNOW

*For the world's more full of weeping
than you can understand.*

W.B. YEATS

G ant's Christmas gift to himself was to lose the crutches. He'd
practiced all day using the cane and finally mastered it. Of course
Dr. Sebastian had warned him not to rush matters. "You can do some
real damage to that leg if you hurry things. And if you're on it too
long at a time now, once you're off the crutches, you're just asking for
trouble."

According to the doc, he was going to be lame for the rest of his life
anyway. Not bad, but he'd have enough stiffness in his leg that he'd
limp a bit. If that was the case, the sooner he got rid of the crutches,
the better. He was becoming dependent on the things, and that had
to end. If limp he must, then he'd limp with a cane for the time being.
Not that he intended to use *it* forever either. But for now there was no
ignoring the fact that he needed it. *But only for now.*

He took one more turn around the front room and then went to
look out the window again. Still snowing. It even *looked* like Christmas.

He rubbed the back of his neck with his free hand. He wouldn't
have known it was anywhere near Christmas had it not been for Doc
and Gideon Kanagy. The doctor had mentioned it before he left town
to visit his son. And then yesterday Gideon had showed up with a

teeming basket of food, including some homemade jam and just about the best snickerdoodles he'd ever tasted.

"Christmas Eve special," the lad had said with a grin as he brought the basket inside. "Mamm and Rachel have been baking for a week or more now."

The boy wished him a good Christmas before leaving, and Gant had awkwardly returned in kind.

Most years Christmas was just another day for him. Usually he spent it on the river if it wasn't frozen, at his house if the weather was fierce. It was always just he and Asa, Asa cooking what he referred to as a "civilized" meal for the two of them. But other than eating too much and, in later years, maybe going to church or at least saying a prayer or two, he didn't pay much attention to Christmas or any other holiday.

The thought of Asa made the worry start grinding in on him again. Where would he be by now? The good Lord willing, he hadn't run into too much bad weather along the way.

He'd hated sending him off on his own with Durham's runaways. It just worked better and was safer, if at least two went together on these trips. What with the bounty hunters always on the prowl and some of the rugged, wild country on the trek north, there was no such thing as safe passage.

He turned and went to plop down in the big rocking chair by the window. The next thing he knew Rachel had slipped into his mind.

Nothing unusual about that.

He wondered what she was doing today. How did the Amish spend Christmas anyhow? Or did they even observe it? Obviously they baked. He had enough food left over from yesterday's dinner basket to last him another day or two.

It was probably a big family day for Rachel and her kin. It would be nice, having a family to spend special days with. Most likely they would all eat together and then sit around the table and talk. It would be a good time.

When he lived in Brooklyn and worked at the shipyards, every year Will Tracey, the owner, invited a few of his men to Christmas dinner at his home. The year Gant went, he'd been miserable, feeling out of his station the entire time. The Traceys ate fancy, and back then Gant hadn't known a butter knife from a butcher knife. The water glasses—*goblets,* Mrs. Tracey had called them—had been paper thin and looked so fragile he would have choked to death on a dry throat before picking one of them up for a drink.

When they invited him again the next year, he'd declined, pleading "other plans."

He cracked a grim smile to himself. Those other plans had included too much rum and a cold slab of ham from his Brooklyn landlady's pantry.

But that was before Asa. And before Asa taught him what Christmas was all about.

Fannie trudged down the road, kicking snow as she went. Rachel had her bundled up so snug she had to struggle to kick at all, much less kick as high as she would have liked. Even so she was still able to raise a pretty *gut* cloud of white on the way.

She was thinking about Captain Gant. She couldn't even imagine what it must be like not to be able to use one of your legs. She figured he was the type of man who would enjoy being outside in the snow too. He had lots of fun in him, in spite of his gunshot wound. He seemed to like making her laugh. And he could make Rachel laugh too, though Fannie could tell her sister usually tried not to.

She didn't like to think about the captain leaving the People soon. She wished he wasn't an *auslander,* so he could stay a long time. Maybe forever.

So absorbed was she in plowing through the snow and thinking about Captain Gant that she didn't hear a sound until the boys were almost upon her.

There were four of them. *Englisch* boys, not so big or as old as

Gideon maybe, but not little boys either. They circled her, quickly blocking her from moving in any direction.

Fannie stood very still. She had never been around more than one or two *Englischers* at the same time, and then they were usually small children she happened to meet in a Riverhaven store or on the street. Her heart raced, but she tried not to show that she was afraid.

It was still snowing, big puffy flakes falling slowly and silently. But the snow had lost its storybook prettiness for Fannie. Now it seemed more enemy than friend, for she knew it was too deep to run quickly enough to get away.

They don't mean me any harm, she told herself. *They aren't going to hurt me.*

But in the corner of her vision, the dark shape at her right moved closer, and then closer still.

Thoroughly bored, Gant decided to see if his fiddle was ruined altogether.

To his surprise—and thanks to Rachel's forethought in emptying his suitcase and laying his things to dry—he discovered that it didn't sound half bad, not at all. It was a bit scratchy at first, and he needed to resin the bow and tighten the strings, but at least it still worked.

He worked on it for a half hour or so, and this time when he began to play, it sounded considerably sweeter.

This was one of the few things he had left from Ireland. His chum Liam Brody had taught Gant to play the fiddle and then pressed it into his keeping just before he was jailed for distributing illegal pamphlets in protest of the oppression of the British Crown.

Liam, God rest his soul, had eventually died from a vicious beating at the hands of a prison guard, leaving the fiddle as his only legacy.

Over the years Gant had discovered that the music that wafted forth from the old instrument, albeit at the rough hands of an amateur like himself, could go far in easing his soul and soothing his mind, even in the worst of times.

These weren't the worst of times, of course, though as he glanced down over his injured leg, he had to concede that they weren't exactly the best either.

"Well, lookit here," the boy standing directly in front of Fannie said. "It's a little Amish piggie."

He was a heavyset boy with red cheeks and yellow hair sticking out below his dark cap.

"Where are you going, little piggie?" he said, grinning at her.

The other boys snickered and crowded in closer. Fannie wanted to look away. She wanted to *run* away, but she kept her head up and looked directly at him. "I'm going to see Captain Gant, who lives right down there." She pointed in the direction of Dr. Sebastian's house, where the captain was staying.

"Oh," the boy said, drawing the word out, still grinning. "This little piggie isn't going to market. She's going to see *Captain Gant!*"

Without warning he reached over and grabbed Fannie's bonnet as if to yank it from her head. When he found it tied, he tugged it forward and pulled it free, dangling it by the strings in front of her.

"Give me that!" Fannie cried, reaching for the bonnet. "It's mine!"

He held it higher, swinging it back and forth, laughing at her.

Fannie felt the first burn of tears in her eyes but blinked against them.

"Say 'please,'" he taunted her.

She almost choked on the word, but Mamma would be upset if she came home without her bonnet. "Please!"

Without warning he pushed it in her face, temporarily blinding her. Someone shoved at her back, making her stumble forward, and the boys on either side of her began to push her, first to one and then to the other.

She tried to break away and run, but they circled closer, trapping her in their midst. Each time she lunged forward, they moved in on her, shoving her, laughing at her.

Fannie thought she would strangle on the fear lodged in her throat. She was crying in earnest now. She tried butting her head against the boy with the yellow hair, hoping to push him out of the way, but he was like the trunk of a tree, unyielding and rooted in the snow.

"Aw, now look what you did, Hank. Made the poor little Amish piggie cry," one of the others sneered.

Fannie's breath was coming in painful stabs now. She shouted one long shriek, but even as she did, she knew no one would hear. There was nothing along this part of the road on either side except a few farm houses, all of which were set too far back for anyone to hear her call for help.

They kept shoving her, jeering and laughing at her. In desperation Fannie covered her face with her mittened hands. Her tears felt like frozen rivers on her cheeks.

Suddenly someone planted a vicious kick to the back of one knee. She stumbled and went down, face forward into the snow. She tried to push herself up, but one of them kicked her, hard, in the back, knocking the breath out of her.

A blow to her head was the last thing she felt as the world went white and totally silent.

⇥ 23 ⇤

WAITING FOR FANNIE

Lord, give me faith!—to leave it all to Thee,
The future is Thy gift, I would not lift
The veil Thy love has hung 'twixt it and me.

JOHN OXENHAM

Rachel went to look out the side window of the kitchen again. She wasn't exactly worried about Fannie—at least not yet. At the moment she was more impatient with her.

Her sister knew she wasn't supposed to be out in such cold weather for very long, especially in rain or snow. Fannie seemed to have what Dr. Sebastian called a "predisposition" toward pneumonia and bronchitis. She could get sick so easily—and *stay* sick for such a long time. Then it would take weeks, sometimes even months, for her to make a full recovery.

Fannie was a good child, ordinarily obedient and thoughtful. But she *was* still a child. And at nine years old, who could claim a great deal of self-discipline? No doubt she'd either gotten involved in talking with Gant and lost track of the time—she had taken quite a liking to him from the beginning—or else she was having herself a good and lengthy play in the snow.

Most likely it was a little of both.

But it was still snowing and simply too cold and wet for her to stay outside any longer. Rachel was beginning to wish they hadn't given in to the child's coaxing to invite Gant to dinner.

Truth was she felt an uncomfortable pinch of guilt. If Fannie got sick again, it would be as much *her* fault as her sister's. She'd given in too easily to the girl's urging—because *she* was also missing Gant and wanting to see him again.

Mamma came up beside her just then, and Rachel saw, at a glance at the tight lines around her eyes and mouth, that she was more than impatient. She was worried.

"If your sister doesn't show up in a few minutes," her mother said, "I'm going after her. It's been nearly two hours now."

"I'm sure she's just visiting with Captain Gant, Mamma. She's been missing him. No doubt she's forgotten the time."

"That might be, and I hope you're right, but I gave her to understand that she was to come right back. You and Gideon talked me into letting her go, so one of you can just go with me to bring her home if she isn't here in the next few minutes."

"Well, I'll be the one to go, then. Gideon is still over to the Esches' having a look at the new foal."

Mamma frowned and pressed her lips together. "Well, isn't this just fine, now? Christmas Day, and my children are everywhere but where they ought to be, which is at home. I should have put my foot down with *both* of them."

Rachel put a hand on her mother's arm. "Gideon will be back soon, Mamma, and I'm sure Fannie will too. We'll all be here for Christmas dinner."

Her mother cast one more look out the window and then turned and went to check the oven.

Having seen her mother's concern, Rachel felt her own apprehension grow even darker.

Gant thought it was about time to help himself to some of the leftover treats from the food basket Gideon had delivered the day before. But first he went to throw another log on the fire.

Instead of heading for the kitchen, he went back to the window. The snow was coming down harder than ever, and the wind was blowing, moaning down the chimney. The winter sky had darkened. An involuntary shudder seized him, and not for the first time, he was grateful for the large fireplace in the front room and the generous supply of wood Doc had laid in before leaving last week.

Something caught his eye up the road. He couldn't see all that well through the blowing veil of snow, but there was something dark against the white bank of snow at the side of the road.

He stood watching for a moment, but seeing no movement, he left the window and went to punch up the fire. He chilled easily ever since he was shot, and he stood for a few minutes more, letting the warmth of the flames seep through his bones.

Finally he again crossed the room to the window. It was still there. Something about the size and shape of it stirred an uneasiness in him. He went to the door, thumping the snow away from the threshold with the head of his cane as he looked up the road, hooding his eyes a little with his hand to block the wind.

What was he seeing? An animal that had been hurt, more than likely. Probably dead since there appeared to be no movement.

Any other time he'd have been out on the road by now, having a look for himself. But even with boots, he'd never make it through this snow with a bum leg and a cane. There was nothing for it but to leave it alone, but the thought twisted a knot of anger in him at his helplessness.

Frustrated he slammed the door and limped back to the fire.

Clearly Gideon wasn't going to convince Phoebe Esch he could go home the same way he'd come—by walking.

"No, and you will *not* walk home in this, Gideon Kanagy! Malachi has to hitch up the wagon anyway. I'm sending some food down to Captain Gant, as I'm sure he's all alone, and another basket to Sarah Bender as well. I packed them both some nice baked ham and an apple cake. Neither of them is strong enough to venture out of the house yet, I'm sure. Malachi can drop you at home afterward."

"Actually Fannie was going down to invite Captain Gant to dinner with us," Gideon put in. "I'm to pick him up later."

"Oh, that's good of Susan! She has such a kind heart. But I'll send his basket with you all the same. He can always use it tomorrow."

She turned to look at Malachi. "From the looks of things out there, husband, I'd say you'd best be going."

Malachi nodded, grinning at Gideon as he started for the kitchen door.

"Here, Phoebe," Gideon said, "I'll take the baskets and go on out to the barn with Malachi, so he won't have to come back inside."

He had stayed quite a lot longer than he'd intended. The whole Esch family had gathered for Christmas dinner, and after seeing the foal earlier, he'd gone back inside to visit with everyone, quickly losing track of time. Mamm was most likely going to give him a piece of her mind when he got home.

But she wouldn't be too put out with him. Not on Christmas Day.

As they trudged down the lane to the barn, he wondered if Fannie had talked Captain Gant into coming for dinner. "Hey, Malachi—if Gant is planning on coming to dinner at our house, do you mind if we just pick him up now and take him along?"

"*Ja*, sure, we can do that. No need having to make any more trips out in this snow than you need to."

It looked as if it were about to stop snowing, but in the meantime Mamma was pacing the floor, stopping every minute or so to look out the window.

"It's so bad out," she said. "Fannie wouldn't stay out so long in this. And I can't think your *bruder* would either. I don't know what to do." She looked at Rachel. "Something's happened. I know it has."

Rachel went to her mother. "You can't know that, Mamma. But you *do* know how Gideon will take on over that new foal. And he'll visit with the Esches. We should have talked him out of going in the first place."

Her mother turned from the window to look at her. "As if we could talk Gideon out of anything, once he's set his head to doing it."

Her mother was right. Her brother had a mind of his own, and it was a right stubborn mind most of the time.

"I'll get my coat and boots and stop at Phoebe's for Gideon. We'll go find Fannie. And I have a feeling we'll find her playing in the snow."

Rachel did her best to sound positive for Mamma's sake, but she was worried too, even frightened. She could just shake Gideon for not coming back sooner. It was bad enough to worry about Fannie, but they didn't need to be fretting about Gideon as well. He was a man now. He ought to be more responsible.

"No, I don't think you should go out in this alone, Rachel," her mother said. "At least wait until Gideon gets back, so he can go with you."

Shaken by the tremor in her mother's voice, Rachel tried to think what to do. Mamma simply didn't get rattled. She and Gideon were a lot alike that way—steady and thoughtful, practical and not easily excited. But there was no mistaking the fear in her mother's eyes. Moreover, Rachel thought it probably mirrored her own growing apprehension.

If Gideon didn't come soon, she would go.

Gant kept going back to the window to look out, straining to see up the road. Something pressed in on him, clamping about his chest like a vise every time his gaze settled on the dark form in the snow.

He was no stranger to dread, had felt its icy fingers on his spine more than once. And now, in this instant, he felt its chilling touch again.

He had to do something. He had to find out what was out there.

Something was wrong. He could feel it. He knew it. Something was very, very wrong.

His decision made—foolish though it might be—he struggled into his boots and coat, glanced down at the cane in his hand. No, that wouldn't do any good at all.

He still had the crutches in the other room, but they'd be next to useless in this snow.

He went to the kitchen pantry in search of something sturdy enough to use as a support.

Nothing.

Finally he opened the back door, his gaze skimming over a few random items tucked in the corner. Almost immediately his gaze came to rest on a big, heavy-looking shovel.

That ought to do it.

✦ 24 ✦

THE SUMMER CHILD

Hopes, fears, prayers, longings, joys and woes—
All yours to hold, O little hands!

LAURENCE BINYON

The shovel made a better support than Gant would have guessed. With the blade digging down into the crunchy snow, he was able to grip the broad handle with one hand, throwing most of his weight on it, and use the cane with the other hand. It was almost like having an extra leg—one that worked. He managed to make his way through the snow fairly well, so long as he ignored the pain that radiated up his bad leg with every step.

Too bad Mac wasn't here to help. He would have used his nose as a plow and made a tunnel through the snow. He did miss the big hound, but Mac would do a lot more good on the road with Asa and the others than moping around here doing nothing. He was more than a dog and a companion—he was a guide and a guardian as well. If anyone tried to mess with Asa or his passengers while Mac was anywhere nearby, he'd bring a bucket of trouble down on himself.

The snow had almost stopped, except for a thin, icy drizzle. Gant hoped he wasn't playing the fool by venturing out. As much help as the shovel had turned out to be, it wouldn't do him all that much good on ice. But the urgency driving him was more than curiosity now. It was like an insistent buzzard riding his back, grasping at him and driving him forward.

It seemed an interminable length of time until he came close enough to realize what he'd seen from the window—a still, partly snow-covered form sprawled along the side of the road. His heart slammed against his chest, his pulse running thin and fast. He stumbled, managed to right himself without falling, and then stumbled again just before he reached the small, motionless bundle lying in the snow.

The big gray gelding had no problem clogging through the drifts, though he was taking his good old time. Surprised by how much snow had fallen since he'd first arrived at the Esch farm earlier in the day, Gideon was now grateful for Phoebe's determination that he ride along with Malachi rather than walking home.

The afternoon was quiet, soft, and cushioned by the snow. Malachi wasn't much of a talker. The only sounds were the chink of harness and the clomp of the big horse's hooves on the road.

As they neared the crossroads, Malachi slowed the horse's pace even more and turned. "It'll be icy tonight, for sure and for certain. Already drizzling."

Gideon nodded, his attention caught by something ahead, off the side of the road. If he didn't know better, he'd think it was Captain Gant, out there huddled against a snow bank.

Malachi had seen too. "Who's that in the road, I wonder? What's he doing?"

As they drew closer, Gideon stood up in the wagon for a better look. "That's Gant."

"You sure?" Malachi strained to see. "What's he doing out in this weather? Why, he'll break his *good* leg in this snow."

Gideon leaned forward still more. "You suppose he fell? Wait… he's holding something…"

They were almost upon Gant now. He was sitting against the bank, his bad leg shoved out in front of him as he cradled a dark-clad figure in his arms. Incredibly the man didn't even have a coat on. It was—his coat was wrapped around—

Gideon stared, his blood setting up a roar in his ears. "What—"

Before the wagon came to a complete halt, he jumped, slipping and skidding as he landed. "That's not—"

But it was. "Fannie?" he choked out. "Is that *Fannie?* What happened to her? Is she all right?"

"She's unconscious," Gant told him. "I saw her from the window. What's she doing out here anyway?"

It sounded like an accusation, but Gideon was too panicked to get his back up. "Malachi—we need one of those lap blankets from the wagon!" he shouted over his shoulder.

He dropped down to his knees. "She's *unconscious?* But—she was coming to invite you to Christmas dinner. That's been two hours or more. How long since she left your place?"

Gant gave him a look of surprise and then shook his head. "She hasn't *been* at my place."

Malachi appeared then and dropped the blanket around Gant's shoulders.

Stunned, Gideon dragged his gaze away from Gant and passed a hand gently over Fannie's face. Cold…she was so cold. A large, dark lump had risen on the right side of her forehead. Just below it was blood. Blood from a jagged cut.

"Fannie…Fannie, it's Gideon. Do you hear me, little sister? Fannie…"

There was no response.

"I don't understand," Gideon said. His mind felt thick with webs. He found it nearly impossible to think. "She was supposed to go to your place…ask you to dinner. She wanted to play in the snow too, but she knows she can't stay out in the cold for long. She gets sick…"

He stopped, shooting a look toward Doc's house where Gant was staying. "Doc…"

"He's not due back until tomorrow." Gant's voice was thin and tight.

They took her home and brought Gant with them after he asked if he might go. Gideon admitted that Doc's house was closer but opted for home. Clearly the boy wanted to get Fannie to their mother and to Rachel as soon as possible.

It was a bad moment when they carried the lass inside. Gant hung back at the door, hugging the blanket around his shoulders. He was keenly aware that this was a family time. Yet he had a strong need to be close to the family, especially Rachel, in case he might somehow be of help.

He felt Rachel's shock, her horror, and her pain as if they were his own. And when her eyes met his just before following Gideon down the hallway with Fannie, the raw fear Gant saw looking out at him cut into him like shards of glass.

He had the sense that Susan Kanagy was holding herself together only by the most rigid effort. But hold together she did. A strong woman, that one. There was no missing the iron in her spine.

He stayed behind, leaning on his cane, and watched Rachel, her family, and Malachi Esch disappear down the hallway and into a bedroom. Then he turned and pulled up a chair close to the potbellied stove, needing badly to take the weight off his leg. The pain, arrowing up all the way to his thigh, was excruciating, though he was sure it was nothing compared to the pain he'd seen in Rachel, her mother, and young Gideon. At this moment he would have given anything to have the right to take Rachel in his arms, to somehow absorb her pain into himself and comfort her.

Instead he could only sit here in the front room like a great dolt, feeling altogether useless and ineffective. He supposed he shouldn't even have come. But in truth he didn't think he could *not* have come—not only because of Rachel, but just as much because of Fannie herself.

He'd grown that fond of the girl in the weeks he'd been confined to Rachel's house. It seemed that to Fannie he hadn't been so much a stranger as a new friend. Whereas everyone else had eyed him with suspicion, if not outright distrust, Fannie had simply warmed to him and accepted him. She was that kind of child.

A *summer* child. Warmhearted, light-spirited, sunny-natured.

How could this have happened?

Guilt set in then. From what Gideon had told him, the lass had been on her way to ask him to Christmas dinner. The very idea made him feel more special than he could remember feeling in a long, long time. Even though the thought doubtlessly had been triggered by sympathy—pity for the lonely stranger, he expected—he still felt less an outsider for it.

He even let himself wonder whose idea it had been. Susan Kanagy's? Fannie's? Surely not Rachel's, though he couldn't help but wish it *had* been Rachel's. Whoever had initiated the idea, no doubt she was regretting it now. If Fannie hadn't left the house to invite him to dinner, she'd be enjoying her Christmas Day with the rest of her family, not lying unconscious in bed.

He glanced around, aware only in the vaguest sense of the house. It was a lot like Rachel's. Plain, simply furnished, wooden floors with a rag rug here and there. The good smells of food baking and roasting hovered and clung. No real adornments, nothing frilly or fancy or expensive.

Yet it was a *home.* A warm, sheltering kind of place where comfort and peace seemed to be part of the furnishings.

At least until today, when tragedy came calling.

At the sound of footsteps on the wide-planked floor, he looked up to see Malachi Esch. He started to get up, but a sharp blast of pain pinned him to the chair again. "How is she? Has she come to yet?"

"No." Malachi shook his head. "She looks to be in a bad way. She must have taken a terrible hard fall. Could sure use Doc right now, we could."

Gant nodded. He'd already thought the same thing. As it was he could only hope the snow wouldn't delay the doctor's return the next day.

"I must be getting home," Malachi said. "Phoebe will be worried, her not knowing where I am. And I need to tell her about Fannie. And you need dry clothes, man. Do you want me to drop you back to Doc's place, then?"

Gant thought about it but shook his head. "I'll stay here for now."

"Well, you can send word by Gideon when you want to leave. We'll get you home whenever need be."

After Malachi left Gant sat wondering about the "terrible hard fall." In truth it would have to be a hard fall indeed, to knock the lass out entirely as it had.

Something stirred inside of him, an uneasiness, a sense that something didn't seem quite right, that things were not as they seemed to be or as they ought to be. And he knew in that moment that the feeling was going to eat at him and dog him until he could get at the truth, whatever it was. In any case Fannie would be able to fill them in on what had happened, once she regained consciousness.

Please, Lord, let that be soon...

25

AN INNER CIRCLE

For where two or three are gathered together
in my name,
there am I in the midst of them.

MATTHEW 18:20

Susan Kanagy could think of other times over the past few years when she had urgently wished for the presence of David Sebastian. But never with the same intense desperation as today.

Sitting at the bedside of her youngest daughter, holding Fannie's small hand as she watched her child's silent, motionless wandering in the unknown place to which her mind had taken her, Susan knew a helpless fear that ripped at her heart of hearts. She had done all she could think to do, all she knew to do—plumped hot water bottles all around Fannie's slender form, had Gideon bring in more wood and punch up the fire in the front room and kitchen, bathed the child in warm water, and put warm stones wrapped in towels at her feet.

And still her daughter remained unmoving, silent, her lips tinged with blue, her skin so pale it was nearly translucent.

Across from her, on the other side of the bed, Rachel sat holding her sister's other hand, watching Fannie as closely as if she were trying to memorize every feature, every breath. "Oh, I wish Dr. Sebastian were here!" Rachel murmured, echoing Susan's thoughts. "He'd know exactly what to do."

Susan nodded but said nothing, lest she say too much. So great was her desire for David's quiet strength, his steady hands, the confident gentleness and care with which he went about treating a patient, that she feared it might be a palpable thing, that others could not help but sense her terror and her need.

Gideon stood at the foot of the bed, his eyes locked on his little sister, his gaze burning and searching as if he could drag her back to consciousness by the sheer strength of his will.

If only David were here...

Susan squeezed her eyes shut for an instant, shaken by the realization that, for too long a time now, she had placed far too much faith in a man. Had she angered the Lord God by this misplaced trust? Her faith—*all* faith—should rest in God. All healing power was in His hands and not in a mere man's, no matter how excellent a physician that man might be. It pierced her spirit to think that she might be in danger of crediting David with a power that belonged to the Lord God and to Him alone. And David himself would no doubt be the first to remind her of that treachery.

"Gott, forgive me," she whispered in her spirit. She prayed then, softly to herself, the ancient prayer that was one of the bulwarks of her faith—in truth, a vital key to the faith of all the Amish people. It was the first prayer she had learned as a child and the first prayer she had taught her own children when they were ever so small. And those children, now adults, heard her murmurings and began to pray with her...

"Our Father, which art in heaven..."

It seemed an age before Rachel came down the hall and stood in front of him. The afternoon had worn on, casting a melancholy pall over the front room and the deepening day outside the window.

Gant watched her face, quickly saw that there was no news.

"She's still...sleeping," Rachel said. "But she feels warm now, not so cold. Here, I brought you some dry clothing."

She handed him a folded bundle of clothes. "They're Gideon's. They'll be too small, of course, but perhaps they'll work until I can get your own things dry. I'll hang yours in the kitchen, beside the stove."

A faint blush crept up her face. "The trousers will be much too short, I know, but at least they're dry." She paused. "Mamma wanted me to come and thank you—from all of us—for what you did. And she thought that after you change, you might like to come and sit with us, to be closer to Fannie."

"I did nothing. If only I *could* have done more. If Gideon and Malachi hadn't come along when they did—"

"No...Jeremiah."

His name on her lips shook him like a wind roaring down from the mountains. And to think he'd never held with his name, never felt that he should wear it, never felt as if it quite belonged to him, not at all.

"If you hadn't seen her," Rachel went on quietly, "if you hadn't gone out to the road and tried to help her...I can't bear to think what might have happened. I believe we owe Fannie's life, if the Lord God sees fit to *spare* her life, to you and your courage. You could have been badly hurt yourself."

Again Gant shook his head, humbled and uncomfortable with her gratitude. "I've been sitting here wishing Doc hadn't gone to Maryland."

"Oh, I think we've all been wishing that! We can only pray he'll be back tomorrow, but what with the snow and all—" She broke off, as if unwilling to voice the rest of her thought.

"Your mother—how is she?"

"Frightened. Very frightened. But Mamma is strong."

He nodded, searching her face. "And you, Rachel," he said softly, "how are *you?*"

She glanced away. "This is...so hard."

When she turned back to him, on impulse Gant took her hand. "Of course it is. She's your sister."

When she made no move to free her hand from his, he tightened his clasp a little. But that slight movement seemed to awaken her awareness of his touch, and she quickly slipped her hand from his.

"I wish I knew what happened to her," she said softly. "If we knew that, perhaps then we'd know better how to care for her."

Gant nodded. "When she wakes up, then we'll know."

"If she wakes up..."

"Don't think that way, Rachel. She *will* wake up."

"You can't be sure of that."

"Somehow I am, though."

And he *was*. In some inexplicable, even irrational, way, he firmly believed that Fannie would be all right. In truth, he *had* to believe it, not simply for Fannie herself but for Rachel. There was something in all this that had gripped his senses, his heart, his every instinct, telling him that for Rachel's sake, as much as for Fannie's, she *had* to wake up. She *had* to be all right.

What accounted for this strange, incomprehensible certainty, he couldn't say. He knew only that it would be as much Rachel's tragedy as her sister's if Fannie didn't revive.

"I should go back," Rachel said. "Please—come join us after you change. Don't sit out here alone."

"You're sure it's all right?"

She nodded. "Yes. It's what we want, Jeremiah."

Inordinately pleased to be asked, Gant hauled himself up from the chair and, with the cane thumping a muffled tattoo on the wooden floor, went to the kitchen to change his clothes.

Late into the night, Rachel realized what an extraordinary thing this was, what with Jeremiah Gant being an *auslander*—an outsider who had become more a friend—sitting among them, bowing his head and praying with them as they prayed, waiting with them, watching and caring.

And Mamma and Gideon not being uncomfortable with his

presence, in fact *wanting* his presence. Even Gideon seemed to warm to the idea of Jeremiah being among them. Every now and then, Rachel would see her brother steal a glance at him, and there was no mistaking the respect in his eyes, albeit a respect mixed with curiosity.

She hoped that somehow Fannie knew "Captain Gant" was here, watching over her. Her little sister had come to like him a lot, had missed him when he moved out to Doc's place—which, no doubt, had prompted her desire to have him over for Christmas dinner.

Now, unless she was badly mistaken, Rachel sensed that he was feeling guilty for that very reason. But Fannie wouldn't want that. Why, if she could, Fannie would be the first to dismiss any feelings of guilt on his part. Fannie always wanted good things for others, especially those she—

Suddenly a small gasp from her mother jerked her out of her thoughts. At the same time, Jeremiah lumbered to his feet, and Gideon moved closer toward the head of the bed to stand beside Mamma. As Rachel watched, Fannie's long eyelashes fluttered against her cheeks, her mouth opened slightly, and she drew in a long, ragged breath, much like a drowsy sigh.

"Mamma?"

The next hour was a flurry of excitement and guarded relief. Fannie seemed to revive quickly, but she was fevered, her breathing sounded harsh and heavy, and every few minutes she would burst into tears.

Gant wondered about the tears—he had a strong suspicion the girl had been badly frightened—but clearly she wasn't up to talking much yet. His heart did a turn, though, when she saw him standing at the foot of her bed and said in a thin, wavering voice, "Captain Gant! You came for Christmas dinner anyway…and I didn't even have to ask."

Encouraged by her alertness and warmed by her words, Gant moved around to the side of the bed where Rachel stood, holding the child's hand. "Why, I wouldn't have missed it for the world, Miss Fannie."

"Captain Gant is the one who found you, Fannie," Gideon put in. "Do you remember falling in the snow?"

Fannie looked at her brother, a questioning look replacing the smile she'd given Gant. Then she shuddered, a movement that seemed to run the full length of her small body under the bedclothes.

Slowly Fannie looked around the room, her gaze traveling to each one of them, meeting their eyes, but finally returning to Gideon and then Gant.

"I didn't fall," she said, an angry flush of red deepening still more the stain of fever on her face.

"Whatever do you mean, Fannie?" said Susan Kanagy. "You fell so hard it knocked the wind right out of you. You've been sleeping for hours."

Fannie studied her mother for a long moment and then turned to Rachel. It seemed to Gant that the child's eyes had taken on an old sorrow, a hurt that went beyond the farthest reaches of childhood.

"Please, Rachel," she said, her voice so soft Gant could scarcely make out her words. Yet he *did* make them out, and he saw that Gideon did also.

"Rachel," Fannie said again. "I need to talk to you and Mamma alone."

26

THE BEST OF INTENTIONS

Broken at last, I bowed my head,
Forgetting all myself, and said,
"Whatever comes, His will be done,"
And in that moment peace was won.

HENRY VAN DYKE

It must have been another thirty to forty minutes before Rachel walked into the kitchen. Her mother wasn't with her.

In the meantime Gant and Gideon had helped themselves to a slice of apple pie and were just finishing up. Even in the dim light from the kerosene lamp on the table, Gant could immediately see that she was shaken. Her skin was ashen, her dark eyes enormous and shadowed.

Gideon, too, was watching her. "So—what was all that about?" he said. "Why did Fannie want to talk with you and Mamm alone?"

She looked from him to Gant and then came to stand at the table, her hands on the back of a chair as if she were bracing herself. "Some boys—*Englisch*—boys cornered her on her way to your house," she said, looking at Gant. Her words came slowly and with obvious difficulty. "They—"

"What?" Gideon shot up from his chair, nearly knocking it over. His hand hit his coffee cup, spilling what was left on the table.

Rachel put a finger to her lips. "Hush, Gideon! She's fallen asleep again, just—a normal sleep this time. She needs to rest."

Gideon pulled out a chair and motioned for her to take it. "And so do you. You look like you're about to fall over. Sit down and tell us what happened."

Something about the stunned look in her eyes, the pain etched in her features, made Gant think of a child who'd been beaten and then sickened from the abuse. He had to squeeze his own hand to keep from taking hers.

"Rachel?" Gideon prompted.

She kept her head down, her gaze fixed on the table in front of her as she spoke. "They teased her. They said—awful things to her, and when she tried to stand up to them, they began to shove her. They kept pushing her and shoving her, and then one of them—kicked her. That's how she fell." She stopped, made a sobbing sound in her throat. "Someone kicked her in the back and also the head. That's all she remembers. Mamma checked. She has a bad bruise on her back."

Gideon's face had turned crimson. Still standing, his hands were knotted into fists. He looked like a thundercloud about to explode.

Gant did everything he could do not to roar with his own rage. He virtually ached to get his hands on those foolish, ignorant boys and do some shoving himself. "Did she know any of them, Rachel?" he asked tightly.

She looked up for the first time since she'd started speaking. "No. She said she'd never seen them before. She thinks they were younger than Gideon, but a few years older than she is."

"Whether she recognized them or not, I'll *find* them," Gideon ground out. "They're going to *pay* for this!"

"Gideon—"

"*Don't,* Rachel! Don't you dare say a word to me about it not being our way. I know it all—I've heard it all before! I heard it when Eli was killed and you—" He stopped, shaking his head so hard his hair flew in front of his face. "I let you and Mamma talk me out of doing anything then—but you won't stop me this time! This time I'm going after them!"

"You will do no such thing, Gideon Kanagy." Susan Kanagy walked into the room at that moment, snapping out the words to her son as if he were nine years old rather than nineteen. Her eyes blazed, her face was lined with exhaustion and gray with sadness, but there was no question as to whether she was completely and fully in control. "What you *will* do is lower your voice right now before you wake your sister.

"Sit down, Gideon," she said, coming to stand at the table.

"No, Mamm. Don't you start with me. I listened to you before, but I was a boy then. I'm a man now."

"Then act like one," she said, her tone sharp, but her voice firm. "A man controls his anger. He doesn't rave and carry on like a child having a temper tantrum." She paused. "Sit down, son."

Gideon hesitated, meeting her gaze straight on with defiance burning in his eyes. But finally he sat down.

"Now you listen to me, Gideon. The way you're behaving is exactly why Fannie didn't want to tell you what happened. She knew how you'd react. And you're proving her right."

"Mamm, it's all starting up again. Don't you *see* that? Abe Gingerich's barn fire—and there were other incidents before that—and now Fannie. They hit her and kicked her like they would a dog. They *hurt* her, Mamm!"

"Yes, they did. They hurt her. And nothing you can do will take away that hurt—not the physical pain or the heart-pain. It will take a long, long time before Fannie will heal."

"That's right! And I know I can't do anything about the pain, but—"

"—but cause her *more* pain."

"What?"

His mother leaned forward, her expression one of entreaty. "Oh, Gideon, don't you see? Fannie is *afraid* for you! She's terrified that you'll be hurt—because of her."

She stopped, watching him closely before going on. "Besides, Fannie completely accepts our belief about leaving justice to the Lord. Just as you should. Vengeance belongs to God, not to any one of us. The *Englisch* may call for revenge, but we believe in forgiveness. Even at your sister's young age, she understands that anger helps no one, that it's a poison. Gideon, you *know* all this. You've grown up with our teachings. Why can't you take it into your heart and live with it? You'll have no peace until you do."

Gideon got to his feet, his face still flushed with passion. "Does Fannie have peace about what happened to her today, Mamm? *Does* she? Do *you*? And what about Rachel? I haven't seen much peace in her since Eli was killed—and his murderers still walking around as free men! Where's *your* peace, Rachel?"

From the edge of his vision, Gant saw Rachel stir and knot her hands in front of her. But she made no reply as Gideon went on railing at them.

"I will *never* understand how you can bear the things that have happened in our community—in our own family—and not seek justice. How can you just—*bury* your anger? How can you ignore what's been done to us? And you, Rachel—" he jabbed a finger at his sister—"don't you dare try to pretend that all you feel toward Eli's murderers is *forgiveness!* They killed your husband! They robbed you of your husband and left you nothing but a broken heart and a shattered life! Don't you tell me you're not still angry!"

She looked up at him, searching his face as if she were looking for something she already knew she wouldn't find. "Of course I still have anger, Gideon. And, yes, Eli's death broke my heart. And it's true that I struggle every day to keep my anger from controlling me. But I also know that there's no chance for healing without—"

He dismissed her words, unfinished, with a chopping motion of his hand. "Spare me the speech, Rachel! I've heard it all before, if not from you, from the church leaders. 'The Amish hold no grudges...our faith allows no place for vengeance...only the Lord God can avenge a wrong.'

"Well, you know what? I *don't* forgive what happened to Eli, and I don't forgive what was done to Fannie today! I don't, and I *won't!* And if cowardice is what's required to be a good Amish man, then I'll never be one! If it means letting the *Englisch* bullies walk all over us and murder us and beat up our children, then I don't *want* to be Amish!"

"Gideon!"

Susan Kanagy shot from her chair, Rachel too, and called after him, but Gideon wouldn't be stopped. Pulling his coat from the peg by the kitchen door, he stormed out of the house, slamming the door so hard the windows rattled.

Gant could see the shattering effect the boy's tirade had wreaked upon his mother and sister, and it sickened him. But after a moment, Susan Kanagy seemed to steady herself. She turned to Gant, and with more dignity than he would have thought anyone capable of in such a situation, she inclined her head toward the door, saying, "I'm so sorry this happened, Captain Gant. I apologize for putting you in such an awkward position."

Gant shook his head and flicked a hand to ward off any embarrassment on her part. "He's young, ma'am, and protective of his loved ones. He means well."

She smiled a little. "You're very gracious, Captain. Thank you for your understanding." She touched Rachel's shoulder, saying, "I'm going back to sit with your sister. Gideon will come back…when he's ready."

"Mamma, I'll stay with Fannie. It's so late—please, lie down and get some rest."

But Susan Kanagy didn't hesitate in answering. "As if I could rest, with your brother on his way to who knows where and our Fannie injured and ill. Don't worry about me, Rachel. I'm fine. With Fannie is where I need to be."

Left alone with Rachel, Gant turned to her. "Your mother is an amazing woman."

She managed a smile. "Yes. She is. And my *dat* was a remarkable man as well. I've been blessed. As for Gideon, though—well, he's a bit of a hothead. I'm sorry that you had to see him at his worst."

Gant waved off her words. "It's as I told your mother, Gideon's young. His intentions are the best."

"Perhaps so, but some of his ways are just so far apart from the faith. I want…better for him."

They sat in silence another moment. "Would you like something more to eat?" Rachel said. "A piece of pie isn't exactly the Christmas dinner we had planned."

He studied her, trying to decide whether this was the time for the question that had begun to nag at him almost from the time he'd first met her. He reached out slowly and covered her hand gently with his own. "What I would like, Rachel, is for you to tell me what happened the night your husband died, and what happened to you."

She looked at him, glanced away and then turned the full intensity of her gaze on him. He could sense the struggle taking place inside her.

"What happened to me," she finally said, "was much like what happened to Fannie today. Except that *I* had someone to protect me—I had Eli. Eli died…because of me."

She told him then, told him of that other time, that night when her husband had been killed. She spoke in a voice so soft that Gant had to bend his head close to hers in order to hear her words. And this time when he gripped her hand, she didn't pull away.

27

RACHEL'S SECRET

I had a beautiful friend
And dreamed that the old despair
Would end in love in the end...

W.B. YEATS

Darkness still shrouded the outside world as they sat in the warmth and dim light of the kitchen.

Rachel kept her eyes closed at first, and the hand Gant wasn't holding she clenched into a fist. Her words came out choked and harsh but evened out some as she spoke. Feeling her tension, Gant couldn't seem to draw an easy breath but let the pressure of their clasped hands come from her, not himself.

"What they did," she said, "what they did was...they beat him. They beat Eli to death."

In spite of his intention to remain silent, a groan escaped Gant's throat.

She looked at him. "Some of the *Englischers* in the area—maybe most of them—don't want us here. They think we're strange because we keep ourselves apart from them and the ways of the world, because our faith is different from theirs, and because we dress differently. Sometimes they do things to mock us, like call us names, and try to frighten us. But until a few years ago, it was just little things they did—they never really tried to hurt anyone."

She glanced at the window, totally dark, as if she were looking down the years into the past. "But then things started to change. Unexplainable things, like mysterious barn fires and wheels removed from our buggies. Our dog was shot." She stopped, her lips thinning. "Eli loved that dog. It gave him a terrible hurt when he died."

Anger flared in Gant, followed by a twist of sympathy. He could almost imagine the pain he would feel if something bad were to happen to his own dog, Mac.

She drew a long breath before going on. "Horses were stolen, and some livestock killed. Even with all this, though, none of us was harmed physically.

"Until the night we were attacked." She tried to clear her throat, but it sounded more like she was gasping for breath.

"Attacked?" Gant echoed.

"Eli and I. We were chaperones for one of the singings. Our young people like to get together at different homes and socialize. They sing songs and talk and just have a good time. It's also a time for courting." She made a weak attempt to smile.

"We were on our way home. It was a nice fall night, crisp but not cold, and we were so newly married it was almost as if we were... courting still. We had had such a good time with the young people, but we were happy to be going home to our own place."

She was having a hard time now, Gant could tell. She stopped again, her gaze going to that place beyond the window—a place where most likely her worst memories still lived. Her hand had gripped his harder, yet he was fairly certain that by this time she wasn't even aware of it.

"They were in a wagon—a noisy old thing—but it was faster than our buggy. There were three of them. Grown men but young. Older than Gideon is now but maybe not by much. They were shouting at us from behind and then pulled up alongside us and yelled at Eli that something was wrong with one of the buggy wheels in back. Said he'd best pull over and they'd help him fix the wheel.

"If only we hadn't stopped..."

She gave a visible shudder. "If we hadn't stopped, Eli would be alive today. But we *did* stop, and when we pulled off to the side of the road, they all jumped down from the wagon and came charging at us. Two of them pulled Eli out of the buggy, and the other one grabbed me and yanked me out onto the road so hard I fell onto my knees."

Gant knew what was coming, and he couldn't look at her. Just for an instant, he had to look away from the raw pain dug deep into her face. She was remembering all of it, and remembering too clearly. It was happening again.

"They knew we don't believe in fighting or in violence. They thought Eli wouldn't fight back. But he surprised them. He *did* fight back. At least he tried. Even though it went against the way he'd lived all his life, he fought them. Because they—they told him what they intended to do to me, and I suppose he couldn't...It was unthinkable that he wouldn't...defend me."

She felt tears burn her eyes, and so she closed them, unwilling to show her weakness. In this, she would honor Eli. Because even though his actions on that awful night went against his faith, he broke trust with his Amish beliefs because of *her,* and she would defend what he did with her last breath.

When she again opened her eyes and continued, she felt only a familiar, haunting sorrow, not anger or grief. "The one who yanked me from the buggy saw that Eli was strong and was actually fighting off the other two, and so he left me there in the road and went to fight with the others. And, of course, then Eli had no chance—three men against one. How much could he do? He told me to run. He kept shouting at me to run and get help, but...he knew...knew by the time I could find help, it would be too late...for him..."

Suddenly Rachel realized she was gripping Jeremiah's hand as if for dear life. All this time she was speaking of Eli and holding another man's hand. She pulled her hand away and locked her fingers together on the table so as not to touch him again.

"I didn't want to leave him…I *didn't*…But he was begging me to go, and when I didn't, he told me I *must* go, that I was his wife, and he *demanded* that I go. I was so torn, wanting to stay with him, but I knew he had no chance alone with them, and I'd be of little help… so I ran…

"*I ran away…*"

Gant heard her voice thicken with guilt, saw her features draw into a mask of self-disgust. He reached for her, but she shook her head almost angrily, keeping him at bay.

He understood. At least he thought he did.

She covered her eyes with her hands for an instant and then knotted them again on the table. She kept her head down now. He saw her try to swallow, watched as she straightened her back and shoulders and then went on.

"I ran to the nearest farm—to Abe Gingerich's place. One of them ran after me but only so far—I think he saw the house and realized I would get there before he could, and so he turned back. Abe and both his sons, Jacob and Luke, went back with me. But it was too late."

Her voice dropped to a whisper. Gant had all he could do not to touch her, to put an arm around her and draw her to him. But he knew she would reject him.

"Eli was already…dead…when we got there. His head—they had beaten him on his head—his neck was broken too. He was gone."

She slumped in the chair. Gant saw her hands go limp. Her face in the lamplight looked gray and sunken. She looked as if she herself had been beaten and broken like an abandoned doll.

"Rachel," he said softly, feeling as if he would choke on the ache in his throat, "I'm so sorry. What a terrible thing for you." He hesitated and then added, "Your husband was a very brave man."

She nodded but said nothing. Gant wasn't at all sure she *could* speak. He thought perhaps all the strength had drained out of her.

"Were the men ever found?" he asked.

She shook her head and finally straightened a little in the chair. "No. The authorities…'looked into it'…but nothing was ever done. And of course we don't believe in pursuing vengeance. We're taught instead to forgive those who wrong us, no matter in what way…so that was the end of it."

"I confess I tend to understand Gideon's difficulty with that part of your faith," Gant said. "What's so wrong about demanding justice when a crime is committed against you? How can you simply ignore something like that?"

She looked at him. "We don't *ignore* it, Jeremiah. We don't pretend the offense was never committed. But we have to give up our desire to punish the wrongdoer."

"But why? *Why* do you believe that?"

"Because of God's grace."

Gant shook his head. "I don't understand."

"It's a lot to understand if you haven't grown up with the belief, if it hasn't been a part of your life since childhood, I know. But it's a belief founded on the words of Jesus, and we take His words in all seriousness. We believe that 'forgive us our debts as we forgive our debtors' means just that—that if we don't forgive, then we won't be forgiven. God didn't exact justice from us but, instead, extended grace, so we're not to exact justice from others but offer grace to them…no matter what they do to us."

Gant sighed. "I don't know that I could ever manage that kind of grace."

She turned around to face him, regret and something else, something akin to anger, darkening her features. "To my great shame, neither can I."

He studied her, seeing now for the first time the battle being waged somewhere deep within her.

"Tell me, Rachel."

"It *shames* me. I'm a poor witness, a poor example of our faith. I've never forgiven those men who killed Eli. I've tried. I've prayed for forgiveness for them. I've *begged* for it—but I still *despise* them!" She stopped and looked away from him. "And I despise myself just as much. Because I can't forgive myself either."

"For *what*, Rachel?" Gant touched her shoulder, and she turned back to him. "What do you mean, you can't forgive yourself. You did nothing wrong."

Her eyes sought something from him, but seemed not to find it. "I *ran*," she said, her voice shaking. "I ran away. I should have stayed. I might not have been able to stop them, to save Eli, but it would have been better if I had died with him. Instead I ran away."

He clasped both her shoulders now, making it impossible for her to look away from him. "You ran for *help*, Rachel! You didn't run away from Eli—you ran to get help for him!"

She slumped under his grasp. "Yes, I know. That's what Mamma told me, and Dr. Sebastian and the bishop—that's what everyone told me. But it doesn't help. And still today I betray my faith by not being able to forgive—those men or myself."

Gant could have wept at the pain that burned through her loveliness. "Oh, Rachel, there's nothing to blame yourself for. Don't you see? There was really nothing you could have done. And in all likelihood the reason you can't forgive Eli's murderers—if indeed you believe you should—is because you blame yourself as much as you blame them."

"I should have stayed with him—I should have *died* with him! And you've no idea how often I wish I had."

Her words seemed torn from a far place, a place deep inside of her, a place Gant had never sensed before this moment. He eased his grip on her shoulders but didn't release her. "And *you* have no idea," he said softly, "how glad I am that you didn't."

Her eyes grew wide with surprise.

"I don't know what in the world we're going to do about this, sweet Rachel," he said, "and maybe I also need to ask your forgiveness because the truth is that I have…feelings for you that I don't know what to do with."

She tensed, staring at him, and Gant saw something flicker in her eyes that struck him like a blow, something she would no doubt deny if he faced her with it. But he knew. He *knew.* She felt it too, this…*attraction,* whatever it was…that was drawing them together, that indeed had been drawing them together almost since that first evening.

"Don't, Jeremiah…You know it's impossible. Don't say this. Anything between us is impossible."

"Tell me you feel nothing for me, Rachel." He held onto her. He was going to hold onto her, no matter what.

"I—I can't tell you that. I care about you…you're my friend."

"No. This isn't friendship, Rachel."

"Jeremiah—it's forbidden. It's impossible."

But she was no longer tensing herself against his touch.

Carefully, gently, he pulled her closer and coaxed her head against his shoulder. He rested his chin on top of her head, against the starched little white cap she always wore and he had come to fancy, even though it did mark her as "forbidden" to him.

"Nothing is impossible, Rachel. Nothing."

But he knew this wasn't the time to talk about it. Not now. Not after everything she'd been through today and after what he'd learned about her husband tonight. She was clearly exhausted, depleted.

Besides, he had to think. There had to be an answer to all this somewhere. The last thing he had expected at this point in his life was to meet someone like Rachel. It was even more incredible that he would fall in love with her and that she was falling in love with him—he had absolutely no doubt.

But for now he knew he had brought her as close as he dared, so when she eased herself away from him, he didn't protest.

Even though every instinct in him begged for her return.

⇢ 28 ⇠

ASA

God give us men! A time like this demands
Strong minds, great hearts, true faith and ready hands...
JOSIAH GILBERT HOLLAND

Three days after Christmas, Asa and his passengers were still stuck at a farm in northern Tuscarawas County. Here they were to wait for the new conductor who was to take Asa's place and lead his passengers the rest of the way to Canada.

Asa daily praised God that this station belonged to a prosperous farmer who had added a well-hidden secret room to the main house for the sole purpose of sheltering runaways and their guides. Here they had found a warm shelter with plenty of food, clean bedding in the form of quilts and mattresses on the floor, and kindhearted folks who kept watch over them as if they were members of their own family.

But when there was still no sight of the new conductor, who was to have arrived at the farm two days before Christmas, Asa feared the worst. He also realized that his responsibility wasn't going to end here as planned. Instead it seemed that he would have to be the one to take his charges the rest of the way.

He was thankful the women and children were all in good health—Mattie's baby included—but their supplies were nearly all used up, and the money the captain had sent with him was getting low as well. He didn't like asking for help, but if he was to take his people the distance, he had no choice.

The Lord bless him. Mr. Walter Eberhardt, an aging German immigrant and their "host," was quick to offer whatever assistance they needed. "You've only to tell me what you require. I will gladly replenish your supplies and see to your money needs. But you and your people are welcome to stay here as long as necessary."

"We appreciate your kindness, sir. We surely do," Asa replied. "But we both know that the longer we stay in one place, the more we risk being caught. It's been five days now, and I'm thinking we had best be on our way by tonight."

The other nodded. "You tell me what you need, and Mrs. Eberhardt and I will start getting things together for you."

Although Asa felt a certain reluctance in leaving that night, he suspected the women and children hated to leave even more. To go from a warm, seemingly secure shelter, where there was no hunger and never a harsh word from their benefactors, back onto the road again, into the cold, raw night where there seemed little or no protection, came as a hard shock. They had enjoyed comfort and security for days.

Nevertheless, Asa had to give them credit—even the children scrambled into the wagon with little in the way of whining or complaining. As for the two women, perhaps it was because both Dinah and Mattie were so set on freedom, for themselves and for their children, that they seemed to maintain a cheerful outlook on whatever might lie ahead.

Asa's concern, as they drove away, was twofold. He feared being discovered by the slave hunters that prowled the state—even a free state and one removed from the South. He also held a fair measure of anxiety about how Captain Gant was getting along with his injury and handling the uncertainty of Asa's whereabouts.

He tried to reassure himself with the reminder that the Amish folks seemed to be good people. Hadn't they demonstrated a generosity of spirit by taking them in during the middle of the night, sending for their own doctor to care for the captain, and through it all not treating two strangers as lesser men but as human beings who needed help?

Still the captain wasn't their responsibility. It was for Asa to protect this man who had purchased his freedom and risked his own life for him, and he did not take that role lightly. God had brought Captain Gant into his life when he was most desperate, and he meant to repay his Lord and the captain in any way he possibly could.

So tonight, as was his way *every* night, Asa prayed for the safekeeping of his good friend—his *only* friend other than Jesus his Lord—and for grace to be extended by the ones who looked after the captain in his absence.

And, of course, included in his nightly prayer was the continuing plea for Ariana, wherever she might be.

✦ 29 ✦

DR. SEBASTIAN'S RETURN

He's heart-sick with a longing sweet
To make her happy as she's fair.

COVENTRY PATMORE

D r. David Sebastian made it safely back home to the farm in spite of the snowstorm, but he arrived three days later than he'd planned.

Tired and somewhat irritable after the long train ride, he unpacked quickly and then went to Riverhaven, first to check on Gant. He found his tenant-patient in good condition, albeit with a head cold. He wasn't surprised the man had a cold once Gant filled him on the events that had transpired in David's absence.

Neither did he waste any time on conversation after hearing about Fannie Kanagy. He proceeded to rebutton his coat even while he continued to question Gant. "So have you heard anything about her since then?"

Gant nodded. "Gideon stopped by this morning. He said she's still coughing a lot and doesn't seem all that well, but her fever is gone."

David let out a quick breath. "Well, that's something then." He picked up his medical case from the table, where he'd set it upon entering. "And Susan and Rachel? Are they all right?"

"Worried, I'm sure, and anxious for you to get back. But otherwise I expect they're fine."

"Well, I'll go there right away." He took a close look at Gant. "Have a care with that cold. You don't need it going to your chest. You're not entirely well yet, you know."

Gant shrugged. "The worst of it is already gone."

"Do you have enough food laid in? Anything you need?"

"No. Rachel and her mother sent enough for two men the day before Christmas. I have plenty. There is one thing, though—"

"What's that?"

"I need to get to a bank and a telegraph office reasonably soon. Some things I have to take care of."

"I need to go into Marietta myself. I was planning on going tomorrow. You can go with me if you like."

Anxious to be on his way to see about Fannie, David left after a hurried goodbye.

Susan Kanagy could have buckled with relief when she opened her front door and saw David Sebastian standing there.

"Oh, David! You can't imagine how glad I am to see you!"

He smiled. "Under other circumstances that kind of greeting might give me a swelled head," he told her. "However, I just came from talking with Gant, so I expect I know why you've been wanting to see me."

Susan had no intention of admitting that she was always happy to see him—*too* happy. Instead she stood aside to let him enter, taking his coat and hat and hanging them on the peg by the door.

"How is she, Susan?"

She put a hand to her cheek, quickly lowering it when she realized she was trembling. She hadn't slept well since Fannie's attack, and it was all she could do to force a few bites of food down. Consequently, she sometimes felt weak and even a little lightheaded.

"I've been putting poultices on her chest," she said, "but her cough is deep, and she says it hurts. I've tried to do everything you've taught me to do when she's like this—the poultices, the steam tent—but other than her fever breaking last night, I don't see much improve-ment. She's going to be glad to see you. So will Rachel—she's over at Phoebe's right now, but she should be back soon."

She turned to start down the hall, stopping when David put a gentle hand to her arm. "Susan—Gant told me what happened. I couldn't be more sorry that she went through that—that *you* had to go through it, as well."

She nodded. Weak as she was right now, David's kindness nearly undid her. "I'm just so thankful Captain Gant saw her and went to her. I can't imagine how difficult that must have been for him, going out in the snow like that, with his leg injured."

"He's a tough fellow. No worse for wear, from what I've seen, other than a head cold."

"He's a good man, David."

"Yes, he is. A very good man."

One look and David knew that Fannie was a very sick little girl. But her eyes, dulled by the illness, brightened considerably when he walked into the room, and her smile was wide enough to warm his heart.

"Dr. David! You're finally back!"

He ruffled her hair. "Indeed I am, Fannie. And I brought my bag of medical tricks with me. Are you ready to get well?"

She coughed and then rolled her eyes. "Yes, please. I don't like having to stay in bed."

"That's because you're always such a busy butterfly, flitting around doing this and that."

She smiled again, but there was a sadness about the child that squeezed David's heart. Even though he'd been with her only a moment or two, there was no mistaking the obvious—Fannie had lost something precious on Christmas Day. A part of her innocence, her genuinely sweet and openhearted view of the world, had been spoiled, tainted by the cruelty and ugliness borne of bigotry and ignorance.

Being Amish, Fannie and her family would forgive the bullies who attacked her.

But for his part, David wasn't so sure he could.

❖ ❖

After his visit with Fannie, David took Susan up on her offer of coffee. In the kitchen he stood near the stove, his mouth watering as he watched her pour coffee and set out a tray of apple bread and strudel.

"Sit, David," she said, gesturing to the table. He hesitated, but he hadn't eaten anything since breakfast that morning, and the aroma of her coffee and pastries was simply too fetching to refuse.

"So, David—what do you think?"

He took a sip of coffee before replying. "It's not pneumonia, Susan."

She put both hands to her face and let out a long breath. "Oh, thank you, Lord *Gott*. Thank you!"

"But we'll have to watch her closely," he cautioned. "She has a chest cold. Your nursing has made a considerable difference, I believe. The bruise and cut on her head will heal naturally. I examined her back, and there's no swelling in her kidney—we can be grateful for that."

He paused and then went on. "I think she'll be fine, Susan—physically. But you know, some of our hardest blows strike the heart with more force than the body. Those...bullies...hurt her heart badly. But because Fannie is the kind of child she is—bright and alert and outgoing—I'm hopeful this isn't going to do any real emotional damage. Even so, we'll need to keep a close eye on her for a while."

He stopped for a bite of strudel. "Because she can count on a wonderful family and several friends in the community—everyone loves Fannie—she doesn't have to go through this trauma alone. And that can make a significant difference."

Susan was watching him closely as he spoke, nodding and squeezing her eyes shut once or twice as if in relief.

"We'll take good care of her, Susan. She's going to be all right."

"If you say so, David, I believe it. I'm so grateful to you."

"Well. I'm also grateful to you. This is the first good food I've had in days. My daughter-in-law is a lovely girl, but she can't cook at all." He shook his head. "Terrible."

"Oh, shame on you, David. I'm sure it's not that bad." She pushed the plate of apple bread his way. "Help yourself now. I'll fix some things for you to take home."

"I'm not too proud to accept an offer like that." He studied her for a moment. "Tell me how *you* are, Susan."

She reached to touch her *kapp*. "Oh, I'm all right. I just need to get the pictures out of my head—the thoughts of those boys treating Fannie like that. I can scarcely bear to think of what they did, and yet I can't seem to *stop* thinking about it."

He nodded. "Do you have any idea who they are? Did Fannie recognize any of them?"

"No. Not a one. All she knows is that they were *Englisch*. Oh, David, they hurt her so!"

Gant had told him most everything that happened, but David didn't indicate as much. He went on listening to her, sensing her need to talk through it again, perhaps with someone a bit more "clinically" minded than Rachel or Gideon.

At the moment, however, he didn't feel all that professional. He felt like going after the young thugs with a club.

"I think it was awful hard on Rachel," she said, her voice trembling. "It brought back everything...with Eli and all..."

Her voice broke, and David reached to cover her hand with his own. But only for a moment. He didn't dare touch her at length.

He stayed for quite some time, longer than was justified. Even though his Amish families always insisted on feeding him after a visit, he didn't try to fool himself—it wasn't the food that kept him at Susan's table, nor was the excuse of waiting to say hello to Rachel all that credible. The truth was that he simply didn't want to leave.

He didn't want to leave *Susan*—a problem that was becoming all too common.

All the way home he thought about how he had missed her while he was away. Of course he missed her any other time as well. Whether he went for only a day without seeing her or several days, he missed her.

He'd done a lot of thinking about that during his trip, about the way he craved the sight of her, the ache that invariably started up in him when he was away from her. Ordinarily he wouldn't allow himself the indulgence of thinking about her too much or too often. But lately he couldn't seem to discipline his thoughts as he once had.

Consequently he'd found his mind following paths he'd never traced before. Ideas taunted him, danced in front of him with possibilities he'd never allowed himself to consider until now. At times he daydreamed like a lovesick schoolboy. Other times he forced himself to abandon thinking of her altogether.

But those times were becoming fewer and fewer. His thoughts seemed bent on betraying him when he least expected it.

In any event he had more thinking to do, more praying to do. He needed to figure out if he'd abandoned common sense altogether, or if it just might be possible that God was trying to present him with some answers to the prayers he'd already prayed…and he was simply too dull-witted to hear Him speak.

He gave a long, weary, and frustrated sigh as he turned onto the lane leading up to his house. Was there ever a more foolish man than a man hopelessly in love?

Well, yes. An *Englisch* man in love with an Amish woman—now *there* was a foolish man indeed.

⇢ 30 ⇠

NO GOODBYES

Man is caught by what he chases.

GEORGE CHAPMAN

This was a Sunday without services. The Riverhaven Amish had preaching services every other Sunday in different homes or sometimes in barns. There was no permanent church building, a practice which harked back to the days in Europe when the People were hunted down, persecuted, and even martyred for their faith.

On a Sunday when there was no preaching, they most often used the time to visit with family and friends. But because of Fannie's condition, it had been a quiet day at home for the Kanagys.

That night, quite a bit after her usual bedtime, Susan sat in the front room reading her Bible. Rachel had gone back to her own home earlier in the week, and Fannie was already asleep for the night. The child tired easily these days. Although she was showing improvement, she still had a wearying cough and needed a lot of rest.

When she heard the kitchen door shut and the familiar sound of Gideon's footsteps, Susan breathed a silent prayer of thanks that he was home. It wasn't unusual for the boy to spend a night in town every now and then with an *Englisch* friend, but this was the first time he'd stayed away so long without her knowing his plans in advance.

When he first walked into the front room, Susan tried to settle a stern look on him. But so relieved was she to see him safely home, she couldn't pretend a pique she didn't feel. She merely watched him over the top of her eyeglasses and said nothing.

He seemed surprised to see her sitting there and stopped in the middle of the room, giving a little lift of his shoulders. "Mamm. You're usually in bed by now," he said.

Susan put her Bible down on the table beside her chair. "I've been staying up later every night, tending to Fannie—and hoping to see my son come home."

He looked at her, as if trying to judge her mood, but glanced away when she met his gaze. "I've been at Orson's."

Susan nodded. "I thought as much. Why, Gideon? With your sister hurt and sick, why would you leave for so long a time instead of staying here at home? We didn't even know where you were."

Still he didn't look at her but stood staring down at the floor. "I just needed...to get away."

"You chose a poor time for that, son. You were needed here."

Without warning he whipped around, and it was then Susan saw that the impatience and frustration that had flared in him days ago still burned. He ran a hand through his hair. "I might as well tell you, Mamm—I'm leaving. I just came home to get some of my things."

Susan stared at him in disbelief. "What do you mean, you're leaving?"

"I can't do this anymore, Mamm. I can't go on pretending to be something I'm not." His voice was strained and not all that steady, as if his words didn't come without regret.

"Gideon—say what you mean. I don't understand."

The eyes, usually alight with good humor or a hint of teasing, went dark, and for a moment the tall, broad-shouldered man her son had become took on the uncertain expression of a little boy again. "I'm not Amish, Mamm," he said. "Not in my heart, that is. And I don't want to be Amish anymore."

Had he struck her, he could not have hurt her more. Truth be known, Susan felt as if he *had* delivered a blow. She couldn't find her breath, and the pain in her chest nearly made her double over.

For a long throbbing moment, she stared at her son. He stood there, his eyes downcast, his large hands doubled in fists at his sides. She had seen that look before, at times when he'd set his head to something he either wanted or didn't want to do and knew he was going to meet opposition.

Susan gripped the arms of the chair, fighting for calm. "Gideon, you don't mean that. You're still upset—I can see that. But sit down and listen to reason—"

"No, Mamm," he said sharply. "I've had enough of everyone sitting around and reasoning but not *doing* anything. No one around here ever does anything but *talk*. We talk and talk and talk and don't accomplish a thing. Well I'm through with all the talk. I'm not going to live like this anymore."

Susan's hands trembled. This son of hers—he who had ever been her rebel, who had been filled with questions ever since he was a small boy, yet so often refused to accept the answers—stood there looking as if he hadn't the faintest idea that he was ripping away the very lining from her heart.

And of course he *didn't* know. What did children know, really, about the pain they could bring to a parent? They could never completely understand the love of a mother or a father until they had children of their own.

But, oh, she did love him! She loved him too much to lose him.

"Gideon, you don't just stop being Amish—"

"There are those who do, Mamm. Some seem to have no choice but to stop. I think maybe I'm one of them."

"You're still young, son. Still in your running around years. Give yourself time. That's what this period in your life is all about, finding what you believe, which road you mean to follow."

"I'm nineteen, Mamm. I'm a man, even if you can't see me that way. And I may not know for sure and for certain what I *do* believe, but I know what I *don't* believe. I don't believe it's right to stand by and do nothing when someone beats up little girls or sets fires to other people's property or steals things that don't belong to them. And I don't believe it's right to just look away and pretend you see nothing when those you love are being hurt."

His voice was clear and even, and Susan had the sense that he had thought about these things for a long time. It struck her that he was so like his father in this way. Amos too had been a thinker, a man who gave his questions and his ideas a great deal of thought and didn't simply react to things. Rather, he kept his silence until he was ready to speak or act, often surprising his family with the direction his thoughts had taken—and the decisions he made as a result.

"Mamm, listen now—I'm not going to just disappear. I'm not going to stop being your son. But I've got to find out for myself just who I am, what I believe, how I want to live. I have to live *my* way. I confess that I'm not sure anymore what that way is. That's why I have to do this. I have questions but no answers. And I'm not finding the answers here, among the People."

"Oh, Gideon—please, don't do this! Where will you go, what will you do—"

"Karl's going to let me rent the vacant room above the shop for now. I make enough to pay him rent and still help you out some too, Mamm."

So she was right—he'd been thinking about this for some time. He had it all worked out. "Surely you'll speak to the bishop first. He won't take this lightly, Gideon. You need to talk with him."

"They can't shun me, Mamm. I've never joined the church. There's nothing the bishop can do."

He sounded so sure of himself. So—decisive. "But do you really want to bring the disapproval of the community down upon you, Gideon? You have friends here too, you know, not just among the *Englisch*."

"Those who are really my friends will stay my friends."

Even as he spoke, Susan could feel him slipping away from her, as if the slender cord that bound them as mother and son was sliding, inch by inch, out of her hands. "I felt sure that sometime soon you'd be joining the church and making your vows..."

"I never gave you any reason to believe that, Mamm. Anyway I've known for a long time that I'm not ready to make that kind of commitment. I don't know if I'll *ever* be ready. There are…things…I have to do first. Before I can even think about that."

Silence hung between them, and a terrible knowing settled over Susan. "You're going to try to find them, aren't you? The ones who hurt Fannie. Oh, Gideon, it's wrong! So wrong! Revenge isn't up to us—you know that! Revenge is for the Lord God only. Are you really going to try to accomplish God's work for Him?"

Gideon's chin lifted, and his gaze was unwavering. His words came quietly but with the firm assurance of one whose mind is fixed with relentless determination on one objective. "Someone out there killed Rachel's husband—they *killed* Eli! Who knows what they might have done to Rachel if she hadn't got away. And now look at what's happened to Fannie."

Anger again flared in his eyes. "And, yes, I'm going to find them. I don't care how long it takes or what I have to do, I'll find them. They're not going to get away with what they did. I know you don't approve, and I suppose you don't understand. But it's what I have to do."

Susan studied him—the strongly molded features that never failed to hold a touch of gentleness for his mother and sisters, the powerful masculine build that marked him as a man, no longer a boy, and the fire in him that burned for justice, not for himself but for his loved ones. She wanted desperately to reach out and hold onto him, so he couldn't get away. But she knew if she tried to hold him, she would lose him for certain.

She stood and moved close to him, looking up at him to meet his eyes. "I know I can't stop you if you're determined to go. And you're right that they can't shun you since you've never joined the church. So you can still come home, Gideon. Whenever you want, whenever you need to, you can still come home. Promise me that you'll never be too proud or too stubborn to come home."

He looked at her and then bent to touch his cheek to hers. "I promise, Mamm."

"You won't leave until you tell Fannie goodbye, will you? And Rachel?"

He shook his head. "I'm going tonight, Mamm. I have to. I'll come back soon and talk to Fannie and Rachel. But I'm leaving tonight."

He was upstairs for only a few minutes. When he came down carrying his father's old beat-up travel case, Susan was still standing in the middle of the room.

He stopped and looked at her, but she turned away. "Just get it over with, Gideon," she choked out. "I won't say goodbye to you. I can't."

He hesitated another moment and then turned to go.

The sound of the back door closing behind him sounded like a door closing on her heart.

31

CHECKERS AND
A CHALLENGE

Whatever the wealth of our treasure-trove,
The best we shall find is a friend.

JOHN J. MOMENT

The latter part of January showed no sign of release from winter's grip. Temperatures often hovered several degrees below zero, and in some places snow had been on the ground since early December. Old-timers were fond of saying it was the worst winter they could remember.

David Sebastian wasn't so sure but what they were right, though he didn't have access to the statistics. Whatever the records might show, all he knew was that he was tired of it and that spring couldn't come soon enough to please him.

That was his tirade as he stamped the snow off his feet. He arrived at his house outside Riverhaven intent on inviting himself to supper with his tenant and patient. He often dropped in on Gant when he didn't feel like slugging through the treacherous road conditions to get home to the farm. Between the two of them, they usually managed to throw together an edible meal.

Surprisingly the friendship, which had developed between him and the Irish riverboat captain since back in November, seemed destined to last. Against all odds they got along exceedingly well. He liked Gant, was comfortable with the man, and had come to look forward to their conversations and highly competitive checker games.

Gant opened the front door for him while David was still pounding the snow off his galoshes. "I heard you grousing to yourself about the weather all the way inside," Gant said with a grin. "I suppose it's to be expected. You Brits have never been a very hardy bunch."

"I'd say it's more the fact that our survival skills never evolved to the point of enjoying Arctic winters," David shot back, following Gant into the front room.

Not for the first time, he silently admired the repair job his Irish friend had done on the massive rocking chair that sat near the fireplace. David had all but discarded it, but with the help of a hammer and a few small hand tools, Gant had salvaged it by fashioning new rockers and replacing the front and rear stretchers.

After hanging up his coat, David stood by the fire a moment to take the chill off and then eased himself into the rocking chair. Looking around the room he immediately saw that Gant had been busy over the past few days.

"You stained the table," he said, regarding the formerly scratched pine table in front of the sofa. In fact not only had the table been restored to its former rich walnut hue, but Gant had polished it to an almost satin finish.

Perched on the leather hassock across from David, his injured leg stretched straight out in front of him, Gant nodded. "I was hoping you wouldn't mind my puttering about with your furniture. I get a little crazy here with nothing to do."

"Mind? Why would I mind? I never seem to find time to do anything around the place—or out at the farm either for that matter. Just have at it till your heart's content. You obviously have a way with fixing things."

"I like wood. I like working with it, handling it. I even like the smell of it."

"Does that come from your days of working in a shipyard?"

"Most likely. But even as a boy, I was always trying to fix this or that. Or build something. I made a lot of useless stuff." He paused.

"And that reminds me. You've a number of things around this place that need shoring up. I could do that, if you like."

"Such as?" David was aware of some needed improvements, but he was coming to learn that Gant saw things he never would have noticed.

"Your back porch for starters. It needs support. And the roof over the porch ought to be replaced. And then those steps down to the cellar. Someone's likely to break a leg on them." Gant paused. "And there's more."

"If you want the job, I'll pay you."

"No. It's my way of paying *you*. Room and board."

David studied him. In fact he studied him for such a long time that Gant appeared to squirm under his scrutiny.

"Well?" Gant said.

"It's just that I'm curious about you," David confessed.

"I can't think why. I'm an open book."

"For one thing I know for a fact that education is hard for most of the Irish to come by—impossible for some—and yet it's plain as can be that you've had more than an adequate education. And then your obvious ability with what you call 'puttering,' yet your occupation is navigating a steamboat."

At the other's shrug, David added, "Oh, yes, I've noticed the books lying about—the ones you've been pulling from my shelves. Not exactly primers. And then there's the fact that you don't seem to be in the least concerned about money, yet it's been nearly two months since you've been able to work." He stopped. "At the risk of meddling, I have to ask just who, exactly, are you, 'Captain Gant'?"

The other lifted an eyebrow and cracked that somewhat cocky grin of his. "I expect I'm just a self-educated tinkerer who loves the river but always fancied himself a carpenter of sorts. As for the money part—I own part of a shipyard in Brooklyn, thanks to my former employer."

David stared at him. "You own part of a shipyard?"

Still grinning, Gant gave a quick nod. "Did I mention that it's been a very *successful* shipyard? Of course when I took Will Tracey up on his offer to invest some of my hard-earned money in the business, I had no way of knowing just how successful it would be. I was a bit of a gambler in those days—that was before Asa converted me—and it seemed a worthwhile venture."

Abruptly he thumped both hands on his knees and hauled himself up from the hassock. "Oh—and I also own another riverboat that mostly deals in ferrying some fairly expensive cargo back and forth from Cincinnati and Kentucky to the South. So, no, I don't worry much about money. Besides I don't need much. There's no family, no one depending on me, and my needs are simple."

David couldn't have been more surprised. "Well," he said, "I believe I'm impressed. To answer your question—I'd be perfectly delighted if you'd like to relieve your boredom by fixing the place up. But, one condition...no, make that two."

Gant looked at him.

"You simply can *not* be on that leg an excessive amount of time yet. You've done remarkably well—"

"Thanks to your good doctoring," Gant said with a friendly sneer.

"Yes, well, that goes without saying. In any case I'll not have my fine workmanship undone by your impatience. Do as much as you like but pace yourself. Don't do any damage to that leg. And no ladders. Absolutely no ladders. You do only what you can manage at ground level." He paused. "I take it this means that you'll be staying around here for a time."

"Aye. I'm hopeful Asa is all right, but whatever has happened, I'll not leave here without him. You remember the wire I sent a few weeks ago to one of the station masters on our route, asking him to try to get word to me about Asa?"

David nodded. By now Gant had filled him in on the "Underground Railroad" system and his part in it. Strange business. Foolhardy to a fault too, though apparently well-organized. All the same, those involved in it placed themselves at considerable risk, including the possibility of jail sentences and extravagant fines. He had to admire them for what they were doing in spite of what they stood to lose.

"I haven't heard anything yet, but I'm hoping that's good, that it simply means there's been a change of plans and Asa had to take his passengers farther north than we'd planned. I've no way of knowing how long it might be before he either shows up here or I at least get word of when he'll be back. So puttering with things around here will give me something to do while I wait."

"Well, let me know what you might want in the way of materials. I'll be glad to get whatever you need."

David thought for a moment. "A bit of a gambler, eh? Now *that* piece of information doesn't surprise me."

After supper they sat midway into their second game of checkers. "So Susan tells me you've stopped by their place," David said.

Gant nodded. "Fannie seems well now. Though I can tell she misses her big brother. Have you heard anything about Gideon?"

"Not a word. His employer is one of my patients, though, and he says the boy is well and works hard." David waited until Gant made another jump. "Are you this ruthless at everything you do? You seem to take great pleasure in humiliating me."

Gant cracked a self-satisfied grin. "When else does an Irishman get a chance to condescend to a Brit?"

David pulled a face. "You were singing a different tune last week, as I recall, when I won three games straight."

"The Irish have always appreciated a worthy opponent," Gant said with a smug smile.

They stared at the board for another moment. "So you visit Susan and Fannie often it seems."

Gant shrugged. "I suppose."

"Do you realize how unusual that is? If the entire community didn't credit you with saving Fannie's life, Susan would have been taken to task long before now for 'socializing' with you."

"I figured as much. And if it ever appears that I'm causing her any trouble, I'll stay away. But I do enjoy their company. Mrs. Kanagy is a fine lady."

"Yes, she certainly is. And so is Rachel." David waited a beat. "Do you see much of her as well?"

Gant took on the shuttered expression he almost always wore when Rachel's name was mentioned. That it was a defensive measure, David understood all too well.

When Gant made no reply but pretended to be studying his next move, David said, "Not seeing her as often as you'd like, eh?"

Gant's heavy-lidded stare remained completely impassive. "I see Rachel from time to time. When she happens to be at her mother's." He waited and then added, "They were both awfully hurt when Gideon took off as he did."

"To the Amish, one of their children refusing to join the church and leaving the community is almost as bad as a death in the family."

"I've heard about this shunning business. Will that eventually happen to Gideon?"

David made his move and then sat back to see what Gant would do to counter. "Gideon hasn't been baptized, hasn't joined the church. He'll still be able to see his family and friends, although some likely won't have much contact with him."

Gant shook his head. "What do they hope to accomplish by casting out one of their own? Seems to me that would only drive the one being shunned farther away."

"Well as I understand it, shunning isn't related to punishment of any kind. It's meant to be redemptive. It's a practice meant to bring the one shunned back into the fold. It's a terribly difficult thing for an Amish individual—and his family—to experience."

"Does it do that—bring the one shunned back to the community?"

"Actually, sometimes it does."

"So…Gideon won't go through that, but someone such as Mrs. Kanagy—Susan—or Rachel *would?*"

"Oh, yes. They've made their lifelong vows. They'd be liable to shunning if the offense were serious enough."

David noticed that Gant's mind seemed to wander for a few minutes after that. Clearly, for him the game had lost its allure.

Unfortunately, he wasn't without his own understanding of why the subject of shunning might be of special concern to his friend. "You...think highly of Rachel, don't you?" he said carefully.

Gant looked up, and for once the mention of Rachel didn't cloud his features to the point of a blank stare. "My folly, I know." He looked and sounded utterly miserable.

David leaned against the back of his chair. "We can talk about it if you like."

"There's no sense to it. None at all," he muttered. "I wouldn't expect you to understand."

"Oh, I might understand better than you think."

Gant's eyes burned through any facade David might have previously tried to set in place.

"Rachel's mother. Of course. I think I suspected as much," Gant said quietly.

"As you said—'my folly'," David replied.

Gant let out a long breath. "Does she know?"

"That I'm a total fool about her? I hope not. Though since I revert to an addlepated schoolboy every time I'm with her, I fear she may have her suspicions." He stopped. "What about Rachel?"

Gant gave a small, dry laugh that held not a trace of humor. "Oh, she knows."

"And?"

"In truth, I think she feels the same. But no doubt she regards it as hopeless entirely. Perhaps even wicked, my being...an outsider." He cast an inquisitive look at David. "In your case, though, I don't see why it couldn't work between you and Rachel's mother. The people here seem to treat you as one of their own, not as if you're any different from them. They obviously have a great liking and respect for you. Why wouldn't they accept you into the community?"

David gave a vigorous shake of his head. "They accept me as their *physician,* even their friend. But if I were to admit to any sort of romantic interest in Susan, I'd immediately be as much of an outsider to them as you are. No man but an *Amish* man can ever be an acceptable suitor for one of their women."

Gant thought a moment about that. "But you're not all that different from the Amish, are you?"

"Whatever do you mean?"

"All you need is one of their hats and a beard, Doc, and you could pass, it seems to me."

"If that's supposed to be funny—"

"It's not. What I mean is that I see in you most of the same things I see in these people. You're a quiet, peaceful man. If I'm not mistaken, you *crave* peace. You live simply. You seem to need little in the way of material things. And it's been my observation that you're happiest when you're helping others. To my way of thinking, that definitely makes you a candidate for the Amish life."

David made a lame attempt at a laugh. "If nothing else, it makes me sound like a dreadful bore."

"You know better than that," Gant said, holding his gaze. "Haven't you at least considered the idea?"

Oh, yes, he'd considered it...but what did that say about his faith, if he were to change to a different religion, an entirely different way of life, so he could marry the woman he loved? And yet could Gant possibly be right? Would the Amish way of life really be all that different for him?

"What I consider is that this probably isn't the most sensible topic of conversation for either of us," he said, trying for a casual tone. "Make your move."

Gant shot him a knowing grin. "As it happens, Doc, I think it'd be a sight more interesting to see you make a move of your own."

32

A MORNING SURPRISE

Our feet on the torrent's brink,
Our eyes on the cloud afar,
We fear the things we think,
Instead of the things that are.

JOHN BOYLE O'REILLY

David didn't sleep more than an hour that night in part because his mind kept sorting through some of the things he and Gant had talked about. But more to the point, he lay awake wrestling with a jumble of ideas and questions he'd been asking himself for weeks… for *months* now.

At the forefront of every thought was the same question: How could he continue to live out his lifetime with any reasonable degree of sanity or contentment if that life were to be lived without Susan? If his love for her was to be forever unrequited and unfulfilled, he could only envision himself as a dry and empty husk of a man.

He loved medicine. He had been a physician in his heart ever since his boyhood. After Lydia's death, caring for his patients and raising his son were many times his only incentives for putting one foot in front of the other and trudging through the days. And after Aaron was grown and had left home for university and then marriage, his responsibility to his patients, his love of medicine in general, and his faith had been motivation enough to survive.

But then with Susan, there had come a gradual, subtle turning. It wasn't that he cared less for his practice or his patients, and it wasn't that his faith became less important or more tenuous. It was more that Susan opened places in him he hadn't known existed. Little by little the chamber of loneliness inside him seemed to expand and beg to be filled. The face of the future loomed closer, and he could almost imagine himself as an aging widower limping along without direction, without purpose, without companionship, without any real warmth or comfort, but simply marking time.

And he knew that kind of life would never be enough. He had reached the point of needing her as much as he needed to breathe.

Somewhere near the hour of dawn, he made his final attempt to court sleep. Flinging the bedclothes aside, he hit the floor on his knees and poured out his heart with an abandon he wouldn't have thought he was capable of.

"I cannot imagine living life this way forever, my Lord. I simply can't. Perhaps that makes me a weak, pathetic man…but I am a man. The woman I love is forbidden to love me in return, and yet my need for her, my wanting her, my loving her, is driving me to desperation. I believe I must do something—make a decision, take a step—something. If this is the way I'm to spend the rest of my life…If this is indeed what you truly want for me…then give me the strength to endure it…or else show me a way to change it."

He continued to pray until daybreak spilled its first light through the window. By the time he got to his feet and began to dress, the way of change for which he had prayed began to form a web stretching outward from the chambers of his heart.

Susan Kanagy usually spent her mornings baking and setting bread to rise, doing laundry or cleaning, and sometimes, on a not so busy morning, tending to small tasks such as tidying drawers and cupboards. Staying busy was never a problem, and she had her days ordered as strictly and precisely as the spices and other staples in her pantry.

That's how well-managed her life had once been. Late on this Tuesday morning, however, she sat at her kitchen table, looking around the room at the chores awaiting her attention but not getting done.

Ever since the attack on Fannie Christmas Day, Susan's routine seemed to fall apart. She would start one task and then move on to another before finishing the first. Sometimes she even forgot which day of the week it was, and when she remembered, she would realize she had worked at Wednesday's chores on Tuesday and Thursday's chores on Wednesday.

What was happening to her mind?

She would like to have blamed her preoccupation and distraction on the nursing needs and, later, the continuing concern for Fannie, not to mention the apprehension about what might happen next to someone in their community. But she knew there was more to it than that.

She was also worried for Rachel, who had been different...and distant...ever since that day. It was no surprise that what had happened to Fannie seemed to have brought back the worst of her older daughter's memories. Truth be known, how could it *not* affect her?

But there was something else working on Rachel, and Susan feared that she knew what it was. Captain Gant. She had seen the looks that passed between them on the few occasions when Rachel had been here and Gant stopped by to visit. He was welcome here, of course, after all the time he had spent among them and especially after saving Fannie's life. But the obvious attraction between him and Rachel never failed to make Susan's heart clench with dread, for she knew the pain a romantic involvement with an outsider would surely bring.

After all, hadn't she felt at least the tip of that same knife of pain herself because of David Sebastian?

Gant looked at Rachel the way David sometimes looked at *her*. And perhaps the look in Rachel's eyes when she glanced at Captain Gant resembled the look in her own eyes when her gaze rested on David.

Verboten. The very word gnawed away at her conscience.

Yet she had to trust Rachel's good sense. She was no child, but a woman—a woman who knew well the rules by which they lived. She knew the anguish that would accompany any entanglement with an *auslander*. Surely she would avoid anything of the kind. Rachel loved her family, her community. She had never rebelled against the Plain life as some young people did, had never seemed much interested in the *Englisch* ways, even during her running around years. In fact Rachel hadn't taken full advantage of that period of her youth but, instead, had wasted little time in making her vows and joining the church.

Surely now she wouldn't risk a faith that she had followed since childhood, an entire way of life, for a forbidden romance.

Oh, that Gideon possessed even half the good judgment of his sister...

Susan shook off the thought. Of all the things that distracted her from her work and any semblance of peace, the worry over her rebellious son nagged at her the most viciously. She would not allow her mind to wander there today. Too much waited to be done, and she was alone to do it. Fannie had spent the night at Rachel's and would no doubt stay most of the day with her. She could ask them both to come and help, of course, but she almost welcomed the list of tasks that awaited her. More than anything else, keeping busy helped her not to think too much.

Today she would use the good judgment with which she credited her daughter. Today she would keep herself so busy nothing would distract her from her work.

She was still dwelling on that promise to herself when she got up from the table and glanced out the kitchen window only to see David Sebastian driving up the lane to the house.

Now that he was actually here, David suddenly was gripped by an almost numbing attack of cold feet. He couldn't remember a time when he'd ever been so close to simply turning and running away. His every instinct told him he shouldn't be here.

But he *was* here and with a goal in mind. And just in case Susan had already seen him approaching, he could hardly do anything other than get out of the buggy and go to the door.

If his legs would support him.

He clenched his fist to knock but hesitated for one last moment.

What in the world was he thinking, coming here like this? She'd probably suspect he'd lost his senses and ask him to leave.

And she'd be perfectly within her rights to do just that.

He reminded himself that only hours ago he'd been convinced that God was giving him clear direction to bolster himself and take the initiative to *do* something. Nothing ventured, nothing gained, and all that.

But there was always the very real possibility that if he shocked her too much, it would be the end of their friendship—a friendship he had come to deeply cherish and depend on.

But what if he was right about what he thought he'd seen in her eyes on the rare occasion she met his gaze straight on? What if he hadn't imagined it?

What if she cared for him too?

But there was still the unavoidable reality that she was Amish…and he wasn't.

He would never know if he didn't confront her. And if he didn't confront her now, he probably never would.

So he forced himself to knock. He knocked so loudly he startled himself.

She was wearing what he seemed to remember her calling a "choring dress." As she stood looking at him, she struggled with a strand of dark blonde hair, trying to tuck it under her *kapp* from which it had fallen free.

She appeared flustered and flushed. And she looked absolutely lovely.

"David?"

His gaze traced every angle, every soft line of her face, and he had all he could do not to scoop her into his arms.

That's it, go ahead and frighten her to death…At the least that will put a quick end to this madness…

"I…ah…Is this a bad time, Susan?"

She gave him a blank look. "A bad time for what?"

"For us to talk."

"Talk?"

"Yes, but if you're busy, I can come back…"

Coward. If you leave now, you'll likely never come back.

"No. I suppose—no, this is fine."

She glanced around their surroundings as if to see if they were being watched.

"Are you sure, Susan?"

She seemed to recover then. The familiar welcoming smile slid into place, and the warmth that usually filled her eyes at the sight of him reappeared. "Of course. Though if you've come to see Fannie, I'm afraid she's not here. She spent the night at Rachel's."

Even as she spoke, she stepped aside for him to enter and stood waiting to take his coat and hat.

He'd entirely forgotten about Fannie! He couldn't have possibly carried on the conversation he intended had the child been here. What was he thinking?

Well that was clear enough. He wasn't thinking. Indeed it was all he could do to string a few words together. He was very nearly incoherent. No, he was most definitely not thinking.

"Actually I came to see you about something else," he said. His unsteady voice belied his attempt at a casual tone.

"Oh." Her expression took on that questioning, uncomfortable look again, but Susan being Susan, she was as gracious as ever. "All right then. Come in, and I'll get us some coffee."

Yes, a cup of coffee would be good. He needed something to hold onto…

→ ←

The intimacy of the two of them alone in the kitchen at this time of the morning unsettled David more than he would have thought possible. At any ordinary time, he would have relished the experience of sitting here at the table across from her, drinking her coffee, and being able to study her face. But now, nervous and uncertain as he was about what he wanted—needed—to say, he couldn't even enjoy being with her. The only thing that seemed to matter at the moment was getting the words out, getting this over.

Susan caught him off guard by speaking first. "I'm glad you stopped, David."

"Are you?"

Good grief. Was he going to be this inane throughout the entire conversation?

She nodded. "There's something I'm concerned about. I think, if you're willing, you might be able to help."

He hadn't expected this, but if something was bothering her, naturally he'd do whatever he could. "Of course. Are you still worried about Fannie?"

"No, not Fannie so much, although sometimes I still sense a kind of...sadness in her. Maybe even fear. But, no, it's Rachel I'm worried about." She looked at him as if she wasn't certain of her next words. "You and Captain Gant—you've become friends."

"Yes, though I suspect it's been a surprise to both of us, we have."

"I wonder, if you don't mind telling me, has he ever said anything that might indicate he has an...*interest*...in Rachel? A *romantic* interest?"

Whatever David might have expected to hear, this wasn't it. And after the conversation he'd had with Gant only last night, he wasn't quite sure how to answer it. He wanted to be truthful with Susan, but he didn't want to break a confidence with Gant.

"Do *you* think he does?" he said, deliberately delaying any real answer until he could decide just how to reply.

She nodded. "I do. The way he looks at her—and the way Rachel looks when she's *with* him—I think maybe they care for each other.

I thought you might be able to talk with him, explain how it is with us." She stopped. "This isn't good, David."

"No?"

"Well you understand why, don't you? Nothing can ever come of it, with Rachel being Amish and Gant being an *auslander*. It can only bring her pain and, if I'm right, pain for him as well. I don't want that for either of them, though of course Rachel is my first concern. She's been through enough as it is. Any thought of a relationship between them needs to be quenched. It can never be."

A sinking heaviness settled over David's heart. The words that only an hour ago he'd felt compelled to speak now turned to dust and died in his throat.

❖ 33 ❖

THROUGH EYES OF LOVE

My heart is like a trembling leaf
carried by the wind.

ANONYMOUS

He tried not to show the cavity that had opened up inside him at the significance of her words.

He made a desperate attempt to find his backbone and feign a steadiness he didn't feel. After all it wasn't as if she'd said anything he wasn't already aware of. It was just that hearing the words from her lips, the finality ringing through them, jarred him into a realization that the idea he'd been so intent on broaching with her was now little more than a flight of fancy. This wasn't anything new. It was nothing he hadn't known all along.

"David? Is something wrong?"

He blinked, even managed a ragged smile. "No. Well—I understand what you're saying, but I can't help but wonder if there isn't some way..."

His words weakened and faded away unfinished.

She was watching him closely. "So Gant *is* taken with Rachel. I thought so."

"I—Susan, I can't speak for him. It wouldn't be right."

She nodded. "You don't have to. I can tell. It's written all over your face."

"No, what you think you see has nothing to do with Gant and Rachel!" he blurted out.

Immediately horrified by his outburst, he tried to cover his mistake. "I mean—it's not what you think."

Still she studied him, her eyes filled with questions. "Then... what?"

He looked at her, pain clamping his chest until he could scarcely breath.

"David, are you all right?" Susan started to stand, but he put up a hand to indicate that he was fine.

Her look was skeptical, even fearful.

He had to tell her. That was all there was to it. He had to risk everything and tell her why he'd come here this morning. He thought he couldn't bear the look of rejection that was sure to follow what he had to say, but the pressure building inside him simply would not allow him to stay silent any longer.

But where were the words to make her understand?

✦

"What I came to tell you...is the very thing you fear for Rachel and Gant. I love you, Susan. I've loved you for so long I don't even remember when it began. I'm sorry to tell you like this, but I simply cannot keep my silence another day..."

The words continued to ring in Susan's ears long after he spoke them. She felt as if she were suspended in a dream, for surely this couldn't be real.

But it *was* real. She felt his hand clasping hers, holding it as if he feared she might jump from the chair and run away.

"Try to understand," he was saying in a voice that didn't sound like David's voice.

"I had to say it just once. Please don't hate me for what I can't help, Susan. I've carried this with me for so long. For years now."

She didn't dare look at him. But she *did* look at him—she had to. And there it was, the love he'd just a moment ago professed, a love shining in his eyes but clinging to her like an embrace. Truth was he might just as well have been holding her, for the strength of his gaze had drawn her in and wouldn't let her go.

"Susan—say something or I'm going to die right here at your kitchen table."

"Oh, David, what can I say? You know there can't be anything between us. It's impossible!"

He was gripping her hand so hard she almost told him to let go, that he was hurting her. But she didn't *want* him to let go. So she said nothing.

"Susan—will you tell me just one thing?"

She waited.

"The truth now—forget for a moment that I'm an *outsider*—do you have feelings for me? Do you?"

She tried to swallow against the knot lodged in her throat but couldn't. He knew. But how did he know? She'd been so careful...

"I—oh, don't ask me that! Don't! Surely it shows...every time I look at you. That's why I so often *don't* look at you."

His eyes lighted. "So you *do care for me.*"

"We can't talk about this, David. We can't be together...like this... or talk about our feelings. We *can't.* I could be shunned for this!"

"Listen to me, Susan. Just...listen for a moment."

He tightened his hold on her hand, and Susan winced.

He saw her reaction, gentled his touch, but didn't release her. He lifted her hand to his lips and brushed a kiss over her fingers. "I hurt you. I'm so sorry, I didn't mean to. I would never hurt you."

Susan's head swam. She had never passed out in her life, but in that instant she thought she might.

"What if I were to convert to your faith?" he said.

His question came as though shrouded in a fog. "What?"

He smiled a little. "Gant said something last night—he was teasing, but after I thought about it, I'm not so sure he was all that far off the mark."

He paused and then went on to explain. "He told me I don't seem that much different from the Amish, that he sees many of the same things in me that he sees in the Plain People. I attempted to laugh it off at the time, but later when I thought about it, I had to concede that he might have a point."

"You're not serious. Would you do that? David, you mustn't think that way!"

But even as she challenged him, Susan felt a spark of hope ignite and begin to burn.

"Oh, I realize there's much more to becoming Amish than merely adapting to your lifestyle. I've been close to you and your people too many years to think it would be easy. But, Susan, you need to know this isn't the first time I've thought about the possibility."

She looked at him and saw no hint of anything but the truth looking back at her.

He leaned even closer to her across the table, still holding her hand, still holding her with his eyes as well. "The truth is I've thought about it *many* times, Susan. There's much about the Amish life that holds a strong appeal for me—much besides *you*, I mean. What do you think? Could I make it happen? Would I be accepted?"

He seemed to genuinely need an answer, but she couldn't think with him holding her hand and looking at her...that way. Gently she slipped her hand out of his and tried to consider a truthful reply to his question.

"Honestly, David, I don't know. The bishop and our leaders would have to give their permission. They like you—everyone in the community likes you and respects you—but it's hardly ever that anyone from the *Englisch* world is successful at becoming Amish. I know of a few who tried, but they gave up after only a few weeks. They found our ways too hard and too different from what they were used to. There was one man and his wife who managed, but it took them a long time—nearly two years."

"Two *years?*" David's eyes widened. "Why so long?"

"There's so much to learn—including our language. It's required. Of course, smart as you are and as often as you've heard it spoken over the years, you probably wouldn't have all that much difficulty. But you'd also have to learn our ways—the *Ordnung* and all the tenets of our faith—everything. And you'd be on a kind of 'trial' throughout the whole time. You'd have to live among us, and you'd be watched for any failures or slipups."

She thought for a moment. "I think they'd probably let you go on with your doctoring, although you'd not be allowed to practice among the *Englisch* again."

Other than his initial surprise at the length of time it might take, he seemed unfazed by her explanation. When she'd finished, he again reached for her hand.

"And once this 'trial' is over, Susan—will you marry me?" he said, his voice low. "Will you?"

She searched his gaze with an intensity that almost hurt her own eyes. "You're serious, aren't you?"

"I think you know I am entirely serious."

Unexpectedly she felt tears fill her eyes. Perhaps it was because his sincerity and the unmistakable depth of his emotion overwhelmed her. Perhaps it was because she finally realized that her own feelings just might not be completely futile after all. Or perhaps it was because she had tried so hard to repress those feelings, to bury them in some safe place where no one would ever know. But now that she knew how he felt, she couldn't go on trying to deceive him—or herself—any longer.

"I can't let you turn Amish just so we can be married…"

"Nor can you *stop* me. Susan, listen carefully to what I'm about to say. I believe that last night the Lord Himself gave His blessing to this decision."

"David—"

"No, wait. I've thought about it for months now, and in all honestly, I can tell you that there's much about the Amish life I want for myself. It's true that I want *you* more than anything else. I won't deny it. But I also crave what you and your people so obviously have. I've committed the sin of envy more than once when I've been among the People."

He stopped, squeezed her hand but with great care this time. "You still haven't answered my question."

Susan closed her eyes and then opened them to find his gaze still locked on her. "David, if you're willing to do all that...and if the bishop gives his permission...yes, I'll marry you. But you understand it will be a very long wait. And we'll be watched. *Closely.*"

He smiled. "Then if you'll allow it, I'd very much like to kiss you now, while there's still no one watching."

She felt the heat of a blush stain her face, but she nodded her consent.

✦34✦

THE GIFT OF FORGIVENESS

And forgive us our debts,
as we forgive our debtors.

MATTHEW 6:12

Rachel enjoyed having her little sister stay overnight, but she thought maybe she'd best be sending her home later today. Fannie had spent the past three nights at her house, and no doubt their mother was missing her.

Although they'd had a good time together, Rachel was still concerned about her sister. Physically, Fannie seemed to have healed well from the attack, but it was the girl's emotional well-being that worried Rachel.

She was quieter, more contemplative. Too often a hint of sadness darkened the eyes that had once fairly danced with eagerness and delight for life in general. Rachel longed to help but so far hadn't been able to get Fannie to open up.

Truth was, Rachel understood all too well how difficult it was to confide in *anyone,* even one's own sister, after an event of this nature. In her case it had been Dr. Sebastian who had finally managed to draw some of the details about her attack from her and at least start her on the road to healing. But perhaps because Fannie was so young, she didn't feel comfortable sharing her emotions, even with their physician and family friend.

Maybe if Gideon hadn't left home, he would have been able to gain her confidence, but his leaving had left Fannie confused and hurting. Even after Gideon returned and attempted to explain the reasons for his departure, Rachel could see that Fannie didn't understand. All she knew was that she missed her big brother terribly and wanted him to come home.

So did Rachel. She was so used to him stopping by in the mornings or evenings to see what odd jobs she might need done or simply helping himself to whatever she might have baked that day. She had no idea how many times she looked out the window, expecting to see him loping across the field on his way to her door.

His leaving had left her torn. She thought she understood Gideon's frustration and at least some of his reasons for feeling the need to get away. Gideon had never accepted the Plain life easily, had always had his own firm ideas about how things should or should not be handled. Yet Rachel had always believed he would eventually make peace with their Amish faith and turn to the church.

Now she had to wonder if he ever would.

With Gideon gone Rachel felt even more than ever that Fannie needed to talk about her feelings. So after they ate their lunch, she deliberately lingered at the table, making light talk as she waited for an opening to move their conversation to a more serious level.

"So what do you think about our mamma and Dr. Sebastian?" she said. She thought this would be a safe subject to broach with Fannie because she was fairly certain her sister's feelings about their mother's astonishing news were the same as her own.

After the first shock of learning that the doctor and their mamma had found love together and were hoping to eventually wed, Rachel was genuinely happy for them. She had seen Dr. Sebastian's affection for Mamma for a long time, and lately she'd begun to suspect that her mother returned his feelings. She had worried about what the situation might mean to them, but with the doctor's decision to convert to the Amish faith, surely things would all work out just fine.

"Well," Fannie said, "I love Mamma, of course, and I like Dr. Sebastian a whole lot. So I think it's wonderful-*gut* that they're going to marry."

"It will be a long time, though," Rachel cautioned. "There's much the doctor has to do after he gets the bishop's permission."

"Bishop Graber *will* give his permission, won't he, Rachel?"

Fannie's features pinched to such a concerned frown that Rachel reached to smooth her forehead. "I can't imagine why he wouldn't. He has great respect for the doctor—as do we all. I'm sure he'll allow him to become one of us. Don't you worry about that. It's going to be all right. Let's just be happy for Mamma and Dr. Sebastian."

"Oh, I *am* happy for them! And won't it be a fine thing to have Dr. Sebastian around all the time instead of just once in a while?"

After another moment Fannie made a remark about hoping Gideon would come to visit soon, and Rachel saw her chance to deepen their conversation. "Are you worried about our *bruder,* Fannie?"

Her sister thought for a moment and then said, "I miss him—a lot. But I don't worry about him, at least not very much. Gideon's really smart and strong. He'll be all right. I just wish he still lived at home."

Rachel watched her. "Then what *are* you worried about, sister?" she said softly. "Something troubles you, I can tell. Are you still upset about those boys who hurt you?"

Fannie glanced away. "No. Not so much."

"What then, Fannie? You can tell me, you know. You can tell me anything."

Fannie turned to her, searching Rachel's features as if looking for reassurance. "It bothers me that some folks are still so angry."

Rachel took her hand. "What do you mean, 'angry,' Fannie? No one's angry with you!"

"No, not with me. But they're angry with those boys—the *Englischers.* And I feel it just as much as if they *were* angry with me." She cast another look at Rachel. "You're angry. I know you are. And Captain Gant too. I can tell. Even Dr. Sebastian is angry. And Phoebe and Malachi—though they don't say much, I can feel it. And Gideon—Gideon is *awful* angry."

Rachel sat back, momentarily bewildered. "What do you mean, you can 'feel it,' Fannie?"

Her sister's young face appeared drawn, intent on gathering her thoughts and forming the words to explain exactly what she meant. "When people are angry, it feels like the room gets smaller and darker. It makes me feel...closed in. And sad."

She paused and then added, "If it makes *me* sad, it must make Jesus even sadder."

Rachel waited, saying nothing because she didn't want to chance distracting Fannie now that she was finally opening up to her.

"Mamma and Bishop Graber always say that Jesus loves all of us— Plain people and *Englisch* people and even not-so-*gut* people—and that we're supposed to love like Jesus does. And that means forgiving them like He does too. But if we stay angry with someone who does us a wrong—even if it's a really *bad* wrong—then we're *not* loving or forgiving like Jesus, are we? And I think that must make Him really sad."

She stopped, but the combination of unhappiness and confusion that had been so evident in her for weeks still looked out at Rachel. "I guess I don't understand why people don't just do what Jesus says. When we don't, everybody seems to hurt a lot and stay angry and awful sad."

Rachel studied the thin little face with the enormous eyes, now so serious and intent, and felt her own emotions struggle behind a wall of conflict. "What about you, Fannie?" she said, her voice little more than a hoarse whisper. "Have you forgiven the boys who hurt you?"

Fannie looked at her, her gaze steady and clear, and nodded. "At first I couldn't. But, truth be known, Rachel, I was never really mad at them. I was mostly scared—and hurt. But the more I thought about it, the more it seemed that they probably didn't even understand that what they did was wrong. I mean how can you know you're doing something wrong unless you know what's right?"

With a shake of her head, she went on. "I think mostly the people who do mean things to us think we're bad because we're different from them. People like those boys—and those men who hurt you and Eli—they must not know about Jesus. At least they don't know that He loves everyone the same way, including them. Otherwise they might not do the things they do. But no matter *what* they do, we're supposed to forgive them, just like Jesus does."

Fannie uttered a small sigh. "I think maybe 'forgiving' is called that because it's like a gift that you give someone. Even if they've done bad things to you and don't even say they're sorry—even if they just don't like you at all and you know they might hurt you again—you're supposed to forgive them anyway. If that's not the way it's supposed to be, then why does the Lord's Prayer say 'forgive us as we forgive our debtors'? Doesn't that mean that if we *don't* forgive them, Jesus won't forgive us?"

Her voice dropped so low Rachel could scarcely make out her words. "I'm still afraid of those boys. And my back and other places where they hit me still hurt sometimes. But ever since I forgave them, my *heart* doesn't hurt. And that was the worst hurt of all."

Shaken, Rachel felt a great stillness surround her as her heart cried out within her at the simple, piercing truth of Fannie's words. And she suddenly knew that her nine-year-old sister had just handed her the healing ointment for her own wounded spirit and hurting heart.

Much later that afternoon, after Fannie had left for home, Rachel knelt before her Lord and wept and prayed, emptying herself of the bitterness, the resentment, and the debilitating anger that had enslaved her for so long. In so doing she discovered that the gift of forgiveness had been near at hand all the time. She had only to claim it and give it.

When she finally rose from her knees, it was to realize that, like Fannie, her heart—the worst hurt of all—didn't hurt anymore.

35

A Meeting in Riverhaven

Mind moved yet seemed to stop
As 'twere a spinning-top.

W.B. Yeats

Toward the end of February, the area was visited by a surprisingly mild day. The snow had mostly melted, and after weeks of bitter cold, the early morning sunshine brought a sigh of relief and teasing thoughts of the spring to come.

Rachel hadn't seen hide nor hair of Gideon for days. Concerned for him and feeling a restlessness brought on by the nice weather, she decided to take the buggy into Riverhaven and visit him at work.

Had Mamma and Fannie not promised to spend the day helping Rebecca Knepp at her house, she would have asked them to go with her. Rebecca had broken both her wrist and ankle on the ice a week ago, and though her daughter Emma and the two younger girls were good to help, Mamma had volunteered herself and Fannie to lend a hand today and give the children a respite. The two of them would do some baking and housecleaning, as well as take care of whatever mending and sewing might have accumulated since Rebecca's accident.

On the way into town, even though she would have liked her mother and sister's company, Rachel had to admit she was enjoying the solitary buggy ride. It was too early yet to see any real signs of spring, but the warm sunshine, deceptive though it was, at least allowed her to *pretend* winter would soon be bowing out.

As she pulled up in front of Karl Webber's carpenter shop, she hoped Gideon wasn't too busy to talk for a few minutes. Mr. Webber had always been patient and generous in allowing family members to drop in, so she wasn't worried about getting him in trouble at his job.

After she saw her brother, she hoped to make a quick trip across the street to the general store. She intended to check on an order of sewing supplies for Mamma and some paint for her birdhouses that should be in any day. Spring always brought an increased demand for the birdhouses, and she wanted to get ahead on the orders she already had waiting before she received any more.

The thought of visiting with Gideon combined with a trip to the general store put Rachel in an almost giddy mood. Eager to share her lighthearted frame of mind with her brother, she got out of the buggy, tethered Slowpoke—so named by Gideon—then hurried into the building.

She was surprised to find her brother alone, and more than a little relieved to see that he was still dressed in his plain clothing. At least he hadn't completely turned his back on their Amish ways. Rachel was also pleased to note that his expression brightened when she walked in.

But not for long. Only a moment after they exchanged greetings and brought each other up to date about things at home and each other, Gideon's mood seemed to change.

He indicated she should sit down on one of the finished chairs opposite where he was working. "Karl won't be back for another hour or so. He had an appointment of some kind."

"You don't look so happy, *bruder*. Is something wrong?"

"Karl's selling the shop," he said without preamble, his tone leaving no question as to how he felt about the matter. "They're moving back to Cleveland. His wife's parents are elderly, and they need care, so they're leaving as soon as he gets a buyer for the shop and their house."

"Oh, Gideon, I'm sorry. But surely whoever buys the shop will keep you on. I should think they'd be pleased to have someone with your experience."

He lifted one shoulder in a quick shrug. "I sure hope so. I like my job pretty well, you know. I'd hate to lose it. But I hate to lose Karl as an employer too. He's been real good to work for."

"Well don't lose heart. I'm sure the new buyer will want you to stay. Anyone would be foolish to let such a good employee go."

He smiled, but it was a little wobbly. "So—how's Fannie doing?"

"She's well. But she misses you."

He glanced away. "I'll come see her real soon. I miss her too."

Rachel hesitated. "You can always come home to stay, you know," she said quietly.

He looked at her. "No, Rachel. This is where I need to be. At least for now."

Rachel didn't want to spoil their visit with an argument, so she merely nodded in a gesture of acceptance. "I hear Dr. Sebastian came to see you with the news about him and Mamma. Were you surprised?"

"Definitely. But after I thought about it, some things started to add up. Looking back I'd say he's been sweet on her for a long time."

"I think you're right." She paused. "Mamma's really happy, Gideon. I think this is a good thing for her—for both of them."

"Seems strange though. Mamm married to Doc. Hard to take it in."

"Are you glad?"

He seemed to consider her question. "I think so. Doc's a good man. But like I said, it's strange. It'll take some getting used to."

"Well," Rachel said while getting up, "you'll have plenty of time to get used to it. Mamma said it might take as long as a year or two before Dr. Sebastian can be baptized and join the church."

He nodded. "Has the bishop approved it yet?"

"No, they haven't heard anything. And I think they're both getting really nervous."

They both smiled at that. "I should let you get back to work," Rachel said, not really wanting to leave him. She did miss her brother, even more than she'd thought she would. Still, he had work to do, so she told him goodbye and started for the door.

Before she left, she turned back with a reminder. "Remember, you said you'd come for a visit soon."

"I will. You take care going home now."

Rachel wasn't sure, but she thought she sensed a sadness in him as their eyes met. She didn't like to think of Gideon being unhappy. All the same she couldn't help but hope that he missed them. At least a little. Maybe that would prompt him to come home to stay.

Rachel was just paying Mr. Whitlock, the manager of the general store, for her order when the bell over the entrance door announced a customer. She turned to look, swallowing a sharp breath of surprise when Jeremiah Gant walked in.

Even though he had to lean slightly on his cane and his limp was pronounced, he was still one of the tallest men she'd ever known.

He was also the most handsome man she'd ever known. In his severely tailored black coat and what Fannie called his "captain's cap," a lock of dark hair escaping to fall over his forehead, he very nearly took her breath away.

He saw her at once, and Rachel felt herself flush when his eyes widened with obvious pleasure at the sight of her. He stopped just past the threshold, standing to one side until she'd finished at the counter.

After thanking Mr. Whitlock, she started toward Jeremiah. He met her before she could reach him, the smile in his eyes like a touch.

"Rachel," he said softly, removing his cap. The way he said her name made it hard to breathe. Moreover, she seemed unable to find her voice.

"I've been hoping to see you," he said, "but I never imagined running into you here."

"How—how did you get here?" Even when she finally managed to speak, her voice didn't sound like her own. At least not to her.

If he noticed her strangeness, he made no sign of it. "I came in with Doc. He needed to see a patient, and I had some things to take care of, so I rode along." He paused. "Later we're going to go see about a horse for me."

Rachel stared up at him. "A horse?"

He nodded. "Apparently he knows a fellow with a couple for sale. Said he'd introduce me."

"You—can ride? I mean, with your leg as it is..."

"Well, Doc's not keen on the idea, but I convinced him I'd settle for a nice, gentle old nag if need be."

Something twisted deep inside Rachel. "Are you—" she could hardly bring herself to ask—"are you leaving?"

He frowned. "Leaving? Oh—no! No, I just need a way to get around every now and then. I'm tired of depending on Doc, and I expect he's tired of it too."

The relief that poured over Rachel made her go weak. She knew he would leave eventually, knew she shouldn't care—but she *did* care. She cared more than any Amish woman should ever care about what an outsider did.

"You came into town to shop, did you?" he asked.

"Shop? Oh, yes—well, to pick up some things I'd ordered for Mamma and me. But mostly I wanted to visit Gideon."

"How is he?"

"He's...all right, I suppose. A little down in the mouth this morning. It seems the shop where he works is being sold, so he's concerned."

"About his job, you mean?"

"Well, yes. There's no way of knowing whether the new owner will keep him on or not, and Gideon likes his job a lot. And he's enjoyed working for Mr. Webber too."

"I planned to drop by and see him today too. Maybe I can cheer him up a bit. I predict the new owner—whoever he is—is going to want your brother to stay put."

"Oh, he'll be glad to see you, Jeremiah! He thinks highly of you."

Still smiling, he studied her, and the softness in his eyes was like a caress. Two women came into the store just then, both casting curious glances in their direction. It occurred to Rachel that an Amish woman talking to an obviously *Englisch* man was an uncommon sight, to say the least.

Suddenly uncomfortable, she shifted from one foot to another, knowing she should leave, yet loath to do so. "I suppose I should go..."

He glanced around. One of the women turned back to look at them again. As if he sensed the situation would be a discomfiting one for Rachel, he stepped in front of her to block her view from the other customers.

"I need to talk with you, Rachel," he said, his voice low. His earlier smile had faded, his expression now uncharacteristically solemn.

"We best not. I think I should leave now."

"Because we're attracting attention." He said it as a statement, not a question.

Rachel nodded. "We shouldn't...be seen like this. You understand..."

His mouth turned down. "No, I don't think I do. But I don't want to make you uncomfortable. Fine—I'll stop by your house later this evening, so we can talk."

"No!" she blurted out. "I mean...that isn't a good idea, Jeremiah. We can't do that."

His eyes narrowed. "Then let's go someplace right now, somewhere we can talk."

"We *can't!* Try to understand. I shouldn't be seen with you at all, Jeremiah. I need you to accept that."

"Well, I *don't* accept it." He kept his voice low, but his words spilled out like hailstones, cold and hard and slashing the air between them. "I'll be discreet, Rachel, but I need to talk with you, and I'm going to do just that. You can expect me to stop by your place this evening."

Without another word, he walked away, leaving Rachel to stand and stare in frustration as he headed toward the other side of the store.

→ ←

After the two women paid for their purchases, Gant paid for his quickly and started for the door.

He already regretted his sharpness with Rachel. She probably wouldn't even come to the door this evening. She'd probably hide from him instead. But he'd meant what he said. He *had* to talk with her.

He looked around when he stepped outside the store, but there was no sight of her. Drawing a long breath, he finally crossed to the other side and started for the carpenter shop.

When he walked in, Gideon looked up in surprise. Gant was glad to see no sign of anyone else around. He extended a hand to Gideon, who regarded him with a studying look for a second or two before offering his own hand.

The boy grinned. "Just so you know, Captain—the Amish aren't much for shaking hands. It's fine with me, though."

"It seems I have a lot to learn about the Amish."

"Truth be known, even the Amish have a lot to learn about the Amish, sir."

Gant laughed. He did like this boy.

"How are you doing now that you're on your own, Gideon?"

A sheepish look crossed the other's features. "You know about my leaving home, then?"

"Your little sister told me. She misses you."

Gideon drew a long breath. "I didn't want to hurt anyone. Especially not my sisters or Mamm. But—I had to get away."

"I think I understand," Gant said. "I also hear your mother had a surprise for you."

"Doc told you?"

Gant nodded, smiling. "He talks about nothing else these days. She's made him a happy man. And he ought to be. Your mother is a fine woman."

"Yes, sir, she is. And I'm glad to see her marry again if it's to a man like Doc. They don't come any better."

"Rightly said."

Gant paused, watching the boy. His leg was bothering him some, and he leaned on the cane now with both hands. "I understand you've had other news as well. I ran into your sister at the general store."

"Oh. She told you about the shop being sold."

"She did. She seems to think you're worried about keeping your job."

He shrugged. "I need the work, but it's not just the money. I like it here. Karl's a good man to work for, and he's taught me a lot. So, yeah, I'm worried about my job. I'd really hate to lose it."

"You're not going to lose it, son."

The boy looked at him. "Pardon, sir, but you can't know that."

"Actually, I *do* know that. About an hour ago, I signed the papers to buy this place. I'm your new boss, and I say you're keeping your job."

36

BREAKING THE RULES

Somewhere there waiteth in this world of ours
for one lone soul, another lonely soul…

EDWIN ARNOLD

B efore Gant left for Rachel's house that evening, he and Doc had a conversation that bordered treacherously close to an argument.

Doc accused Gant of being stubborn and unable to think beyond the moment. Gant accused Doc of being overly cautious. "But then that just seems to be something in the Englishman's blood, I've noticed."

"In the first place, you've no business riding around after dark on that horse," Doc groused. "One good fall, and you risk breaking your leg. And isn't that just what you need? A break to go with a bullet."

"You took the bullet out," Gant reminded him.

The look Doc shot him would have withered a cactus.

"Now you listen to me carefully, you hardheaded Irishman. I told you just last week that you are going to have a bad leg for the rest of your life. That bullet shattered your bones so severely that you could have lost the leg altogether. It took some doing to save it, and let me emphasize that I didn't save it so you could abuse it as you like."

Doc stopped only long enough to emphasize his next words by stabbing the air with his index finger. "You need to be extremely careful for the next year, at least, not to take a fall—and that includes being thrown from a horse."

When Gant started to speak, Doc ignored him.

"When I agreed to introduce you to Roger Forsythe so you could have a look at his horses, it was with the understanding that you'd use that thick head of yours and take no foolish chances. The only reason I kept my silence when you bought the gelding in the first place was because Forsythe assured us the animal was well-trained and gentle—and because I thought you had the good sense to be cautious. But you can take a fall with even the mildest nag if it steps into a hole after dark or somehow gets spooked. You're not used to that horse yet—you've ridden him, what, a total of ten minutes?"

Again Gant tried to get a word in, and again Doc cut him off.

"You simply cannot subject that leg to any sort of punishment. You could still lose it. And even if you don't care, *I* don't like you playing light with my hard work. So you'd better take me seriously and do as I tell you, or you'll pay for it. You surely will."

Gant took him seriously all right, though he didn't much like Doc having the last word. "Are you finished?" he said.

The other shot him a look of disgust—conceivably as nasty a look as Doc was capable of. Gant assumed an expression as innocent as *he* was capable of, made a deep, exaggerated bow, and uttered a solemn, "I hear you, Doc. And I'll make you proud. Indeed I will."

At that point Doc muttered something under his breath that sounded like another jab at the hardheaded Irish before stamping out of the room.

In the end Doc cooled off enough to insist that Gant borrow his buggy to go to Rachel's. "I'm bunking here tonight anyway," he said. "Tomorrow morning is my meeting with Bishop Graber—and whomever else I'm to be subjected to—so you'll just have to put up with me until then. In the meantime you might just as well use the buggy."

So that was why he was in such a testy mood. Not wanting to provoke the man any further, Gant swallowed the sarcastic comeback he was tempted to make and accepted the offer of the buggy.

Before he managed to shrug into his coat and get out the door, however, Doc decided to issue what sounded suspiciously like a warning. "You be sure you know what you're doing, man. Don't you dally with Rachel Brenneman. You're in a position to bring down a mountain of trouble on her. And while you might be able to walk away scot-free, Rachel will pay a cruel and bitter price."

Gant stopped and looked at him, any trace of sarcasm or insolence now gone. "You're wrong, Doc. It's long past the point where I could walk away from Rachel, scot-free or otherwise."

For a long moment he thought she wasn't going to answer the door. This time he pounded harder, glancing around to make sure no one was about.

Finally the door creaked open, though not all the way. She stood there, those big dark eyes of hers wide and wary, the head covering she called a *kapp* all starched and neatly in place. She had never looked lovelier.

Gant wanted to grab her up in his arms and carry her off.

That'll endear you to her, all right. What woman wouldn't want to be abducted by a grizzly bear?

"Rachel," he said.

She stared at him, clearly debating whether or not to let him past the door.

"Jeremiah, I don't think—"

She stopped, her eyes locking with his. Then, as if she'd seen something in his face that told her he wouldn't be denied, she sighed, eased the door open, and stood aside as he entered.

She watched him take his coat off, almost snatching it from him, at the same time saying, "You can't stay. Not long."

But apparently she'd seen Doc's buggy parked out front. "I suppose, though…anyone who might be nearby will think it's Doc who's here." She paused. "Not that that would be acceptable either."

"But not as unacceptable as I am, right?" he said.

She ignored him, hooking his coat and cap on the peg by the door before turning to him with obvious reluctance. "Would you like some coffee?" she said.

That was his Rachel. She never forgot her manners.

"No, Rachel. No coffee or tea. Nothing right now. Though later, if you don't throw me out, you might talk me into a slice of pie."

He watched as she swallowed. It seemed to take a long time and a good deal of effort.

"May I sit down?" he finally asked, determined not to carry on the intended conversation while standing just inside her front door.

"Oh—yes. All right."

Even though he'd declined her offer of coffee, she led him straight to the kitchen.

No doubt she felt safer with a table between them.

Gant didn't believe she was actually afraid of him. More likely she was afraid to be *with* him, afraid of the repercussions that could come if they were known to be alone in her house after dark.

Or any other time.

He hated that, hated that she had to guard against being seen with him. But he had things to say to her, things he was determined she should hear. He hoped that just this once she could get past her reluctance to break the rules, her fear of the consequences if she *did* break the rules...and hear him. Really hear him.

He waited until she sat down and then instead of sitting down across from her, as she probably expected him to do, he pulled up a chair beside her.

She drew back a little, eyeing him as if he were trespassing on private property.

And in a way, he supposed he was.

✦ 37 ✦

FORBIDDEN LOVE

What if the dream came true?

PADRAIC PEARSE

He sat so close to her that Rachel caught the clean scent of his soap, felt the radiating warmth of his body. He extended his hand, palm up, and after staring at it for a few seconds, she placed her hand in his. He held it tightly—not so tightly as to hurt her, but more as if he feared she might try to pull away from him. She felt the callused strength of his grip and, at the same time, felt her resistance to him drain away.

"Rachel?"

She looked at him, his smile drawing her into the deep blue pool of his eyes, so that she couldn't quite bring herself to look away.

"You know I'm in love with you?" he said quietly.

That was his way, she realized. Always direct, even blunt. Never wasting time on idle talk. Jeremiah believed in coming right to the point.

It was both infinite joy and unspeakable agony to hear those words, to know that she was loved by such a man...and to know an almost annihilating grief because the love was futile. *Verboten.*

"I know you think there can be nothing between us," he said.

She nodded.

"I have to believe you're wrong about that, Rachel."

She darted a quick look at him. "Jeremiah—"

He put a finger to her lips to silence her. "Just…hear me out. Please. I have to say this to you. Right now, tonight, there are things I have to say."

Rachel heard the slight unsteadiness in his voice, felt a fleeting tremor in the hand clasping hers. But more than anything else, she saw his love for her, too tender and too deep and overflowing to be anything but real. She had seen it before, and she saw it again now. She could have wept at the cruelty and bitterness of such a love…such an incredible, wondrous kind of love that could never be anything more than a reflection in the eyes, a longing in the soul.

A forbidden love.

Her heart felt as though it were bleeding.

"I know what you're thinking, Rachel," he said, his voice hoarse and unsteady.

She looked at him.

"I know what you're thinking," he said again, "but you're wrong. You and I, we're meant to be together. We belong together. And I believe that somehow we *will* be together."

"Jeremiah, don't do this! You know it's hopeless. The only way we could ever be together is if I were to give up being Amish, abandon my family, my entire way of life…"

"I'd never ask you to do that," he said quickly. "I know you *couldn't* do it."

"Then *why*, Jeremiah? Why did you even come here tonight? You're only making it harder. Soon you'll go away. You'll go back to your old life, and in time, we'll put all this behind us as if it never happened. It's insane—it's not right—to stir up feelings that can never be more than dreams, to pretend there's a future for us when we both know—"

"I'm not leaving, Rachel."

His words, the quiet finality in them, brought Rachel up short. "What?"

"I'm not leaving. I'm not going anywhere."

"But your boat—your work—"

"My boat was torched, remember? Well, there's another boat, but it's strictly for cargo." He smiled a little. "All kinds of cargo."

"Your work with the runaway slaves..."

"That will go on. But in a different way." He paused. "According to Doc, my traveling days are pretty much over."

"Oh Jeremiah, I'm sorry! I didn't know."

He shrugged. "I can still work with the railroad, but in a different capacity. There's no reason I can't help with shelter for the runaways—and supplies. I've already laid the groundwork for that. But Doc says no more living on the river or trekking miles at a time through the woods. Not with my leg as it is, and he seems to have no great hopes it will improve much more than it already has."

Her heart ached for the disappointment this must be to him. His love for the river and his life on that river had been transparent every time he talked about it.

Immediately she wondered what he would do now. He wasn't the kind of man to handle idleness well. "Is Doc absolutely certain of this?"

He nodded. "I argued with him, of course. We both enjoy a good argument now and then. But I know he's right. I already had my suspicions before he gave me the facts in his own inimitable way."

"What will you do?"

"Well, as it happens, I have a new line of work. I bought Karl Webber's carpenter shop. Signed the papers just today."

Her mouth actually dropped open. "You *didn't!*"

He nodded, smiling at her surprise. "I did. In fact I had just come from meeting with Webber and his attorney when I ran into you at the store. Webber is a patient of Doc's, you see, and when Doc found out the shop was going up for sale, he told me about it right away, knowing my inclination toward woodworking."

She studied him. "I didn't know that about you—that you liked to work with wood."

He drew a long breath. "I expect there are a number of things you don't know about me, Rachel. I intend to remedy that yet tonight."

"Does Gideon know—about your buying the shop?"

Again he smiled. "He does. We had a nice chat after you and I parted. I'm not too sure how he feels about working for me, but he did seem pleased to know his new employer has every intention of keeping him on."

"Oh, Jeremiah. He's probably thrilled!"

"He may not be for long. My crew always found me somewhat of a hard taskmaster on the river. But we'll see."

He raked a hand down the side of his face. "There's something I want to make perfectly clear before I say anything more. I'm not staying here because of my leg, Rachel. I had already made the decision to stay before Doc forced me to face reality about my bad leg and what it means for my future."

Rachel tried not to read too much into his words, but she couldn't help but ask. "Why...did you decide to stay?"

"I'm thinking you already know the answer to that. I planned to stay because of you."

"Even knowing I wouldn't leave the Plain life?"

"Aye, even knowing that as I did, I also knew I couldn't leave you. I have to be close to you, you see."

Slowly and with no small measure of frustration, Rachel shook her head. "I don't understand. When you know there can never be anything more than friendship between us..."

"I happen to believe there can be a great deal more between us, Rachel. That's why I'm here."

Unnerved by his searching look, Rachel glanced away. This was so hard, knowing that he loved her and that he cared enough to stay, simply to be close to her—oh, she couldn't listen to anything more! The hopelessness of it all was crushing the life from her heart. What could he possibly think to achieve by telling her all this?

And then a thought struck her. *But, no, surely he wasn't expecting that...*

As if he could read her mind, he released her hand only to tilt her chin with one finger and search her face with a questioning look. "What?"

"You're not thinking I'd have a…an *affair* with you?"

His eyes went hard. "No, Rachel. I want marriage. Children. A lifetime."

"Stop it! You're just being…stubborn. Stubborn and foolish, and you're hurting me! What if I told you that *I'd* want those things too—if it were possible? If it weren't forbidden. Don't torment me with the thought of something we both know we can't have."

One dark eyebrow lifted in what appeared to be an expression of dry humor. "Do you know, that's the second time tonight I've been called stubborn? I'd hoped for better from you, Rachel. On the other hand, it takes a certain measure of patience to be truly stubborn. And where you're concerned, I'm prepared to be as patient as necessary to resolve our…difficulties."

"What are you getting at, Jeremiah?" His wry demeanor and his attitude of calm and cool reason were beginning to exasperate her.

"Just tell me this, Rachel," he said. "If you weren't Amish or if I weren't *Englisch,* would you marry me?"

✦ 38 ✦

KNOWING JEREMIAH

Judge not the Play before the Play is done;
Her Plot has many changes; every day
Speaks a new scene; the last act crowns the Play.

FRANCIS QUARLES

She stared at him in disbelief. "That's a totally ridiculous question. I *am* Amish, and you're *Englisch*."

"Irish, actually. Even so, if we were on equal ground, do you love me enough to marry me?"

"Really, Jeremiah, I'm not going to dignify that with an answer. In the first place, I hardly know you—"

"—you've known me for months, Rachel."

"We've been *acquainted* for months. But I don't *know* you, not really. Why, I don't know anything about you—"

He leaned back, crossing his arms across his chest. "What do you want to know?"

Her annoyance with him gave way to confusion. "What do I—well, for one thing, I don't even know how old you are."

"Thirty-six. Does that really matter?"

She studied him. "You look older."

Both eyebrows shot up. "Why, thank you, Rachel. Pardon me while I remove the arrow from my back."

"Would you *stop* it?"

"Stop what?"

"Stop being so...just stop it, Jeremiah. The thing is, I don't know anything about your family—your parents, if you have brothers or sisters—nothing. You can't possibly love someone you know nothing about."

His expression sobered. "My father died when I was still a boy. I scarcely knew him. My mother died before I left Ireland. My two younger sisters are still in Ireland. They're married and have children."

"I'm sorry—about your parents," she said.

"What else would you like to know?"

Truth be told, there were only two other questions she felt compelled to ask him. But did she have the right?

He started this, she reminded herself.

"You remember that I unpacked your travel case when you and Asa first came to Riverhaven—"

He frowned. "And?"

"There was a photo. A young woman. A very lovely young woman. Is she someone who's...special to you?" Almost as soon as the words were out of her mouth, it occurred to Rachel that she was acting as if she had the *right* to pry into his past when she didn't, not at all. "I'm sorry, I shouldn't have asked—"

He waved off her apology. "It's all right. The photo is of Asa's sister."

"Asa's...sister? But she looks—"

"—white?" He nodded, a smile that wasn't really a smile creasing his features. "She's half-white. Asa's parents were both slaves, brought here from some island or other. But Ariana's father was a white plantation owner." He paused. "A slave has no recourse. If the owner wants her, he simply takes her."

Sickened by the thought, Rachel said nothing else.

"Apparently, during a photographer's visit to the plantation to take family photos, Ariana caught his eye, and he snapped a couple of pictures of her as well. Asa and I each carry a copy with us because we keep hoping to find her."

Rachel looked at him. At her unspoken question, he explained. "Ariana tried to run away from the plantation. The owner was showing a little too much interest in her. Asa did his best to protect her—she's much younger than he—but there *is* no real protection for a slave. She was caught before she got far, and as her...*punishment*...the owner sold her into a brothel." He stopped. "She was sixteen years old at the time."

Rachel gasped. "That's awful."

"Oh, you'd be surprised what some slave owners are capable of. Anyway, after I bought Asa's papers and hired him on, we searched for her everywhere we went. We were able to track her to a house in Louisiana once, but by the time we got there, she was gone. That was the last we ever heard of her. But we keep her photo with us just in case someone might recognize her. It's been hard for Asa. He never got over what happened to her. He blames himself, but there's nothing he could have done."

He stopped. "In truth, if there's any blame, it's mine."

"What do you mean?"

He sighed, dropped his arms away from his chest, and splayed both hands on top of the table. "Asa doesn't know this, but I found her once. He wasn't with me—he'd stayed with the boat while I went into Charleston for supplies. As usual, I showed Ariana's photo around, and a storekeeper happened to recognize her. He told me the name of the brothel where I could find her.

"She was there all right. She'd aged badly—there was no missing how hard and jaded she'd become. I told her to stay put, negotiated with the owner of the place to buy out her...'contract'...and went to the bank to get some money. By the time I got back to pay her way out, she was gone. She left word with one of the other women there to tell me not to come after her or try to find her. She said she didn't want to 'leave the life.' But I think the truth was that she was ashamed of what she'd become and didn't want Asa to know."

He framed his head with his hands, and Rachel didn't know which bothered her most: the tragic story of Asa's sister or the look of total dejection that now enveloped Jeremiah.

"I shouldn't have left her alone."

She put a tentative hand to his shoulder. "It wasn't your fault, Jeremiah. You tried to help her."

He lifted his head and the look of pain and defeat in his eyes made Rachel catch her breath.

"I never told Asa how close I came to getting her out of there. To this day he doesn't know what happened. I don't know how he'd feel about me if he were to ever find out, but I do know how hard it would be for him to lose his hope of finding her again."

"I can't imagine anything changing Asa's opinion of you," she told him. "He's completely devoted to you."

"And I to him. Asa's the reason I can call myself a Christian and not feel like a total hypocrite."

"Asa?"

He nodded. "Asa told me the truth at a time when I wasn't sure there *was* such a thing as the truth. I owe Asa more than I've ever owed any other man in my life. And I've repaid him by withholding information about his one surviving family member. Information he's entitled to know. I never thought of myself as a coward, but in this case, there's no other name for it."

"You're no coward, Jeremiah. You simply don't want to face hurting a friend. But maybe at some point, you ought to tell him after all."

He nodded. "I know. And I will. I just…keep waiting for the right time. And the right time never seems to come."

He made a visible effort to collect himself then, straightening in the chair and adopting his earlier, lighter mood. "So—what else, my beauty? Any other secrets you want to pry out of me?"

"There is one…"

"Have at it, then. I can't seem to refuse you anything."

She could feel the heat of embarrassment already creeping up her face. "The scars on your back—who did that to you?"

The look he gave her made her wish she'd never asked the question. He said nothing, but Rachel knew that *he* knew just how she came to be aware of those scars.

"It would seem that I can have no secrets at all where you're concerned. Ah, well. Those scars are old, Rachel. I've carried them since I was in my teens. I owe a British landlord for the lot of them. He... took issue with my lifting a loaf of bread for my mother and my sisters. It was winter, we were hungry—near to starving if truth be told. My father was dead by then, and we'd been evicted from our cabin. There was no work. No matter where I looked, there was nothing to be had.

"One morning I spied a loaf of bread airing on the landlord's kitchen windowsill, and in truth I didn't think twice—I made off with it. Unfortunately the son of the house saw me. I lost my bread and my dignity all at the same time."

"They *beat* you over a loaf of bread?"

His insolent grin didn't quite manage to conceal the hurt pride and the flint of old anger in his eyes. "I'm sure they merely meant to teach me a lesson I wouldn't forget." He paused. "And do you know, it worked. I never stole so much as a leaf from another man's tree after that."

"I'm so sorry that happened to you."

He shrugged. "I expect my pride was hurt worse than my back, love."

Rachel knew he was making light of the pain he must have felt, but she sensed it was a subject best left untouched.

For her part, she couldn't quite ignore the endearment, though she tried not to cherish the sound of it on his lips. *"Love..."*

When she looked up, she found him watching her. "Any other questions, Rachel?"

Rachel shook her head. "No," she said softly. "None."

"Then let's get back to *my* question."

Rachel said nothing.

"That question, as I recall, was: If you weren't Amish or if I weren't *Englisch,* would you marry me?"

Her impatience with him returned. Or maybe it wasn't so much impatience as frustration with the futility of his question. Why did her answer *matter?* It wasn't as if her loving him would actually change anything. It only made their situation worse.

"All right, I see you're not willing to answer me yet. Even so, I have something to say to you, and I want you to hear it exactly as I mean it. I don't make promises unless I'm reasonably convinced I can keep them. So when I say this to you, it's with the self-assurance...and God-reliance...that I'll find a way to make it happen."

He reached out and took both her hands in his. "I'm going to find a way to marry you, Rachel. Somehow, some way, I mean to make you my wife."

When she started to protest, he silenced her with a look.

"Now I've been thinking a lot about this, and frankly I've come to wonder if perhaps I'm not just as capable as Doc when it comes to making radical changes in my life. Though I have to tell you that, even if I were willing to make such a change, I question whether your people would accept me. I can't think it's all that much of a stretch for them to accept Doc. They know him, and they trust him—indeed, I believe they love the man—so it's not likely they'll turn down his request to convert."

He released a long breath. "But as for me—well, I expect that's a decision that would require a great deal more dialogue and debate, don't you think? More than likely, the only thing they see in me is *trouble.*"

"That's not true, Jeremiah—they think you're brave and trustworthy."

It was plain that he didn't intend to be diverted. "For whatever it's worth, I want you to know that—in time, and if I sense the good Lord is behind the effort...and if your people will allow it—I expect I can follow in Doc's footsteps."

Rachel knew astonishment had to be written all over her face as he continued.

"Oh, I mean it all right, Rachel. I'll become the most Amish of all Amish men. You have my word on it."

Her head swimming, her heart racing, Rachel attempted to find reason among the confusion closing in on her. If she had any doubt whatsoever as to whether he was in earnest, the unflinching glint in his eyes told her he was deathly serious.

"You can't...you mustn't...promise such a thing, Jeremiah. You haven't given this enough thought..."

"I have given this more thought—and more prayer—than you'll ever know, fair Rachel. I have thought about it until my head hammers. Now, are you going to answer me or not? If I were an Amish man, *would you marry me?*"

Rachel was finding it impossible to answer him because her breathing had stopped. All she could do was nod her assent.

He tugged at her hands until she was in his arms. He kissed her then, so carefully, so gently—almost as if he thought she might shatter under his touch.

He eased back for a moment, just enough to search her eyes. Apparently he saw what he was looking for, because he brought her back into his embrace and kissed her again, more deeply this time, as if he meant to claim her as his own and seal the promise of their love for all time.

SONG OF THE PEOPLE

Take my life, and let it be
Consecrated, Lord, to Thee.
Take my moments and my days;
Let them flow in ceaseless praise.
Take my hands, and let them move
At the impulse of Thy love.

FRANCES HAVERGAL

April, 1856

On this fine spring day, Rachel took time out from the food preparation to stand on the porch and watch the activity in the yard.

Dozens of horse-drawn buggies had lined up in neat rows just inside the property line and along the road. The People—at least a hundred or more, men, women, and children—had been arriving since sunup. While young boys rushed about carrying supplies, the men, divided into groups, worked on the new house for Maryann and her husband, John. As was often the case, the young couple had been living with Maryann's parents at the Plank family farm during the first few months of their marriage.

It was nearing noon, and by now many of the more experienced men were busy setting the roof rafters while others worked on installing the windows. The younger men who hadn't yet gained much training in building or carpentry busied themselves with clearing the brush away from the side of the house in preparation for the root cellar.

The women were inside the Plank's kitchen putting the last-minute touches on the food. On such a beautiful day as this, they would be able to eat outside. Tables were already set up, waiting for the men to stop their work long enough to enjoy a hearty noon meal.

Rachel looked forward to these times when the whole community got together. There was always a lot of laughter and good fellowship, which made the hard work seem to go faster.

Englisch friends often commented on how the Amish could raise a house or a barn so quickly. This was easily explained. When an entire community joined together to help a neighbor, much could be accomplished in a brief period of time. Moreover, Amish men had a lot of experience in building—so they knew going into a project what was expected of them and how to do it. They typically accepted no pay when they labored for a friend or neighbor, although sometimes a master craftsman or a professional builder was employed to supervise the work. In that event, fair payment was rendered.

She searched the various groups of workers until she found the face she was looking for. Rachel smiled as her gaze came to rest on Jeremiah. He and Dr. Sebastian stood together talking. Doc wiped perspiration from his forehead with his shirtsleeve, while Jeremiah leaned on his cane and scrutinized the progress of the men working on the rafters.

She had been ever so pleased to learn that Jeremiah was asked to attend today. Although sometimes non-Amish neighbors volunteered to help, it was an uncommon occurrence for an outsider to actually be invited to a house or barn raising unless he was a paid professional whose experience was needed.

Dr. Sebastian, of course, was almost always asked to be present just in case an accident occurred. Rachel had noticed, though, that most often he ended up on a ladder, helping out with the physical labor, not just tending to bruised thumbs, cuts, and scrapes. Also, having secured the leadership's approval to pursue conversion, he was now viewed as a potential member of the community.

But for Jeremiah to be invited—that wasn't so common. However, because he helped order the lumber and other necessary supplies and had proved himself a builder and a carpenter in his own right, some of the more experienced men took notice. He wasn't physically able to do any climbing on ladders or hard labor, but that didn't matter. They were more interested in his advice and ideas.

Jeremiah and Gideon had come together, pleasing Rachel no end. Nor was there any mistaking Mamma and Fannie's excitement to have Gideon back among them.

At community occasions such as this, Rachel often had to take special care in guarding against the sin of pride. The sight of her people working together in such harmony never failed to move her. These were *good* people, unfailingly concerned about the well-being of their neighbors. They were people who put the needs of their families and friends above their own self-interests—people who took God at His Word when He instructed them, *"whatsoever ye would that men should do to you, do ye even so to them."*

She could almost sense a rhythm in the swinging and pounding of hammers, the steady movement of the men's shoulders as they raised a frame or secured a beam. Their conversations, their shouts back and forth, the squealing of children, and the frequent laughter from the women in the kitchen were like music.

Work and worship, love and laughter...*the song of her people,* she thought, smiling at her own fanciful reflections.

She looked back to Jeremiah and saw that he was watching her with what she'd come to think of as an almost proprietary smile. She would have to caution him about being so open with his feelings. Though, truth be known, she couldn't help but delight in the way he looked at her.

Still, no one must suspect that they cared for each other in any way besides the most impersonal kind of friendship. Even if he were Amish, any public acknowledgment that they were in love would be improper. The Plain People kept the act of "courting" and any romantic relationships strictly private, often not even confiding in family members.

Her mother stepped out onto the porch just then, and Rachel

noticed that it took Dr. Sebastian only a moment to start making his way toward the house. Rachel almost laughed at the idea of the doctor and Mamma keeping their love for each other a secret. The way those two looked at each other left little doubt as to their feelings.

And she couldn't be happier for them.

She hoped that some day she and Jeremiah would feel free to look at each other in that same way. As it was, any time they were in the same room, she had all she could do to keep her eyes turned away from him. And it seemed to Rachel that he had the same problem when he was near her.

Here he came now, predictably close on the heels of Dr. Sebastian. Those two had become great friends, though they were inordinately fond of trading insults.

Close behind, with his hands in his pockets and his hat tipped at too jaunty an angle for an Amish male, came Gideon. He was wearing a wide grin as he approached. As Fannie came charging around the side of the house, he grabbed her up and swung her around, laughing at her squeal of pleasure.

Fannie's eyes darted from one to the other among them and she seemed unable to contain her delight. "This is the best day ever!" she cried out. "And I get to spend it with my three favorite people in the whole world, all together in one place at the same time."

Rachel looked around, her heart filled to overflowing as she breathed a silent *Amen* to Fannie's words.

The End

Coming September 2009...

RIVER SONG

Book two in BJ Hoff's
The Riverhaven Years trilogy

DISCUSSION QUESTIONS

1. Dr. David Sebastian is aware that holding a negative opinion of a patient could actually affect his judgment and even the course of treatment for a patient. In spite of that, he has a difficult time with remaining objective about Jeremiah Gant, largely because of his close friendship with Rachel, her mother, Susan, and his other Amish friends and patients. Have you or someone you know ever battled with similar difficulties in being impartial toward another person based, not on fact, but rather on your fear that that person might be a poor influence on or even a danger to someone you care about? If so, how did you handle this dilemma?

2. Phoebe tries to explain to Rachel and her mother her conviction that providing shelter to runaway slaves is God's will, even though it's against the law of the times. Do you think she's trying to align her own motives with God's will, or do you believe there are events that call for the breaking of man's law so that God's will can be accomplished? Examples?

3. Eli, Rachel's deceased husband, is another example of the breaking of man's law, but in this situation it was because he was trying to protect Rachel from attack. Even though he knew he was violating the Amish way by meeting violence with violence, he loved his wife too much not to make a stand against her attackers. How do you, personally, feel about this tenet of the Amish faith—to abstain from violence even in the face of violence being inflicted upon you?

4. How do you interpret Samuel Beiler's behavior toward Rachel? Do you find him protective or manipulative?

5. Rachel indicates in her thoughts that her anger and resentment toward Samuel could be mitigated by his simply talking with her as a friend rather than as her deacon or an adversary. Have you ever had an experience with someone you know well wherein hard feelings or conflict possibly could have been avoided had that person treated you with respect and kindness rather than indignation or censure? How did you handle that confrontation?

6. During his travels with runaway slaves, Asa has discerned that some of

their "helpers" gave them assistance more from a sense of duty or obligation, and with some fear for their own safety, rather than with a willing spirit and true charity prompted by the love of God and a love for their fellow man. When we extend our help to another, in any form, how can we make certain we do so with the right motives?

7. How does the setting—the river, the season of winter, the snowstorm—affect this novel? Did it affect your mood, and if so, in what way?

8. Who do you consider to be the strongest, most memorable character in this story? In what ways do this character's attributes relate to our everyday life, not just the novel?

9. The Amish of Riverhaven are suspicious of Jeremiah Gant at first. What happens to at least partly alleviate their doubts about him?

10. While getting to know the Irish-born Jeremiah Gant, the British-born David Sebastian asks himself: *"The British and the Irish. A case of old wounds that continued to fester, with hope of healing almost beyond imagining. What would it take to end that ancient, bitter enmity?"* How would you answer that question?

11. Rachel's young sister, Fannie, says she believes that "forgiving is called that because it's a gift you give someone." She goes on to say that "…my back and other places where they hit me still hurt sometimes. But ever since I forgave them, my *heart* doesn't hurt. And that was the worst hurt of all." Why do you think that forgiving the boys who attacked her was the key to easing her "heart hurt?"

12. The Amish believe that the Lord's Prayer means exactly what it says: "forgive us as we forgive our debtors." Do you take the prayer literally—do you believe that if we *don't* forgive our debtors, Jesus won't forgive us? Why do you think forgiveness of others is so important to God?

BJ Hoff's bestselling historical novels first appeared in the CBA market more than twenty years ago and include such popular series as An Emerald Ballad, The American Anthem, and The Mountain Song Legacy.

BJ's critically acclaimed novels reflect her efforts to make stories set in the past relevant to the present, and continue to cross the boundaries of religion, language, and culture to capture a worldwide reading audience.

A former church music director and music teacher, BJ and her husband make their home in Lancaster, Ohio, where they share a love of music, books, and time spent with their family.

Be sure to visit BJ's website: **www.bjhoff.com**